Praise for *Such a Good Man*

"Hoffman has written an inventive and thrilling collection about everyday working people that stares directly into darkness without ever abandoning his characters' longing for connection. These wry, expertly crafted stories interrogate labor and masculinity with the skill of a practiced and accomplished writer."

—Marian Crotty, author of *Near Strangers*

"The stories in *Such a Good Man* are formally inventive, heartbreakingly funny, and always deeply grounded in the lives and struggles of their working-class characters. Reading them, I felt like I was flying as close to the edge as Hoffman's characters, whipping down the highway atop a cherry picker, one moment from disaster and, because of that, fully alive."

—Gwen E. Kirby, author of *Shit Cassandra Saw*

"Dustin M. Hoffman's brilliant *Such a Good Man* could easily be titled *Such a Good Woman*, for the female characters show strength and resilience. These stories of hardworking, usually down-on-their luck, characters bring to mind the stories of Raymond Carver and Larry Brown. What a great, strong collection."

—George Singleton, author of *The Curious Lives of Nonprofit Martyrs*

SUCH A GOOD MAN

DUSTIN M. HOFFMAN

THE UNIVERSITY OF WISCONSIN PRESS

Publication of this book has been made possible, in part, through support from the Brittingham Trust.

The University of Wisconsin Press
728 State Street, Suite 443
Madison, Wisconsin 53706
uwpress.wisc.edu

Copyright © 2025 by Dustin M. Hoffman
All rights reserved. Except in the case of brief quotations embedded in critical articles and reviews, no part of this publication may be reproduced, stored in a retrieval system, transmitted in any format or by any means—digital, electronic, mechanical, photocopying, recording, or otherwise—or conveyed via the Internet or a website without written permission of the University of Wisconsin Press. Rights inquiries should be directed to rights@uwpress.wisc.edu.

Printed in the United States of America
This book may be available in a digital edition.

Library of Congress Cataloging-in-Publication Data

Names: Hoffman, Dustin M., author.
Title: Such a good man / Dustin M. Hoffman.
Other titles: Such a good man (Compilation)
Description: Madison, Wisconsin : The University of Wisconsin Press, 2025.
Identifiers: LCCN 2024032649 | ISBN 9780299352448 (paperback)
Subjects: LCGFT: Short stories.
Classification: LCC PS3608.O477666 S83 2025 |
DDC 813/.6—dc23/eng/20240715
LC record available at https://lccn.loc.gov/2024032649

For Dad,
the best man I know

CONTENTS

In Darkness Floating   3
Dad Died in Denim   16
Such a Good Man   19
Essentials   38
Too Bad for Marcel Ronk   44
The Man with the Yellow Hat   51
The Whites   62
Retainer   67
Smoke at the End of the World   82
Eat Fire   87
Orville Killen: Lifetime Stats   95
Mistint   118
God Chooses the Wheelbarrow   131
Privy   140
Bicuspid   155
The First Woman   164
Work from Home   174
This Picture of Your House   187
Every Number Albert Knows   197
The Salesmen Approach   205
The Night the Stars Fell   210

Acknowledgments   223

SUCH A GOOD MAN

IN DARKNESS FLOATING

Dad's drunk and riding the bucket. He's way out there, arms waggling at the top of the cherry picker's extended boom. He begged me to drive him around the country roads so he could be closer to the moon, closer to a more rational clump of rock since this one may have just reelected Trump. They're still counting votes in Pennsylvania, in Arizona, in Georgia, while we freeze in Michigan, waiting. Dad's certain sanity will prevail. I'm not so sure.

So I gave in and got behind the wheel and here I am. I'm only half buzzed on the cheap-ass bottle of tequila we bought. Dos Manos, it's called, two hands. I'm driving with one. Earlier, we passed the bottle back and forth after finishing the Hendersons' gutters. That was the last job we had lined up, and it's slim pickings during COVID. The Hendersons paid us with an envelope on the doorstep. We never even saw their faces. It's been weeks since I've seen any real-life face but Dad's. Without more work tomorrow, we might as well celebrate our doom. We don't know what's next. But we sure as shit know neither Biden nor Trump can stop the no-work dead time of endless snow, which could happen any day now that Michigan has smashed into November. I worry about making rent and heat. Forget about making the late-late payment on the cherry picker we've named Betsy. The repo man has already been sniffing around the house, the neighbors say. But Dad worries about nothing. Usually. He's always had the skill of willing ignorant bliss, but tonight

4 In Darkness Floating

he's drinking like I've rarely seen. Tonight he's aiming for amnesia. I hear him out the open window hooting at the owls, then howling for coyotes, then shouting "tree, tree, tree" at the trees.

I realize he's shouting at me and stomp on the brake too late, and we skid under the branches of a massive oak or maple or who knows what. The autumn-dead leaves clatter a hellish scraping against the bucket, maybe against Dad's face. When the truck finally stops on the dirt road, I'm spilling out the door, wobbling, and I guess I'm a bit drunker than I previously calculated.

"Are you dead, Dad?" I yell at the empty bucket now laced in leaves and branches.

Dad's head pops over the bucket rim. "My heart's pumping from my toes to my nose, darling! What a rush." He howls at the moon again.

"Sure you didn't lose anything important back there?" My head feels wobbly tilted against my shoulders. "Your fucking brains maybe?"

"Your turn," Dad says and lowers the bucket. The boom retracts fast as a snail and emits an electronic whirring, a grind here and there. The night stammers in slow motion. I have plenty of time to enjoy the scenery of nowhere. We're out on a dirt road skirting Mattawan or Paw Paw or maybe even farther off track from home. The clock in the cab doesn't work and my phone's dead, so who knows how long I've been driving. Maybe we've gone so far west that the empty fields might give way to beach, and then we might spill right into the thirty-three-degree Lake Michigan waves.

Dad kicks the bucket door open, jumps to the dirt road. Of course he falls forward on his face, but he does some sort of roll thing, pops right back up, arms outstretched. If there's one thing Dad knows, it's graceful recovery.

"What a night for wonder, my dear daughter." He wraps an arm around my shoulder, swings his head back at the sky. "Where's the bottle?"

I retrieve the Dos Manos from the toolbox, take a long swig, then chuck it as far as I can into the dirt fields. "No more if you're driving."

"You think I'm some kind of irresponsible derelict? I merely want my dear daughter to treat herself, which you did, with a dramatic flourish."

He reaches his hands to the stars, as if to scoop them. "Just like your mother."

"I'm not like her."

"Not in the least," he says. "But you're both brilliant and beautiful and way too good for me. So saddle up, lady," Dad says and saunters toward the cab.

"So now you're fine to drive?"

"I certainly am not." He takes a few steps of straight line, heel to toe, as if walking for the cops. "That's why I'm just going to idle."

Mom would ride the bucket. Mom would for the experience, for her art, for the whimsy, the danger, the passion—no reasons that interest me. Yet I end up inside, and I'll say it's to humor Dad. For him, not me. We've owned this rusty bucket truck for a whole summer. Dad got a too-good-to-be-true great deal, but then the work dried up when the virus got worse. Dad's thinnest summer ever. In Michigan, for contractors, summer is fattening time before the winter famine. We're in no shape to hibernate.

I still barely know how to operate the truck. Betsy hates me, this tangle of creaky steel joints and hydraulic lines. Tonight's no different. Tonight's probably much worse now that my last big tequila swig is flashing through my veins. I'd rather be back in the cab, clutching a wheel, pushing a pedal, a logical machine. Instead, a cramped control panel decorated with buttons and sticks mocks me. I punch a joystick up, and the boom slams down. I jab buttons and flip switches until I'm finally ascending. She bucks and kicks and shrieks. But I persist. I stick around, unlike Mom, who bailed while I was away at school last year. School didn't work out. I got smart and realized a ceramics degree doesn't mean dick to the real world. And once I returned to the nest to join Dad's business—which he'd recently renamed Sky's the Limit, due to the new cherry picker—Mom had flown to Costa Rica. She'd been threatening to leave the States ever since Trump got elected. Now she's painting sunsets on the beach.

The bucket shutters, stalls, and I realize I'm all the way up, the boom fully extended. Below me, Dad has turned on the cab's dome light. His head flicks out the window and he gives me a thumbs up, waits for me

6 In Darkness Floating

to return it. No way Dad can see me in this dark, see me waving him on, ready to go, but the cherry picker lurches forward.

We might be doing ten miles per hour, but I feel like a kamikaze meteor thirty feet aloft and choking on wind. Moon-grayed rows of humped dirt blur beneath me. We blow through an intersection, probably a stop sign, and then it's all dirt again. I can't help clinging to the frigid metal of the bucket rim. My knuckles want to pop out of their skin. This death-defying, half-drunk flying is exhilarating, of course. Dad's known how to do this, how to fake flying, since I was a baby, a year old, and he'd lie on his back, palm my butt in one hand, and rocket me straight up. I've seen the pictures, and Mom oil-painted a scene, just Dad's tanned arm shooting up from the bottom of the frame, his fingers clawlike around my bulging toddler thighs. I hate that I love that painting, love all her paintings. When I was five, I'd superman, my belly on Dad's feet. At twelve, he brought me up the extension ladders, let me straddle the roof peaks— *and now you're above everyone, so high no one can look down on you,* he'd whisper in my ear. By fifteen, I was living on ladders, earning money gunning the power washer. Dad never once worried over me falling, so neither did I. If the ladder legs were going to slip, on the job or in life, I always figured I'd see it in Dad's face first. He's never stopped smiling.

But today he hasn't stopped drinking, and I wonder if it's because he heard the repo man was coming for Betsy. Or maybe because this country could still turn red again. Dad's been laughing for months any time one of the guys at Sherwin-Williams or Menard's talked about Trump. "He stiffs his contractors," Dad said to them. "Done. End of story. No greater sin." And then Dad laughed right through the sliding glass doors under the electric eye.

I wonder if Dad's face has cracked down there. The last year has been a fistful of gravel, and he has to feel the slip of ladder legs this time. But he won't let me see it on him.

Just when I feel my stomach lurching, wanting to spill the beers and On Fire jalapeño burger Dad and I takeout ordered from the Olde Peninsula pub, I look up. The stars steady me. They seem unmoving in their enormity. The Milky Way has ripped the sky wide open. I forget about puking. I forget about Trump and Biden and whether the repo man will be packing a gun tomorrow and if Dad might be stupid and pick a fight. I forget about school, the potter's wheel, my hands aching to cup the buttery silt of clay spinning in my palms. I forget all of it for this sky.

And then there's a power line. I scream for Dad to stop, but he doesn't hear me. I duck into the bucket to await electrocution. Our momentum slams to a stop. My skull smacks into the bucket's wall. There's a pulling, a snap, a twang. We're stopped.

"Darling," I hear below me, "you better be hiding in that bucket and not flung onto the road."

"Your night vision's shitty, old man," I say, and allow him to breathe.

"You ran into a tree, I'll remind you, which is mighty easier to spot than a tiny string of telephone wire floating in the night."

"Where is it?"

"Snapped it clean. And now we better make our escape before someone says my wallet is accountable."

I punch at the controls and, as usual, get nothing but whirring. I do my switch-flipping routine, still nothing. "Stuck. Damn."

Dad gives it a try below on the parallel control panel affixed to the back of the truck. Even from up here, I spot him biting his tongue in concentration, like he does when he's cutting with a paintbrush or caulking a miter. "Been thinking," he hollers up at me.

"Don't hurt yourself."

"Thinking of renaming again, reinvigorating the old DBA down at the courthouse."

"Would be the third time this year," I remind him. Before Sky's the Limit, it was Handy Man Stan, even though his name's Gus. Before that it was Hammering Hank.

"Daughter and Dad on a Ladder," he says. "What do you think?"

It's the first time I've been included in a business name. I'd find the moment a whole bunch sweeter if I wasn't suspended in the bucket that had nearly killed me. I feel the bile rise again.

8   In Darkness Floating

"Hey, Dad on a Ladder, how about you go get that ladder and get me down?" I say.

"Or maybe this: A-A-A-A Handy Dad and Daughter. Then we secure one of those primo first spots in the yellow pages." He's flipping switches as randomly as I do now, as hopeless as the yellow pages are these days. "Tell me, what's the point of having Betsy, if you need to carry ladders?" he says.

So no rescue's coming. I study the boom's dead-drop slope, try to route a path where I could climb down without tumbling thirty feet onto my skull. The boom bends in my drunk vision. My head goes light. I puke over the side. I hear Dad cussing, scuffling out of the path.

When I lift my head, I spot a shadow on the night skyline. Looks like a farmhouse, someone impossibly surviving out here in this dirt ocean. I point it out to Dad.

"Good eye, my floating daughter. Onward to our saviors." He whistles his way back to the driver's seat, and we're off, headed for the only house sprouting out of the hibernating fields.

While we drive, I squat, prop my head against the buzzing bucket, and stare down sky to try and keep my guts inside. It's an impossible image to capture, the night sky, any sky, despite what painters pretend. Fuck *Starry Night*. Mom loved smearing her oils and pretending that, bam, there it was, perfect mimesis, but her blues were never right, her blacks never deep enough. That's the catastrophe of representation. Painters like her, they cover a canvas in darks and stab a couple white dots and think they made night. I chose clay. Give me mud squeezed between my fingers over oily ox-hair bristles. One of us is believing their lying eyes. The other is making something to drink from. Give me water.

The stars slow and my head steadies. Dad has stopped. I struggle up on my wobbly legs. He's already out of the truck, hands cupped around his mouth. He whisper-hisses up at me, "Two shakes of a lamb's tail, darling," and then he scuttles off toward the lonely house I spotted. We're parked on the dirt road, next to their mailbox. I'm eye level with a leafless oak tree. Through the skeletal upper branches, a window spills yellow

In Darkness Floating

light. I have a perfect view of a narrow bed, a wooden crucifix hovering above it. Below, Dad skips toward their barn. Not toward the house, where he should be going to ask for help. He disappears, and I'm left to listen to nothing—no breeze, no crickets, no traffic. This nothing swarms me, makes my ears ring. My breaths are riotous. I look around for anything to distract me. Across the road, a little way down, stands the biggest damn Trump-Pence sign I've ever seen. This behemoth's whiteness throbs in the moonlight. It's a custom job, hand-painted, and the Keep America Great gets cramped and slanted on the "Great" where the artist planned their space poorly.

Through the branches, bodies appear in the window. A woman slaps a man across the face once, slaps him again. He hangs his head. She's yelling at him, but I hear nothing. This Michigan farmhouse is so well insulated against winter, against cold, that a not a single syllable could escape. Not even as her mouth gapes, and I catch the flash of teeth and tongue. His chin buries deeper into his chest. Mom used to berate Dad for his dumb purchases—the cherry picker, brand-new gas-powered paint sprayer, barely used jackhammer, too many rust-abused trucks and trailers, the 3D printer he almost purchased before I talked him out of it. He's a dream spender, but he wept when he saw my first tuition bill, and he immediately emptied his wallet into my hands.

The window woman holds the man's cheeks, is probably scowling into his eyes. At least the man gets this. Mom jetted without farewell. She called once she was in Nosara, Costa Rica. She calls every Sunday now, tells me how her brushstrokes have grown so wide and free. She tells me to visit: *We'll drink margaritas and sangrias on the beach, and the whoosh of waves will invigorate your artist spirit.* She's always believed I followed in her footsteps, became an artist like her, groomed since I could stand with a mini-easel set up next to hers. But I'm nothing like her. When we talk, I click the volume button on my phone, quieter and quieter until she's less than a whisper.

The woman still holds the man's face, and then their torsos collapse together, their arms weaving into a hug. They both wear drab-colored plaid, and from my distance, I can't tell where one body separates from the other. The bile rises again, but I fight it back, force myself not to blink until my eyes burn, until crashing metal clatters from the barn. The bodies break apart, and the man nears the window, peers out at the night where I am, where Dad is. New squares of yellow light up as the man zigzags through his house and down the stairs toward the front entrance.

The door opens, and a body stalks out. As he nears me on the way toward the barn, I identify a gun in his hand. Something long barreled. Dad has never owned a gun. I worry Dad's buzzed enough to do something stupid. I imagine him pouncing from the barn rafters to spin into a sales pitch and then stuffing the man's flannel breast pockets with business cards. So I have to act first, even though I'm trapped up here with the trees. I hoot, like an owl, like Dad was doing earlier. I'm not sure why I don't just say, "Hey, asshole," but I hoot and it works and the man is trudging my way with his gun.

"Bit late to be working the telephone lines." He stands below Betsy's bucket, and he's close enough that I can clearly see what he's packing. It's a crossbow, some fancy fiberglass number with a red laser dot dancing off the scope. A gun I'd feel better about. A gun is a normal by-product of American paranoia. This, though—I wonder if this farmer's pillow bulges over the crossbow he sleeps on. Just in case Biden comes for his arsenal. I wonder if this is the kind of man who might repo part-time when he's not doing whatever farmers do in winter.

"We're not doing anything," I say.

He lifts the crossbow, points it at his house's glowing bedroom window. "Having a little peep?"

"I didn't see."

"Just seems like a lot of trouble." The man scratches his thigh using the crossbow. "Rent a bucket truck, drive it all the way out here, just to see a middle-aged man's skivvies."

"We own it," I say, swelling with stupid pride. I consider spitting on that big moonlit Trump-loving nose. "My dad and me own it. We don't rent."

In Darkness Floating

"Long-term perverts, then. Good for you making a serious go at it," he says. "Now get off my property."

"I'm in the road."

"Get off my road then."

"You don't own this," I say. "It's my right to stay here and look in any window owned by any idiot lazy and stupid enough not to hang curtains." Maybe it's the Dos Manos in me or maybe it's the Trump sign that has me spitting venom. Maybe it's talking to a human in person for the first time in weeks. I'm a lump of clay gone lopsided on the wheel, an unstoppable imbalance.

"I suppose, what I mean to say," the man waves the crossbow in the air, "is I'm telling you to scram."

I wonder how fast an arrow flies. I feel like I might have time to duck if this asshole is truly crazy enough to shoot. Then that arrow would just keep going, arc into a field and plant itself until some other farmer came along and threshed it into horse feed. Two counties over, some expensive thoroughbred's gums will spill blood like a magic trick.

"The stars are pretty," I say. "Think I might stay a bit."

"The hell you will."

"Waddle along, redneck."

"How about you come down and I teach you some manners, missy?"

"She can't come down," Dad says. The farmer and I both turn. Dad somehow snuck up on us while hoisting a massive extension ladder over his head. "Our lift motor's on the fritz. Betrayed us. She's stuck as a duck up there."

"Don't see how that's my problem," he says. "Don't see how that means you get to steal my ladder."

"Just a borrow, my kind neighbor." Dad stands his ground, even though the farmer now faces him, crossbow dangling. We all know it's there. "Then we'll be out of your business and back to ours."

"What business you got so late?" the man says.

"Midnight Painters," I holler. "'Dry before dawn' is our motto."

"Cute." The man shifts the crossbow to his other hand.

In Darkness Floating

"Twilight Fix 'em Upper and Daughter," Dad says.

"Give me a break."

"By sunrise you won't believe your eyes," I say.

"Patch and Clean While You Dream Incorporated," Dad says.

"Made in America," I say.

"Licensed and insured," Dad says.

"Totally legit," I say.

"We pay taxes and have never once filed bankruptcy," Dad says. He must have seen the sign. How could anyone miss it?

The man slings the crossbow over his shoulder, relaxes his posture.

"We could build you a wall around your whole farm," I say.

"It's gonna be hugely super-classy," Dad says.

"We'll even get your neighbors to pay for it," I say.

"Walls Are Us," Dad says.

"We Are the Wall-Rus," I say.

"Wall-Mart," Dad says.

"Wall-mageddon," I say.

"MAGA Walls," Dad says. "Terrific walls. Tremendous. The best."

"Okay, okay." The man waves with his empty hand for us to stop. I can't tell if he's laughing or fuming. "Just go ahead and use the ladder so I can get back to sleep," he says.

Dad props the ladder against the bucket. The man rests his crossbow on the cherry picker's fender. Dad and the farmer seem to be chuckling about something. Dad calls for me to climb down, but I can't do it. It's not that I'm scared of heights or the fall. I was raised on ladders. It's that when I come down, this will be over, this night of drunk stars and floating over the country that just voted, and what if they're all counted now? If Trump won again, then what's down there is no place for me—a dropout ceramicist, a woman worker, hell, a woman. No wonder Mom bailed. Staying stuck isn't my worst option. I sink back into the bucket.

Eventually Dad's wire-brush scalp pops over the rim. He reaches out his hand. Even in moonlight his palms show calluses. When I was four, I used to sleep under my bed. I waited for that moment when Mom and

In Darkness Floating

Dad would whisper and shuffle around the room searching for me, terrified, imagining me gone. I never felt as full in my own body as in those seconds of absence. Then Dad would drop to his belly, his head pressed to the carpet. He'd wiggle his mustache at me and reach out that same sandpaper palm. Shortly after that, the whole world would rematerialize from the night. Rational, tangible dawn.

I take Dad's hand and yank. He climbs into the bucket to join me.

"What the hell you all doing up there?" the farmer calls.

"Sorry, darling," Dad says just for me, just loud enough to hear in this bucket where we sit, knees touching. "Wish the whole world was better for you."

"Hell with the world."

"We've always been okay," he says. "Our little us."

"You don't know how to be alone."

"I don't." He looks me in the eye even though I bet he wants to look anywhere else. "Not since you were born."

"Fuck Mom and fuck Trump."

"They're not even close, my sweet," he says. "Don't lump your mom with lumpy Trump."

I stand and shout down at the farmer, "Wanna buy a cherry picker?"

"No?" he says like a question. I shove the rails and the ladder slides over. There's nothing the farmer can do to stop its crash.

"She's properly drunk, my friend." Dad has popped up next to me. "Sincerest apologies."

"That your sign over there?" I spit.

"If anything's broken—a single rung dinged—you'll receive reparations," Dad says.

"There's never been a better time to buy a bucket truck," I say.

The farmer stares past us to the freezing dirt fields. "That sign just showed up one day," he says plenty loud, as if he's not used to being quiet, to hiding anything. Being surrounded by acres of corn and only a tractor might do that to a person. "Like, you remember hearing about Jesus Christ's face on your toast? A miracle like that just spoils breakfast.

14 In Darkness Floating

No more toast. Every morning that sign blocks the sunrise. Big square of black shadow every morning."

"Who'd you vote for?" I ask.

"At least whoever planted it there will pull it up now," the farmer says, still gazing off. "Who the hell has time to vote?" he finally answers.

"Buy the truck, and we'll throw in a free sign removal," I say.

Dad seems out of jokes. Me too. We're a daughter and father team full of missing—my clay, his wife, my mom, a house painted all white in DC that we didn't think mattered until it suddenly mattered more than anything has ever mattered. I start to laugh anyway. Dad touches my shoulder, and I rock the bucket. We howl into the night. This farmer must be sure we're complete nutjobs by now.

"Before I decide anything," the farmer says, his head thrown back on his hinged neck, his eyes glistening, "I'd have to test-drive."

Dad tosses down the keys. The yellow square of bedroom light back at his house goes dark. He's all night now, just like us. He gets into the cab and rumbles up Betsy's gurgle-gutted engine. He's gentle on the throttle, takes his time pushing out onto the long dirt road that in summer will be flanked by hay, by corn, by soy. Currently, the land stretches barren in waves of dirt. This is a stranger's land, and we're trespassers clouding over every future seed and shoot some farmer will nurse.

We three know he's not going to buy the cherry picker. But he's driving faster. Dad hugs my shoulder, tucks me against his ribs. I watch his face, his lips under that forever mustache of his. These are the parts of my parents I'll never witness: Dad's naked upper lip, Mom painting an un-still life on a Costa Rican beach, my parents ever again together.

The wind picks up. Our driver's flannel arm sails out the window. His open palm surfs the wind waves. He could be taking us out to dump us in the woods. Or he could be just riding the night along with us. Wherever he's driving, we're gaining momentum. Dad's arm leaves me, raises into the night air. Both hands up, fingers spread, catching the wind like the farmer, hailing the night. I'm not quite ready to let go of the bucket. The cherry picker's catching speed, propelling my heartbroken father.

Broken is easy, just pieces to mash back together so long as they haven't dried out. I haven't been out of school too long. Not too late. And I hope the farmer's cheek still stings from his wife's slap. I hope the sound of Mom slamming the door the last time still rings in Dad's ears. All the hurt seems raw enough yet, still fresh enough to mold in our fingers. All those floating votes might yet form a softer world. Dad's on his tiptoes, head back, howling. And I might. I just might let go of the bucket rim and push my hands higher in the air too. Higher and higher. I might. I just might.

DAD DIED IN DENIM

on a second shift, collapsed over a headlight, the same headlight he'd been assembling since 1978, the same five Phillips-head screws. They just kept rolling down the belt and they always did and they always will and they're coming down the belt just now, into Betty Davenport's hands as we speak, which is why she won't make the service. We understand. Everyone understands someone has to screw those five screws. Everyone understands the line can't stop.

Dad owned one suit, back of his closet. We pulled the plastic bag, unzipped a brown number that seemed impossibly small, tailored to fit a miniature Dad even Mom couldn't recall. There was a picture somewhere, our sister Jilly said, of him pinched into that suit and squatting on the hood of an orange Mustang. Mom didn't remember an orange Mustang. None of us did. Jilly dug through boxes and albums but couldn't prove it.

The brown suit sprawled across the kitchen table all night, and when we found that deflated man in the morning, we knew it wouldn't fit our dead dad. No way.

We returned to the closet to shuffle hangers, all holding neatly draped Wranglers and Levi's and Lees. Finding pants formal enough for death was a problem. Dad didn't go to church, and he'd worn blue to all our weddings, all our babies' pageants and baptisms and spelling bees. "Anyplace that don't let me wear jeans, don't need me," Dad always said. But we had an open casket to face, and the mortician was calling again, asking if they could lend some burial garments from their stock or if we'd be bringing clothes over. Borrowing burial garments from the funeral home sounded like a good way to make twenty-dollar slacks cost two hundred, and we knew Dad would've hated that. It would've made him spit, right on the carpet, which he'd done only four times: when the union busted, when the plant cut overtime, when Jilly's husband bruised her jaw, and when Jilly married Janice, but that time he'd done it because he was too happy. Janice was from the factory, from his floor, and he loved her more than he'd ever loved any of us. She cried hardest when we unzipped that sad little brown suit.

Back at the closet, we dug under bright teal and orange sweaters from the '80s and found a pair of threadbare jeans bleached white as a ghost. In a cardboard box labeled with a Sharpie-drawn smiley face wearing a hard hat, we found denim so deeply indigo they'd pass for black, but they were speckled in white paint, streaked in the maroon of Jilly's teenage room, dabbed in the sage green of my kid room, dotted in the gray and purple and red and beige of the rotating colors Mom had demanded for our front door over the decades, splashed in the canary yellow of baby Wanda's room that she got to live in for only three weeks and four days before she stopped breathing one night in her crib.

Jilly liked the idea of burying him in these pants, said it'd be like taking the family house down to the dirt with him, but we knew that just wouldn't be right. You can't go to the grave wearing your weekend work pants. Since we couldn't decide, we resorted to a game. Each of us would pick a pair of jeans at random, eyes closed, all of us good and drunk off the bottle of ten-year-old bourbon Dad had been saving for the most special occasion, and we supposed this was it.

We stumbled into his closet, blindfolded now since we'd decided none of us could be trusted to keep our eyes closed. When it was my turn, I stumbled in, head throbbing because they'd tied the blindfold too tight in their drunken belligerence. It felt like my eyes might roll back into my skull, and I'd show up at Dad's service too blind to read the eulogy I couldn't bring myself to write. But then my fingers found his denim and I squeezed and I crouched to bury my nose in his smell—shop grease and WD-40 and Brut deodorant and Stetson cologne, and behind that fatherly potpourri there was the trace of ammonia he could never quite mask. Dad was a heavy sweater. Even dumping vinegar in the washing machine couldn't cut the stench that made him so self-conscious, a smell we said nothing about even though we all hated it, but we fucking loved him so much and I was glad my eyes were so squeezed behind that blindfold or else I'd cry and he couldn't stand crying because it would get him going. He was as much a crier as he was a sweater—a father who couldn't keep anything bottled up, who poured everything out on the living room and factory floor.

I fanned my fingertips across the dozens of pairs of jeans and said a Hail Mary and an eeny-meeny-miny-mo, and I grasped that pair. This one. Right here. This would be the one we'd bury him in, because could you imagine him wearing anything else?

SUCH A GOOD MAN

They told Eggy they'd be calling the cops soon, if their missing kid didn't appear in the next ten minutes. Eggy knew their type, fussy helicopter parents, the rich kind raised on fistfuls of pills and internet, who could afford to be chronically anxious about terrorism and plastic straws in the ocean and global starvation because they never had to worry about their own empty bellies. Eggy had grown up hungry. She'd tasted worry. She knew Mason and his guns, and now he was two days out of prison and calling her momma's house every two hours.

This missing kid—he was no sweat. She could find the kid before the cops showed. She'd bet all the money in her boot on it. She told the parents, "It's a sure thing," and sprinted off. But then she realized they probably didn't know all what she meant, so she sprinted back, grabbed the mom's gold-bangled hippie wrist—she smelled wonderful like patchouli and brand-new plastic bags—and said, "I'll find your kid in a flash."

It happened. Now and then, when Bouncy Paradise pumped up their inflatable arsenal on a town event, a kid would go missing, and a parent, often buzzed and wobbly, would start bawling, and then they'd recover the kid in a big fanfare of tears and cotton candy. Eggy liked the idea of playing hero. She danced through the crowd, weaving past sticky kid fingers and blind parents staring into their glowing phone screens. This was her crowd, her world, and she'd quickly become an expert. It was probably her best job ever. Sure beat waitressing that truck stop, or shooting meth and blowing hicks and shooting more meth until she spent six months in Leath Correctional and came out pristine clean. Johan, the Bouncy Paradise big boss, loved the tax break he got for hiring felons. Nearly every employee had a tar-stained past, so she never worried about hiding her brown meth teeth. She smiled big as she pleased at parents and kids alike and they smiled back. Everyone was dirty here.

Bruce's Gorilla Punch-Out inflatable loomed in the distance, the gargantuan twenty-seven-foot gorilla head bobbing in a breeze she couldn't feel from the ground. Lucky goddamn ape had the nicest spot in the whole place, plus could probably see every missing kid from up there. She didn't spot Bruce out front. Everyone was dirty here *except* Bruce, who was too sweet for this place, who dearly loved Jesus, who some called Pedophile Bruce, but Eggy figured that was just the torture you got for being a good guy around a bunch of fuckups like her.

Twelve years ago, out on Mason's cracked-concrete patio decorated with brand-new Walmart patio furniture, Mason said, "I know you want a baby. Let me help you out."

But he was her dealer, and she didn't want to screw that up, so she said, "Maybe next time," and tried to smile and then remembered her teeth so didn't.

"No strings." He began mashing a crystal with a magazine from his AR-15. He crushed gentle as if he was pinning butterfly wings. "I'd admire from afar. You'd be your own woman. I believe in that. I believe in women leading their own lives."

"Why the hell would I want a kid?" she said.

"I want to help you put more love in the world." He reached across and gripped the back of her neck. He pulled her head down to the table, to a row of three neat lines. He kept his hand there, light grip, but she doubted she'd be able to lift her head if she wanted. She didn't want. She inhaled the middle line first.

With her head still held down, he said, "And you're pretty, Eggy girl. This favor for you would be doing me a favor. And you're smart. You're a special customer. My favorite."

Such a Good Man

She did the first line second. Through the glass table she had a direct sight of the crotch of his cargo shorts. Below that, the black AR-15, missing its magazine, rested across his bare toes, a black toenail, hairless. This was her view, and she wouldn't be able to break it until he released his hand.

"Think you'd like a girl or a boy, Eggy?" His thumb kneaded the divot at the base of her skull. It wasn't unpleasant. "Me, I think I'd prefer a girl."

She did the last line.

$$\sim$$

Eggy sprinted through the slides, shimmying her body through the twenty-person line. "Official bouncy business," she hollered until she was up the ladder where she scanned the landing, then bombed butt-first down the slide. She dumped herself into the carousel-shaped mini bouncer jampacked with toddlers, tried to yell the kid's name, but already had forgotten it. She settled for "Hey, lost kid," and spied for head turns or that curly towhead she'd seen pictured on the parents' phone. With no luck, she bounded out of that dirty-diaper mob.

She was working up a sweat by the time she reached the Thunder Gauntlet. Sharice looked tired and pissed, her usual look. She'd worked there two months longer than Eggy, and every day seemed like it'd be the one she'd quit. She scowled at the kids, yelped, "Giddyap," when it was their turn to go, and yelled at the ten-year-olds who loitered behind the half-wall rope climb to body-slam the little ones. She'd growl at the little ones, too, if they puttered too long.

"How's business, Sharice?" Eggy asked.

"I'm sweating like a stuck pig and these kids don't listen, and," she leaned low to whisper, "my hemorrhoids are inflamed as a motherfucker." Though she screamed generously at the children, she made sure not to cuss loud enough for little ears.

"Seen a lost one?"

"Looks like?"

"Usual stuff. Blond, four years old, and they said an orange Clemson shirt."

"Oh yeah," Sharice said, "I saw one of them."

"Yeah?"

"Or maybe," she waved open palms at her line, "that describes half the snots here."

"No reason to bust my cunt. I'm just telling you what I know," Eggy said.

"Crummy intel. Worthless."

A sweep of cool air blew between them, and the whole area seemed to pause and bend in the rare breeze. It was too good and too rare in the South Carolina July not to honor a few seconds of relief.

"Hate to suggest what you're already thinking," Sharice said, "but you sniff around Pedophile Bruce yet?"

Bruce was just too nice. Even if there was a touch of truth, she believed in giving everyone a second shot. Hell, every employee here was on their fourth or fifth.

"You shouldn't call him that."

"If the shoe fits, he's gotta be forced to wear it," Sharice said and then screamed at a kid pretending to wrap the rock wall rope around his neck noose style. "We don't have no pink jumpsuits here, so I see value in reminding."

"What if people change? Reformed, and all that."

Sharice snorted, puffed hot air.

"Plus, Boss hates it. Bad for business," Eggy said. "Who's gonna bring their kids back to a place that may or may not employ a pedophile?"

"Tough for Boss."

"Could be tough shit for you when you lose a job."

Eggy knew she had her there, but Sharice couldn't stand to lose an argument. So she muttered "Good goddamn goose" under her breath and then lunged herself through the inflatable tunnel at the Thunder Gauntlet entrance. The kid was strangling himself again and laughing like a dumbshit. But that would stop once Sharice was towering over him screaming, the red worms on her forehead pulsing. Eggy preferred the friendly route, which was probably why Johan planted her in front of the Rainbow Bounce with the little kids. Eggy was one of the nice ones. But none of

Such a Good Man   23

them knew about Mason, his recent parole, the phone calls—the fucking phone calls—how Mason begged for her to listen, was aching to tell her more about what she didn't want to hear, about the kidnapping he'd served time for. Eggy couldn't smother the spark of fear that maybe Mason had come to prove something to her, that the missing kid was with him and it was her fault.

She swerved through the shaved-ice line, the cotton-candy queue, the barbecue pit. She even popped open the smoker, imagining the missing boy's orange shirt hanging from the blackening meat, and then she cursed herself and bit her cheek for thinking so dark.

~

Mason came for her baby when it was eight months old. He showed up on her momma's driveway in his burgundy Jeep with the chains that rattled on the front bumper, and he revved his engine until Eggy ran out in her underwear and a Minor Threat T-shirt.

"Your legs look pretty," Mason said through his open window.

"Neighbors are gonna call the cops on you," she told him.

"All of you looks pretty, Eggy girl," he said. "Baby didn't do nothing to slow you down."

"Hope you don't have any shit in that Jeep," she said. "Momma's probably calling the cops right now."

"Where's my baby?"

"What do you care?"

"I want to take it for a ride. Introduce myself. It'll ride right on Daddy's lap and help me steer and we'll go get ice cream." He formed his hands into brackets meant to cradle a baby's armpits at the steering wheel.

"You're high," she said.

"What flavor he like? Is he a he? I bought both kinds of toys. Dolls and dump trucks."

"Don't think babies are supposed to eat ice cream."

"Don't be a bitch about it." Mason smiled his wormy lips at her, trying for a cute she didn't feel like receiving. "Let the little fucker have some fun."

"He's not here."

"A boy?" Mason honked his Jeep horn three times. A neighbor's light flicked on a yellow square down the road. "Hell yeah. Point me in his direction."

"He's not mine, I mean."

"Who else's could he be?"

"Adopted is what I mean."

Mason punched the rearview mirror and it snapped and shattered and rattled to the floor. His fist was bleeding. Eggy felt the old fear dripping, and she knew Mason well enough to know running inside would rile him. Mason on meth needed to be treated like a wild rottweiler. Run from a rott, you get teeth sunk deep into your calf muscle.

"The fuck's wrong with you, Eggy?" he said. "That's not a choice you make without your baby's daddy."

She longed to tell him all the ways he should fuck off, but she spotted the assault rifle's barrel poking from the passenger-seat floor. He caught her looking at it, and if she didn't play this right, he'd make her do a bump off the barrel like in the old days. She might not be good at saying no.

"I tried calling you, to tell you about the baby, but your old number didn't work."

"Yeah. That's right." He sniffed at the blood on his knuckles, sucked at them. "Got into some heat and had to get invisible."

Her arches hurt from running all day at the diner, waiting first shift, cooking second. If he stayed much longer, maybe she'd ask him to rub her feet or, hell, blow them off with the rifle. She'd have a good excuse for no work tomorrow.

"Well," she said and waited, and still Mason stayed idling in park. He fumbled around for the rearview mirror, found it in the shadows, and tried to stick it back in place. It fell again. "Was a nice surprise, you stopping by and all," she said.

Mason hurled the broken rearview at the passenger-side door. It hit glass like a thunderclap, and Eggy felt her guts cringe.

Such a Good Man 25

"Know what, Eggy?" he said. "It doesn't matter that you're a lazy quitter of a mother. That you stole something important as fuck to me." He was smiling in the dark—something flickering that was shinier than teeth. She never much thought how close a smile was to gnashing teeth until now. "I'm gonna find him. I'll track him down. I'll use my guys. Whatever it takes. That's my love you gave away. And when I find my son, you won't even know. You won't even be a thought. Less than a fart in the wind. That's the kind of mother you are."

He spun rubber in her momma's driveway until she was coughing on burnt tire, and then he was careening down the street as a pair of disappearing red eyes.

≈

Of course, Boss Johan already knew about the missing kid even before she climbed the ladder to the roof. He was perched atop the gutted trailer home they used to transport all the inflatables. He was on his throne overseeing his convicts. She watched him watch for a moment. He picked his nose and flicked it into the sky and then leaned forward on his inflatable throne. He spray-painted it gold once a week.

"Boss," she said, "seen any lost kids from up here?"

"I see everything," he said.

"Blond boy, orange shirt, four years—"

"Wonder why I bother paying you all if I'm responsible for losing kids." He was back at plowing his nose again while he stared into the crowd.

"It's just, the parents are pretty freaked, and, maybe I wonder if you've seen a long-haired guy—" She stopped herself from describing Mason. It probably wasn't him. She couldn't jump to that yet. No reason to blow fire into the worst-case scenario when there was still time. Johan didn't seem to be listening anyway, busy fondling nose hairs.

"Know why I got into this?"

Once Bouncy Paradise was inflated, Johan never came down from his roost. She did wonder, if he wanted so little to do with the crowds. She liked kids, and she figured that had to be why anyone would choose a business venture like this. "Because you like kids?" she said.

"I like money."

"Oh."

"All there is to it." He stopped fiddling with nose hairs and turned to stare her in the eyes. "Money, honey," he said, stretching syllables like he was talking to a slow kid. Her fists balled. She let the urge to punch him flutter off.

"And, I suppose," he said, "I do like a good screw on an inflatable after hours every now and then. What I don't care about is kids or convicts." He turned back to his watching, as if she'd breezed away.

She thought about how they tended to rush Lysol-ing the inflatables. She'd be extra thorough to scrub out the bumper gutters next time. "So you haven't heard anything?" she said. "Sorry I bugged you."

"The parents just called my cell. They're calling the cops now," Johan said, pointing out into the crowd. "I guarantee it'll be one of you who eats shit before my liability insurance. So what I'm saying is find that kid or you're fucked."

Eggy skidded down Johan's ladder and cycled back through the crowd with all the optimism sucked from her lungs. She couldn't even smile at the blue- and purple-lipped kids getting sugar-high on snow cones. The cops would run her name, and Mason would come up. The kidnapping he'd been incarcerated for would flash sirens in their heads. She'd been absolved for her testimony, but the word *accomplice* had been tossed around enough. The cops would suspect her for this missing kid. Even if she'd been innocent before. Hell, she'd been a kind of victim, though no one gave her that label. It had been her boy Mason had stolen from his adoptive parents, after all. She never even got the chance to see him. She got nothing. Less than that. Forced to sweat death deep down all her cracks in court in front of the judge's stare, and they didn't even show a picture of her kid as evidence, like she'd hoped.

But she went free and Mason didn't. He spent ten years locked up, and she got clean, goddamn it. She had truly been clean.

She kicked through the women's bathroom door, stuck her head under each stall and saw nothing but sweat-glistening thighs. She slammed into

Such a Good Man

the men's room, and immediately a white-haired Friar Tuck–looking asshole wearing a tank top stretched skintight over his inflated gut gave her a wink. She scanned the wall of urinals for a miniature man. She considered apologizing to the old-timer on her way out, but he was making a humping thrust with his hips, so she walloped his belly hard as she could on the way out the door.

She was running out of places to look, and Bruce's giant gorilla's smirk was grimacing down on her, but she didn't need to bother Bruce when Mason haunted her mind, a likelier and likelier suspect. Bruce didn't need the harassment. Just last week, he'd told her about his own cocaine problem. He'd lost two houses, three wives, a half-dozen children, and a cat named Bingo he loved more than anything. He used to own a chain of burrito restaurants, all organic, paid his workers a whopping thirteen bucks an hour, and now he, like Eggy, was scraping up Johan's $7.36 per hour.

So when she jogged past the Gorilla Punch-Out, she hardly glanced through the netting. Instead, she checked the dumpster brimming with Styrofoam cups and paper plates smeared in corn dog mustard. She dove into a sea of trash.

≈

After only the third Jeep visit to her momma's house, she gave in, and it was easier than collapsing on the couch after a double shift. She let Mason light a foilie for her. She couldn't remember the last time he made her pay. It was before everything, before she had a baby and let it go. But, of course, nothing was free. She understood that even as she savored the burning-plastic taste that filled her lungs the way no food had ever filled her belly, no love her heart. She contracted every muscle to hold it in. Maybe if she passed out holding it in, holding her breath, let herself become a smoke wisp, she wouldn't have to find out why Mason was smiling so grotesquely.

He flicked the tinfoil clean and loaded up another go, which, turned out, wasn't for him. She'd do it. She'd get as high as he'd let her. She'd already missed her work at Wendy's for the fifth shift in a row. They'd stopped calling. Her hair finally didn't smell like french fries anymore—now like apple shampoo and tar. She'd never eat another french fry.

And Mason wouldn't quit flashing that new gaudy golden grill with fake diamonds sparkling the words Get Fucked. No way any sane women would find it even ironically funny. Then again, she didn't know many sane women.

"What the hell you goofy-smiling at?" she finally said to his sparkly diamonds.

"Been thinking," he said, "planning, I suppose, is how I should put it."

Mason let the room's ghostly gray smoke swirl around his face, his long black hair. She wished he was just more smoke she could inhale before his crazy plans materialized heavy as gelatinous Frosty mix bags.

He said, still stupidly smiling: "We should find him."

"Who?"

"Who the fuck else?" he said. "Don't be dim, Eggy."

"I'm not." She drew the lighter's flame to foil. "I didn't get what you meant. I try not to think about him so much these days."

"Well, Eggy," his cracked, peeling lips closed over his diamonds, "I never ever stop thinking about him."

Of course, she never stopped thinking about him either. He was thirteen months now, and seventeen days. Maybe the red splotchy birthmark shaped like a bunny on the back of his neck had faded. He probably lived in a suburb. He'd probably said his first word, *dad* or *mom* or maybe *dog*, if they had one. Maybe they'd even bought a puppy, a soft yellow one, to grow up with him. It was summer. He'd be doing something amazing she'd never done as a kid, something she couldn't even imagine. He'd never know she'd named him Abel. Only she knew that, and she'd never tell anyone. She took the hit.

"Every single second I'm thinking about him," Mason said. "And it's about time we went and found the little fucker."

Eggy held her breath, held the hit in, pounding to escape her chest, lungs begging for air.

"Let's go rescue him and teach him how to be a little badass."

"Kidnap him?" she said. "I don't even know where he might be."

"I can find him. I can always find anything. You know that."

"Don't do it."

"Come with me."

"I can't."

"You can do anything, Eggy. I always believed in you most."

A cough escaped her, then another, and then she couldn't stop herself. She vomited on Mason's red silk sheets. He patted her back not ungently. She knew she had to stop him, but she couldn't kill anyone. She couldn't. No way. Not with her momma's pistol. Not with the tire iron in the back of her Neon. Not with one of the matte-black rifles mounted on Mason's wall. Couldn't. Couldn't.

But if she didn't, her boy might not ever learn to play lacrosse or how the horse-shaped piece moves on a chessboard.

"Gotta go," she said and hopped off his bed. Mason might've been following her as she left his house, might've been ready to bind her arms with an extension cord and dump her into his Jeep, and then she'd have to go with him. When she got to the driveway alone, she plunged one of Mason's serrated combat knives into his Jeep tire, just to be safe, the hiss following her into the night.

~

She was running low on spots to check now. The parking lot provided a hundred shiny windshields. She searched through a reflection of her face, her graying hair, her skin wrinkled into an unrecognizably old version of herself. No way she could check every car. No way she could stare into herself that many times. She climbed a dusty Bronco's hood and scanned the lot for Mason's Jeep. Just because she didn't see him didn't mean he wasn't there, waiting to pounce and kidnap and crank her full of meth. Or, worse, if he'd already taken this kid, they could be driving toward the Blue Ridge Mountains to get invisible in the nowhere Appalachian fringe.

She didn't want to believe that a pedophile version of Bruce could exist, but she supposed checking with Bruce was better than the horror of

Mason. Bruce was a nice guy, proof you could clean up once and for all, and he didn't need suspicion. Still, her feet moved faster than her hesitation, and suddenly she was standing in front of Bruce's Gorilla Punch-Out. His ponytailed scalp popped from the entrance flap. His face was red. He was panting and smiling.

"Swell to see the one and only Eggy," Bruce said and offered her a high-five. She touched his palm. "What brings you to my neighborhood? That missing kid show up?"

"I've been searching all afternoon," she said, kicking dirt and playing it cool. "I mean, I'm sure he'll turn up. This is the last place I looked. I hadn't even thought of it, really."

"Oh my gosh, Eggy, what a big bummer. I'm so sorry." He reached out and gripped her elbow with one hand, her shoulder with another. Any other guy, this would be a cheap attempt to dig into her panties. But that wasn't the way with Bruce. His touch was sincere, warming. Hell, she wished he was sleazing on her, and then she'd know for sure not to worry about the kid.

"If I don't find him I'm in big trouble," she said.

"I'll say a prayer, Eggy. You can pray with me, if you like. But, of course, you should feel no obligation to. I'm not one of those God pushers." Bruce began to bow his head, but a preteen kid in a football jersey kicked Bruce's shoe and demanded to know why the shit the line wasn't moving.

The image of Bruce stashing a kid inside his inflatable melted away. A woozy nightmare replaced it—the peaks of the Blue Ridges through Mason's windshield. He'd drive as fast as the Jeep would go, the boy bouncing in the passenger seat. Her best bet now was to slink back to the parents, head bowed low, and hope to hell the kid had found his way back on his own. But as soon as she neared, she knew no lucky reunion was happening. Two black uniforms stood in front of the parents, their backs to Eggy. They were cops. Fuck and double fuck.

"Any luck on your end?" she said, touching the mother's back from behind. The muscle in her shoulder shriveled under Eggy's touch.

Such a Good Man

One of the cops, a woman wearing a ponytail so tight it raised her eyebrows into a permanently surprised expression, turned to Eggy. "You the one in charge?"

"I work here."

"This ride?"

"It's more of an experience," Eggy explained. "I mean, they bounce in it."

"We all know how a bouncy house works," the other cop said. He had dopey eyes, a half-opened mouth. The heel of his hand rested on his pistol.

"I haven't found him yet," Eggy said. "But I will."

"Where did you see him last?" the ponytail cop asked, and she realized now her memory hadn't retained the kid at all. A blurry face on a rectangular screen. Could've been anyone.

"Before all this," Eggy said, because lying to cops was always easier than admitting you didn't know. "I guess a few minutes before all this."

"Can you be more exact?" the cop said, and the dad's face was pale, frozen. The mom looked like she might gouge an eye out.

"About what?"

"Don't mess with us, ma'am," the cop with the dopey eyes said and kept his hand on the gun. "No good ever comes of that. Just tell us all you know."

Here was another man expecting her to know the whereabouts of every child. The impossible pressure stoked that old fear, like when she had a dozen grams of Mason's junk bunched into her underwear, sweaty between her butt cheeks.

━

The last time she saw Mason, two days ago, he was fresh out of prison. He wore only silvery track pants, shirtless, yelling to her second-story window from the lawn at 3 a.m. "We need to make this right," Mason was saying. "Let's make another one!"

She was living in her kid bedroom at her momma's house. She stuck her head out the window and tried to shush him, but he was too stoned.

"Let me up."

"Go home, Mason, baby," she said. "You don't feel like it, but you need sleep."

"You're not too old, if that's what you're worried about. I read a thing, said the over-forty age group is popping babies more than ever." He was still yelling, though he looked calmer. She remembered being so high you couldn't tell you were yelling. No control. She never wanted to feel like that again, now that she was cleaned up for the fifth and final time. And, also, she only wanted to feel that no-control frenzy again. She wanted it more than anything in the world. Maybe except for seeing her baby who was not a baby anymore, who Mason got to see for a moment that cost him ten years. Ten years he'd just repaid.

"Let's talk about it tomorrow," she said.

"Let's talk about it now."

"Momma's sleeping. She's old, Mason. She needs her sleep. Please."

"Don't you love me more than Jupiter's big? More than the sun's burning?"

"No, Mason." If she kept saying his name, it seemed like maybe it'd calm him.

"Well, fuck you, bitch."

"You'll be okay, Mason."

He reached down and then heaved a clump of dirt that thumped against the siding.

"We are too old, Mason. And we're too screwed up. This is stupid."

"I told you we're not too old!" Mason would never grow up, would never stop thinking he'd live forever. Why did he need a child when he'd always be one? He threw another clump. She could hear Momma rustling downstairs. Eggy hated him for wasting so much of her time. And probably she would've wasted it without needing him. A paperweight was in her hand, big as a baseball and made of glass, the one with the purple crocus trapped inside forever fully blooming. Her arm pitched it and the glass orb smacked Mason in the thigh. He went down howling.

"Eggy?" the floor said, the muffle of her mother beneath it. "What—"

Such a Good Man

She couldn't catch the rest because Mason was limping toward the little crab apple tree. He pulled at a low-hanging branch.

"Just go home," she hissed.

"I'm gonna yank this tree down and beat you through the window with it." He tugged and the tree swished, but the branch's grip was stronger than anything Mason had to offer. He gave up, threw his fists in the air toward her. "New plan. I don't need your ugly old ass and I don't need your meth babies. I'm gonna go get my own. Go steal a big healthy one."

"Good luck."

He got to the end of the yard, an overgrown wall of kudzu, and turned around. "Come with me, Eggy girl. Come steal a kid with me and we'll teach it everything and we'll drive to the mountains and I'll grow a beard and you can get fat and we'll teach that baby to live off the land."

"You gotta let me be done with you."

"I don't gotta do shit." He kickboxed the air with his shiny pants. "You'll see. And when you see how happy I become, it'll hurt so bad."

~

"You're not going to run, are you?" the cop with the strangling ponytail said.

"That'd be pretty stupid," the dopey one said, and shifted in a way that made more of him seem to be touching his gun.

"She knows." The mom was yelling, pointing at her. "She most certainly knows where he is."

"Do you?"

"Do you?" they were saying.

If it was Mason, he'd want her to join him in the mountains so she could get ruined again. If it was Bruce, that meant no one ever got fixed for good. Both were the worst scenario. It seemed she didn't know anything for sure anymore.

It probably would've been impossible not to run, she admitted to herself as she started running. The cops could easily find out where she lived, find out about her priors, about Mason. She heard the two cops mutter curses, and they'd have to be fast to catch her smashing through the

34 Such a Good Man

snaking shaved-ice line, behind the Big Rapids Bubble Slide, a hop over the generator, where she'd lose them behind Johan's trailer. Then she was sprinting even harder than when Mason had first taught her to shoot into her veins and she'd spent the night running through a field of wildflowers by moonlight that—when she woke up stinking, her bare legs sliced redly raw—she'd realized was a landfill. She had no other choice but Bruce. If it was her or Bruce, then it was Bruce. If it was her or Mason, Mason. No man was worth risking being clean and free. Clean and free felt like air-conditioning, sixty-eight degrees on a South Carolina August day. It felt like funnel cake on an empty stomach, fresh out of the fryer and warm and soft and the sugar light as a ghost. It felt like bouncing and bouncing and no adult to ever demand you stop.

She dashed toward Bruce's inflatable gorilla, risked a look over her shoulder, and saw that the cops weren't tailing anymore. She slowed into the crowd and the heat and let that massive, bobbing gorilla visage pull her like a magnet.

When she reached the Gorilla Punch-Out, Bruce was MIA again and the kids had unleashed anarchy like bullets fired in a bank vault. They ricocheted off the walls, off each other, heads clunking together, blood spattering the bouncy floor and dripping from noses.

The only sign of Bruce was a note taped to the entrance that read, "Attraction temporarily closed. So *so so* sorry. Recovering a missing child. Be back in five!"

She scanned the crowd for Bruce, for the cops, for, perhaps, Mason in a slinky tracksuit carrying an assault rifle under one arm, a kidnapped boy under the other. What she did see was Sharice, still screaming at the prepubescents, but in between her ravings, Eggy locked eyes with her. She pointed a bony finger toward the Jungle Bungle maze and mouthed, *I told you so.*

At her back, the cop with the ponytail screeched her name, her full one, the one Johan must've told her because she never used it and hated the name her deadbeat dad had demanded: Adrina Eugenia Sinclair. But if they were hollering her name into the South Carolina heat fumes, they

Such a Good Man

were still searching, just like her. She still had time to fix this all. She entered the maze.

Inside, the sun was nearly set and the inflated walls decorated in camouflage looked real in the shadows, reminding her of her momma's backyard, how the kudzu eventually swallowed the turtle-shaped sandbox she'd used as a child. In the decade Mason had been in prison, she'd imagined her son flinging sand inside that turtle, if he were ever to visit, which he never would.

Teens loitered in the Jungle Bungle maze, making out and groping in the dead-end corners. She came upon one couple, his hand all the way down her unbuttoned jeans. The girl and Eggy met eyes for a moment, and the girl didn't slow the boy's grinding dry humps. Eggy wished she could explain who would be left responsible for every decision after they zipped their jeans back up, about how this boy would surely disappear and then bounce back only when least convenient. But Eggy was too busy, and the girl wouldn't listen. If some old bouncy-house worker had preached at her when Eggy was a teen, she would've spit in her face.

She wanted to call for the missing kid, but she still couldn't remember his name. Her son—she'd never learned his legal name. She'd hoped to find out in court. Things she also didn't know: the color of his eyes or his hair, if he ever sucked his thumb, whether he was afraid of the dark, if he liked cookies or cake or had preferred Grover to Elmo, if he hated playing outfield, if he'd started liking girls yet, if he'd found out he was adopted, if he imagined her. She often found herself playing the game of all she didn't know about the person she'd made who was living out there in the wild world.

"Adrina Sinclair," bellowed from outside, through the din of the crowd's white noise just beyond the inflated walls. They could be in the maze any minute. She risked calling: "Bruce, you in here?" She held her breath. Waited. The throbbing in her feet inched up her limbs and into her skull, and it seemed nothing could stay quiet for long, even her own body.

"Over here, darling," Bruce said, and she hurried toward the voice. She found him around a corner, dead-ended like the teenagers, kneeling. On

36 Such a Good Man

his knee—a blond boy, young, the right age for missing. His face was puffy, but he was silent. His hair was mussed. The top two buttons of his orange Clemson Tigers shirt were undone. Bruce smiled neatly. One Velcro strip of the kid's shoes was undone.

"Isn't it a miracle, Eggy? Aren't we so lucky?" Bruce said, bouncing the kid on his knee. "He's okay, see. He's safe."

She wanted to ask him questions, but every inquiry that surfaced seemed barbed with accusation. And what good would that do? Here was what she needed, the missing kid that would absolve her and keep her clean and free, so she walked over to Bruce and took the kid's wrist. It was thin, bony, the compulsory fitness of one of those kids probably forced onto an organic vegan diet. A kid deserved to eat ambiguous meat on a stick now and then, battered and fried, smothered in mustard. A kid deserved a face caked in powdered sugar and cotton candy. Eggy could've at least given her boy that.

She walked the kid out through the maze, where her instincts told her the exit might be, away from Bruce, who was machine-gunning his desperate hope at her back: "I mean, first place I looked. I just said a prayer and strutted in here, and there he was. What a blessing. Isn't that a blessing, Eggy? Praise God. The kid was here all along."

Onward, around another bend and another, the kid's face seemed frozen, jaw set tight. She picked him up, and he latched his little legs around her hips mechanically. Bruce still huffed behind them, explaining, bargaining, maybe turning her into an accomplice again. Or maybe he was indeed the blessed hero. Maybe. Maybe. Maybe the next turn would relieve her from the maze, but she met another dead end, another teenage couple groping and fingers too fast for their own good. She spun around to retrace her path, and there was Bruce tugging his eyebrow. "You believe me, right, Eggy? You believe me—that I'm a nice guy, that I love kids, that I'd never hurt them. I know the rumors, Eggy. I know what they say, and they're wrong."

She pushed past him, butting his shoulder harder than she intended, but he'd been taking up the whole path, the only way out. The kid made a throaty grumble at her hip. Sunset was upon them and had dimmed the maze into an orange glow so dull it was almost shadow. Everything seemed to swim. Bruce spoke from behind her: "It's not true. All of those sins are so far behind me and I'm such a good man now. I am, Eggy. I'm nothing but love now."

Faintly, she heard her name beckoning her from somewhere outside the walls. Those walls were just air, after all, just the same air filling the breathless South Carolina nights, the same air inhaled by the blower pump fans and forced through the vinyl walls. In the center was nothing but air. But you couldn't punch through it. That was the genius of the inflatables: such a soft landing, the impression of a cloud, but far too strong for anyone to break by force alone. All she needed was something sharp and she could tear through that vinyl film. If she could find something sharp, she could slash her way to free and clean and emerge the hero. Her pockets were empty, and a missing boy clung to her hips, and she held him back, one arm supporting his weight, her other palm stroking his back. She'd have to try a few more corners. A few more. More. Another. Until she'd reached the last one.

$\approx$

"Difference between us, Eggy," Mason hissed over the phone, an airplane engine rumbling behind his words, "is I got to see him and you didn't. You never will, and I did, if only for a moment. I got to see him and smell him and touch him and hold him, and you didn't, Eggy. You never ever will. He had your long, goosey neck. He has my thick knuckles. Smells like neither of us. Never laughed once, but he knew who I was. He could tell who was who. He knew, and I knew, but you never will."

ESSENTIALS

Big dude walks under the electric eye and through the Bi-Lo sliders. His face is naked, save for a brown goatee dangling like unkempt pubic hair. He wears one of those Don't Tread on Me T-shirts, that angry snake lunging. Its fangs might as well be clamping onto our genitals. We all keep scanning barcodes, that music of beeps that makes us feel like we're getting somewhere, like if we scan stock fast enough, we'll get out of here sooner. Every shift seems like a sprint now. Scan it and bag it and on to the next one before any customer has a chance to make small talk, to spit virus all over us.

Mr. Don't Tread on Me Goatee starts with a cart, but then sees the baskets and ditches his cart. He strands it right in the middle of the aisle where one of us will have to touch it. No way Mr. Goatee washes for twenty seconds. We'll make Nina put away his cart. She's a baby, seventeen, younger than any of us by decades. Babies don't die of this shit, they say. Whereas Robin on checkout seven is fucked, fifty-seven and diabetic and fat-assed. Whereas Maribeth working cigarettes and lotto is fucked, with her IBS and celiac and asthma and always going home early for migraines. Whereas Roy, the only man among us, who chain-smokes two cigarettes every break and survived some kind of cancer and is seventy-five and should be retired but claims he likes the company of us ladies too much—whereas Roy better stay the hell back in stock, throwing trucks and counting boxes until that destined day they find a vaccine. Even then,

Essentials

39

better stay a bit longer. Don't come out too soon, Roy. A heart attack alone in there is better than facing Mr. Goatee out here.

It's busy time at our Bi-Lo, three o'clock, and the heat from our Carolina summer huffs in like a heavy breath with each new customer. Mr. Goatee manages to clear the produce section with his circling. He gropes a cantaloupe, doesn't buy it. A geriatric with a white perm backs her cart away. He swoops his finger over the crescent of a banana, doesn't buy that either. He samples a grape, pops a second, tosses a third in the air and tries to catch it with his mouth but misses, then kicks it under the watermelon pallet. After all that, nothing goes in his basket, which he swings as he disappears behind an endcap.

Maribeth is filling in on the self-checkout station, but she keeps her distance, shouts directions to a customer on how to punch in an avocado's PLU. The customer—a woman in a homemade floral-print mask so big it looks like it's eating her face—just marvels at the avocado as if she can't imagine how it materialized in her cart, on this planet, as if it might be some green alien turd magicked into her hand. Maribeth is going to have to get closer than six feet. At least we got the plexiglass at our POS stations. They speckle with saliva that sparkles in the fluorescent lights. Each sparkle like a bullet. We never realized how much spit we absorbed each shift, our customers' tongues flicking sickness.

Mr. Goatee struts through the cereal aisle now. He studies Cap'n Crunch's nutritional facts, compares to a box of marshmallow-infused Froot Loops. That toucan's humanoid hands have always freaked us out. Once you notice you can't stop looking. Death-doomed Roy says it's based on Greek mythology. Sugar-betes Robin says Kellogg is just trying to mess with us.

While Mr. Goatee is reshelving the Froot Loops, he sneeze-shouts so loud everyone in the store turns. Customers in other aisles bury their noses in their shirts. Another customer in the cereal aisle U-turns their cart and clangs it into a stack of Cheerios boxes that go tumbling.

"Allergies. It's just allergies," he bellows at the retreating customer's squeaking cart.

40 Essentials

He struts to the endcap and gazes up at the aisle signs. "No one can find nothing they need in this store." But there's no one left to hear him. Only us. And Stanley, who watches from the security camera. Stanley bursts through the Employees Only door wearing his satin red necktie that absolutely no one ever asked him to wear. He got promoted to assistant manager three months ago, just after Christmas, before all this started, and now the other managers are dumping every shift on him they can. Stanley's necktie seems to grow longer every day—down to his thighs now—with every additional added shift that he misinterprets as self-importance.

But no one appreciates the tie. All we care about is whether you wear a mask. Stanley's pink nose dangles over the top of his mask.

"This man needs our help," Stanley says over our rows of beeping registers, chugging belts. We don't look up. Mr. Don't Tread on Me Goatee is staring into the red depths of marinara sauces now.

"Can't y'all hear me? This stupid thing." He wrestles the mask off his ears and nears Maribeth. She dodges past him and behind the safety of her cigarette counter. "Is customer service dead? Are we not the heroes of the pandemic? Someone help him, for Christ's sake."

But we all have checkout lines at least four customers deep. The store can't hold staff—eleven of us quit in the last month, and the news anchors on our car radios won't quit tallying deaths, up past one hundred thousand now. Maribeth's next to quit, we bet. She doesn't seem long for the torture of Stanley's spittle showers spurred by his bloated pride.

"Really, no one will help in our country's greatest time of need," he says. "Then I guess it'll be me who steps up." He lowers the mask back over just his mouth, nose still dangling and redder than ever. He strides toward Mr. Goatee, who's poking his finger into Doritos bags.

Stanley's speech in front of us, in front of the customers, probably grew him a partial chubby under that massive necktie of his. But last week Stanley hardly believed we were heroes. He was convinced of a hoax perpetuated by the liberal medical industry. Instead of watching the mandated corporate HR video on safety measures, he made us watch that

Essentials 41

Plandemic documentary on YouTube. When the video got pulled off the site, he paced our checkout lines, panting, *See! See! There's your proof! They don't want the truth out. We gotta shed these masks of fear, and take back our microbial flora!*

Stanley saunters down the chips aisle and tries to catch up with Mr. Goatee looping into toiletries. Soon, Mr. Don't Tread on Me and *Plandemic* Stanley will converge midaisle in an eruption of hidden truths and unfettered American patriotism. The whole store will glow, the lights surging, the freezer aisle puffing out chilled fog. We'll waste our time weighing potatoes and scanning EBT cards while these men fight for freedom.

But Stanley halts a few feet behind Mr. Goatee, who's dipping to peer into an empty bottom shelf in the baby aisle, and he must be flashing Stanley some horrifying ass crack, because Stanley retreats, speed-walking back around through the chips aisle to us.

"He's got a gun," Stanley whispers, in each of our ears, one by one, our faces warming to the heat of his breath, his exposed nose whistling.

Other times, a gun wouldn't've been a big deal. We know guns. Our state is mostly fine with concealed carry. Our townie boys love their guns, decorate their truck windows in rifle racks, fly their rebel stars-and-bars flags stamped with AR-15 graphics from their truck beds. They're good for a laugh, those boys screaming for attention with their rust buckets sporting extra-loud mufflers. But our amusement has changed lately. Just last week, we had six customers threaten to shoot us for wearing masks, calling us un-American sheeples. One asked to face our manager "man-to-pussy," and we sent them to Stanley, of course. He told the customer he sympathized, really, was on the side of the Second Amendment, though yoked under corporate tyranny. They understood, right? Jobs at stake and all? But these men leaned in, yanking his tie, snarling, threatening, before they took their business to Walmart and Amazon.

Good riddance, we say. Fewer customers is just fine for us. But Stanley has lost his nerve when it comes to men and their guns. He's taking a brief break on Second Amendment enthusiasm.

Mr. Goatee heads our way now, toward our cash wraps, his basket empty, coiled snake springing across that bright yellow shirt. Stanley says he should go warn Roy and bails for the back. And poor, dear Maribeth and her irritable bowels become this man's target. He marches toward her, smiling too brightly, handgun knuckling gently against his spine. We know how this will go. We've become the receptacles for your pent-up frustration, your deferred desire to hoist bench weight and ogle women in spandex at the gym, to have your beard trimmed properly, to drink a goddamn beer at the goddamn bar while the Braves blow a lineup of young talent to a weak-armed pitching rotation. We know, we know, and we long for all that too. But we're behind the conveyor belt, behind the register, behind the plexiglass, and you are out there, and corporate says we can't bring our guns to work, no matter what you threaten. At least there's the plexiglass. At least we can keep you warded off with the dappled accumulation of ten hours of customer spittle to meet your glowering.

Maribeth tries to look busy, staring at her screen while Mr. Goatee stares at her and we stare at them, and you, standing in line with your cart full of canned beans and bleach, you notice we rang up the mac and cheese twice, but you don't want to say anything, because you, too, are enthralled by this confrontation. You overheard Stanley and his terror, and we're all waiting for the sign that it's time to switch to full panic. How long can this half-cocked precautionary fervor last? The dam has cracked, and here he comes, reaching behind his back and still smiling.

Mr. Goatee pulls from the waistline of his jeans a fold of white paper. "Excuse me, ma'am," he says to poor ruined Maribeth, who finally must look up. "Can you tell me you got any of this?"

She punches the products into her computer, but she knows. We know. There's no toilet paper. There's no beef. And we've been out of formula for the week.

"When, do you think?" He tries to hold his naked smile. We wait for the gun. We study his waistband, but only the holes in his underwear show.

"I don't know," Maribeth says.

Essentials

43

"No one knows, it seems like. No one knows anything," he says. "I mean, for now, ma'am."

Maribeth touches the folded white paper, slides it across her counter. "Here's what I'll do," Maribeth says. "Soon as it's in, I'll call you. Now, what's your name and your number?"

We got kids too. We got kids or why the fuck else would we still be here while everyone else has been home making the fattest unemployment anyone has ever seen? We fed them from bottles and fed them from our bodies, and we loved them while they slept so soundly and hated how they never let us sleep. And can you imagine it now, you, with your cart full, stocking up bravely, even though you hated to have to come out of your home, though you were also dying to come out into the world again? You, can you imagine a new baby right now?

Maybe they sleep better, these pandemic babies, their parents home with them but scrolling infinitely through their phones, that blue glow their night-light, soft as moon glinting off their parents' knotted faces.

So, let Maribeth call you when this is over, Mr. Goatee, Mr. Formula-hunting Father, when we're ready, when we have what you need, a real reason to reenter the world. Until then, we'll be here punching in, counting the float, thinking of you and your babies at home, safe and hungry and scared as us.

TOO BAD FOR MARCEL RONK

A man is taking out the garbage in the dark, crunching snow underfoot. He clutches an open bag and attempts to study its innards. He has dark gray hair and a daughter, who, three months ago, grew up just enough to leave him alone with his wife. Empty nesters, his friends keep telling him. His wife dyes her hair brown like woven branches, highlights red sections like little surprises of fire. But this man, this one taking out the garbage, this one named Marcel Ronk, doesn't like surprises. He doesn't like fire surprises in his wife's hair dyed brown as a nest. He can't remember her natural color and wonders if it would be as gray as his if she didn't dye it. We know the answer is that her hair would be pale yellow, sun-bleached wheat, gray strands straggling here and there. Her hair would still hold surprises waiting to haunt her husband—gray ghosts instead of red fire.

Marcel Ronk chose not to tie up the garbage bag. Marcel Ronk left it loose so he might spy a secret discard: used condom, new shade of lipstick, hotel receipt, blood-flaked razor blade. He tries to look, but can't look. Marcel Ronk hates surprise. It is *their* garbage after all, but nothing has been simply theirs since his daughter left three months ago. And three years ago, they'd sworn to separate once she was gone. They'd decided to wait until they wouldn't disrupt her life with the consequences of Marcel Ronk's affair with the waitress. We know Marcel's secret, that the affair had meant so little to Marcel Ronk, like tripping over a crack in the sidewalk. Stupid, clumsy, careless. Yet he'd told his wife that it made him feel human, like he had skin and teeth and breathed air for the first time in so many years. We know he lied to his wife, lied because it was easier than explaining the pointless shape of an accident.

They produce only one bag of trash per week between them now that their daughter has left. Not much garbage for a two-bedroom house with sixteen windows and burgundy shutters and a half-acre corner lot. We want Marcel to reach inside his own garbage, plunge his wrist deep into banana peels and tissue wads. Our eyes can't penetrate the thick black plastic, and we need to know. We want full omniscience so badly our phantom fingers curl. We ache to cross them. Since this is impossible, we cross dozens of fingers owned by sleeping infants in Ohio. In the morning, Ohioan parents will lean over cribs and shudder. No longer will they admire tiny fingernails. Instead, dozens of Ohioan parents will marvel at the spontaneous superstition of their babies, and they will be frightened.

We are frightened. Marcel Ronk is frightened. Anything could be inside those garbage bags. All of Ohio must share our fear.

Marcel Ronk fights off curiosity, hurls the bag into his green trash can, slams the lid. He clings to threadbare trust. He loves his wife, Cynthia Ronk, even if he doesn't know her all that well anymore and is terrified of surprises.

She is upstairs now, in her bedroom, with another man. They've been there for over an hour, since the other man knocked on their door, shook Marcel's hand, and then Cynthia tugged his forearm upstairs. The other man is up there now showing her how easy their life could be, how easily these vacuums clean floors and then rose-colored drapes with a quick click of a simple plastic attachment. The attachment is shaped like a T. The other man's name begins with a _T_. Ted, Teddy, Theodore, Theo. Years ago, the other man elected to call himself Theo. In seventh grade, he got kicked in the ribs while twelve-year-olds chanted "Teddy" above the grass dappled with his blood. As Theodore, he was told he seemed overqualified when interviewing for a garbage-collector position; the employer just couldn't imagine his trash being gathered by a Theodore. Theo's father's name was Ted and TED was stamped into the leather of that belt with the painful gold buckle. Theo it is.

Theo finishes sucking the right side of the south window's drapes. He proffers the T-shaped attachment to Cynthia Ronk, smiles, extends it nearer to her slender wrists and the blue-green lace of her veins. Cynthia shakes her head, taps her chin, bites her lower lip. Theo does not understand this secret sign language. Neither do we. Neither does Marcel Ronk, who stands beside the trash can outside, kicking ice chunks off the trash can's wheels. His breath plumes white and thick against the Ohio winter's black-sky evening.

Theo's breath is invisible in the warmth of the Ronk bedroom. He wishes he hadn't gone upstairs with Cynthia, wishes his demonstration never included bedrooms while spouses waited downstairs. But here he is with a client in their bedroom, sucking drapes. Sometimes they try out the T-attachment for themselves. Sometimes they take off their clothes or take off his or put their lips around his penis. They are men and women. They are sometimes attractive, but mostly plain, forgettable faces on soft bodies. Cynthia is striking, like an actress in a black-and-white film. But real life is in color, and striking is not the same as attractive. Theo hopes her mysterious chin taps do not equal sexual invitations. Theo is bad at saying no. No one waits for Theo in his studio apartment where his kitchen and bed occupy the same room. He has only this job, his commissions, and a karaoke bar downtown where he croons the wrong words to Frank Sinatra songs when he is very drunk. His first time singing, a stranger with white teeth and yellow eyes told him he had a divine voice. No one has said that again in 124 stumbling karaoke performances.

We know Theo's voice is lovely. He sings from his diaphragm, from deep inside his stomach. He was born with genetically inherited, splendid vocal cords. His grandmother sang in a touring barbershop group in the 1930s. She flattened her breasts with medical gauze, glued a black mustache to her lip to sneak into the all-male group called Barry's Tones, named after their founding member Barry Hackney. She was their only soprano. Barry secretly loved her as a man. All the other members secretly loved her, too, though they knew she was really a woman. The skewed mustache and taped breasts fooled only Barry. Too bad for Barry, who spent the rest of his life buying blue anti-homosexuality pills from his quack doctor. He eventually volunteered for electroshock therapy and then chemical castration. Too bad for Theo, who never says no and only wants to sell a vacuum and then get very drunk at his karaoke bar.

Too bad for Marcel Ronk, who breathes another thick cloud at the lighted window of his wife's bedroom. He abandons the garbage and its mysteries and trudges back to their front door. He slips on a slick patch of his lawn. His tailbone smacks against the frozen ground and venom sprints up his spine. He is afraid to touch his back, so his fingers fumble through the snow and find the slick. He thumbs something that feels like ice but is actually a magazine buried just under the snow. Marcel Ronk's fingers grip the pages, unearth the magazine. It is a twenty-year-old issue of *Topper*. Inside, he finds nude women with large breasts, backs arched, lips parted, permed hair. They are young women, all of them, much closer to his daughter's age than his wife Cynthia Ronk's age. Coincidentally, the women in the pages are now much closer to his wife's age in real life, but Marcel does not know the magazine's age, didn't check the publication date, only witnesses the pictures. Marcel Ronk flips through a few pages, still lying on his side in the snow, in the dark. On page sixty-seven, he finds a woman with auburn hair. Auburn is not the right way to describe this. Her hair is as red as the terrifying streaks in his wife's hair. The model's body melts off a purple love seat, her head lolling as if her neck is broken. Her eyes are half-closed, mouth half-open. Still lying in the snow, he reaches for his crotch. His crotch feels the same as always. Nothing hard. He feels relieved, as this beautiful, melting woman is also the approximate age of his daughter, looks like his daughter. He closes the magazine, rests it atop his chest. His fingers pet the ripples of the waterlogged cover.

Marcel Ronk is relieved, but we are hypnotized by the magazine and its provenance. Three nights ago, three boys walked down this street clutching glossy pages. It was late, and the boys squinted to see naked flesh. Each streetlight they passed worked like fingers unbuttoning undergarments of night. They slowed their pace under the lights, hustled between lampposts. The shortest boy had stolen the magazine from his father, slipped it down the front of his pants where it pressed against his penis. He'd heard from his older brother about STDs, and now that the magazine had touched him without a condom he imagined his penis gnarling, spitting pus, eventually erupting into something that resembled cauliflower. The tallest boy had waited outside the short boy's house, stood as lookout like a tower, but he only stared at his feet every time a car passed. The middle-height boy didn't care about their efforts. He clenched the pages, let the others look over his shoulder. His eyes hunted nipples, creases of skin between legs, secrets.

Bright lights had flashed across a red-headed woman sprawled atop a purple chair. The shortest boy craned his neck and hissed, "Headlights." The tallest imagined handcuffs and metal bars and his mother's tears. He ripped the magazine from his friend, chucked it into a yard and ran. They all ran. The shortest boy felt the coolness of winter soothing his gangrenous genitals. His not-quite-manhood would not turn into cauliflower. The tallest wouldn't go to jail. They would be boys again tomorrow. Except for the middle-height boy. Tomorrow, he would die in a car accident. We thank any singular or all plural gods who watch over us for allowing him to find nipples and skin creases and secrets on the eve of his death. We are grateful for this mercy, grateful the other boys let him hold *Topper*.

Theo, vacuum seller, clicks the T-attachment back into its holster, demonstration complete. He wonders what comes next—a sale or sex. Meanwhile, outside, eighteen feet down and fifty-two degrees colder, Marcel aches on his sidewalk, stares up at the bedroom, wishes the blinds weren't open so he couldn't see the vacuum seller's stern jaw, his broad shoulders, yet no sign of his wife who could be on her knees fellating or draped over their bed, skirt hiked. *Topper* protrudes from his pullover's pocket. Marcel Ronk crawls to his fence, struggles to a leaning stand,

Too Bad for Marcel Ronk

49

peers through the slats. Seeing only scraps of a secret is the worst torture. We can attest to the heartache of missing jigsaw-puzzle pieces. We admit we don't know enough about Cynthia. We know that no one knows enough.

Marcel creeps into a shadow against the house, puts his ear to the cold aluminum siding. He listens. He cannot hear a vacuum groaning, or his wife moaning, and he wouldn't anyway since they are upstairs. He does hear water churning through the pipes, a load of dishes in the machine. They have just hit the rinse cycle. Hot water rushes through his walls, in between his side of the wall and his wife's side. Marcel Ronk's ear turns cold and red against the siding, but as hard as he presses he won't hear Theo's quickening pulse as Cynthia pats the mattress beside her, as she beckons him to sit. He's done this before, so he shouldn't be surprised. His heart shouldn't pulse. His penis shouldn't press against his thigh as she touches his cheek, his ear, and then she withdraws her blue-green-laced wrist to the mattress. She asks him how many vacuums he must sell this month, how many this year, how many until he can relax. Theo tells her there is no quota, only commission. Sales initiatives are set so the sky's the limit, but even failure won't sink him.

Cynthia says she understands quota versus commission, failure that equates to stasis. Theo smiles, is genuinely pleased, even if he's not sure what she really understands. He doesn't understand how he'll ever be done flourishing the disgustingly clogged dust filter after cleaning a bedroom's drapes. And even when he shows them what's inside the filter—the dust mites and pet hairs and skin particles and insect limbs and allergens—they're so rarely inspired. Everyone's drapes are filthy. No one takes the time to really clean, to scour and search and love one another as they would like to be loved, like his father said they all must always do just before he slipped off the belt branded TED with the painful gold buckle.

But we understand that Cynthia truly understands. She tells Theo to wait on the bed, and she exits the room. While he waits he unbuttons his shirt. He folds his pants at the seam so as to preserve the pleat, leans them over a purple chair. He contemplates his boxer shorts, his black socks, decides to leave them on for now. Downstairs, Cynthia brews coffee for Theo and for Marcel, who must be cold after twelve minutes outside. She gets out her checkbook and scribbles a number high enough for four vacuums. She tears up that check and writes another one for five vacuums. We know how pleased Theo would be that he had to do so little, just his actual job, to earn such a commission. He would find enough joy to sing the actual words on the karaoke screen. He would if he didn't feel such a sting when Cynthia remerged into the room to find him mostly disrobed and half-erect beneath his boxers. She finds Theo beautiful. Her cheeks burn red. She wants to slap this stupid man for assuming sex to be like an accident they could stumble into, like strangers on an ice rink, both falling and flailing against gravity until mutual collapse. Accident is excuse. She wants intent. So that's what she wants.

Cynthia sends him out into the night with a check crumpled in his pants pocket next to his unzipped fly. The sting will wear off in the Ohio winter. Marcel Ronk leans into shadow, watches Theo depart. Marcel studies the flash of white underwear through Theo's fly. So this is payback and now they can get on with quiet lives in separate rooms, and Marcel will never say how truly sorry he is for an affair he is apathetic about, and Cynthia will never say what she didn't do with the other man. She won't say it so much that it will burn Marcel Ronk to ashes.

THE MAN WITH THE YELLOW HAT

The man with the yellow hat dragged his monkey out onto the balcony and locked it inside the wire-walled kennel. He'd reached desperation. The monkey he'd named George had finally followed his curiosity to disaster. The monkey had nearly killed a man. From behind the sliding glass door, he studied the monkey's stillness, wondered what terrifying curiosity it could be conjuring now: a swing from the power lines, steak knives chucked from their sixth-floor apartment.

Cool fingers trailed up the back of his neck, bumping down his hat brim. "Don't you think he's learned his lesson?" the scientist, his girlfriend, whispered into his ear. She joined him at the glass door.

The man clenched the syringe in his pocket. After two years of fostering, the man had become certain that the monkey he'd named George couldn't be trained. The scientist imagined the man kinder, so much more patient. But there was a frailty he hid just as carefully as his balding scalp under the hat. His patience, his compassion for defenseless animals, was rubbed threadbare. So, he carried a fatal needle for the monkey, the quick solution, finally. She was wrong about him. Everyone was wrong.

Before, when he'd taken George on city walks and women followed him on the sidewalk to inquire, the man took pride in claiming he'd adopted a good little monkey who was always just a tad curious. In front of adoring crowds cheering for the monkey's bravery and wit, the man could

52 The Man with the Yellow Hat

fake it and mask his anxiety, just as the victims of George's hijinks replaced their ruddy-faced scowls with forgiveness. The crowd's approval, that pro-simian mob mentality, cooled their ire. George's big, glassy brown eyes and dopey frown won them over. But they never lasted, those resolutions thinner than children's paperback books. He currently had seven small-claims cases going, court dates set with the chocolate factory, the toy store, and the movie theater next month alone.

The man would soon be financially smothered. Thank Christ the zoo allowed him and the monkey to work off damages by volunteering every Saturday to let kids shake the monkey's hand and scratch his ears. In this way, the monkey had eviscerated his weekends, and the man tried his damnedest to hide his disdain while the monkey hooted and danced for the kids. Yeah, sure, everyone thought it was cute when the monkey swung from toy store rafters, doled out ice cream to the kids, or flipped pancakes at the town picnic, so long as the man was around to pay for the damages.

But yesterday, the monkey had almost killed a man, the window washer with three broken ribs and a fractured pelvis. "Acrobatic ape assault," one of the papers alliterated. Another claimed a "monkey menace" and blamed the owner for a "reckless attempt at domestication." Wild is wild and will always be, they chanted in the man's head.

"Take a bit longer, if you need," the scientist said, "but not so long that you miss me." She stepped into the next room to clack at her laptop, filling it with brilliantly undecipherable jargon. Alone, the man peeled off his yellow hat and scratched his scalp underneath. He'd lost most of his hair on his crown, a combination of cruel genetics and stress and the fleas the monkey kept bringing home. He knew the wide-brimmed safari hat was ridiculous, but it shielded him, and once he leaned into the clothes, he couldn't stop; the all-yellow outfits made him mysterious, taller, a memorable character no one could forget, rather than a middle-aged, balding man. The yellow camouflaged him in personality.

He opened the sliding glass door to the balcony and stared down at the kennel where he'd sequestered the monkey. By now, the monkey would usually be sleeping in the child's bed with the polished brass frame the man had bought just for George. The monkey clutched the kennel's wires and stared out at the city, ignoring the man. He checked the water, still full, the bananas' skins, still unbothered. The only change was the turds piled just outside the kennel. The monkey had managed to defecate onto the balcony boards. This seemed to be his one quiet protest.

Each skyscraper outside his balcony reflected a sunset on fire. It was the man's favorite time of the day. All that color of the sunset was just pollutants, poor air quality, a tricky concoction of carbon monoxide and methane and various carbons—that's what his girlfriend the scientist had told him. She had a way of rationalizing beauty that was supposed to flatten the emotional edges but instead had the effect, for the man, of making him more appreciative of such beautiful accidents. Though she was not a fan of sunsets or the man's yellow hat, she'd always liked the monkey. She'd been the one to suggest naming him George instead of Bobo or Kiki.

He hadn't visited her apartment in months. Ending this silly monkey thing would mean more nights with her, more nights removing each other's clothing by candlelight, surrounded by her moon rocks and massive amber Atlas moths pinned to their wall mounts and incapable of causing curiosity-driven property damage.

He sat on the lounger next to the cage and tapped the syringe in his pocket. A main artery would be best, the vet—that ex-lover he'd turned to for advice last night—had told him, but she gave him enough so that he could jab anywhere. He had imagined a violent neck stabbing last night, but now the monkey's eyes glistened and he cooed at the evening view. Goddamn it. Goddamn that beautiful monkey.

It turned toward him then, as if about to speak, as if to apologize, gazing with those big dark eyes. What could the man do but open the kennel hatch? The monkey he'd named George climbed onto the chair's footrest and sat hunching just as a child might. He was an adolescent chimp, runty, twenty-six pounds, the size of a toddler. When they were in college, he and the vet had tried so hard to prevent babies—a trifecta of

54   The Man with the Yellow Hat

spermicides, condoms, pills. Now he and the scientist were trying for a
baby, but it had been years. He often joked about how old he was, pointed
to his thinning scalp that he never let her touch, safely stowed under
the hat that was the last article of clothing he removed, and often he'd
try to sneak it on during sex. The scientist had lectured him numerous
times that the myths about biological ticking-time-bomb ovarian clocks
all stemmed from bullshit Victorian studies, when parents married their
daughters off at the age of fourteen. They still had ample time in their
early forties. He wasn't too old for anything besides maybe hiding under
a giant yellow hat.

But his father had died at fifty-two, which meant that if they had a
baby tomorrow, he might only see it turn ten, fourth grade, still discarding baby teeth, still just starting. The scientist often carried the monkey
around on her hip, and they clung to each other in mock terror while
they binged Hitchcock and John Carpenter and *Twilight Zone*. The man
wondered if she realized how the monkey was slowing them down. Stress-
ing over that monkey probably contributed to his low sperm count.

George rested his palm on the man's ankle. They didn't make eye contact, both staring ahead into the skyscraper-toothed sunset. The monkey
petted his shin as delicately as one might pet a kitten. Maybe the monkey
had finally learned how costly curiosity could be. It was toxic, venomous,
the man knew. His own curiosity had prompted him to ask the scientist
about her past lovers, and she told him how her first husband had died
of colon cancer. Sometimes he thought about the dead husband when
they were trying to make a baby and they'd have to stop and he would
apologize and the room would breathe too cold on his exposed scalp.

The man couldn't allow their lives to be dragged by the whims of a wild
animal any longer. Who knew how long anyone had—cancer or a curious
beast bearing down any second? The man gripped George's wrist with one
hand, reached into his pocket for the syringe with the other. The monkey
he'd named George flinched but didn't turn, as if resigned to this pun-
ishment. Could monkeys feel remorse? The scientist had sent him an
article once about how dogs had adapted a submissive look to placate

their masters. Did they actually care that they pissed on your dissertation or bit your baby's face? They were evolutionarily good actors, tails tucked, ears wilting, eyes upturned for their lord's mercy. It was survival symbiosis—emotional placebo bartered for food and shelter. The scientist had asked him what he thought. She doubted the theory, voting for animal empathy. He'd once imagined in George an infinite tangle of passions, deeper than a jungle's thicket. But now the man worried monkeys were simply smart, even better emotional manipulators than the dogs.

He jerked the monkey he'd named George closer. Maybe he was holding the monkey too tightly, but restraining it was necessary, to make sure this went smoothly as possible, a firm kindness. That was more kindness than the lying monkey had ever shown him.

The sliding glass door shushed open, a sound like gasping. The man's scalp tingled. He slackened his clenched fingers. The monkey remained still.

"Are you boys done moping?" the scientist said from the door. "Nothing good that'll do. Ready to come back inside?"

She wore a yellowed Sonic Youth T-shirt, one of his ancient souvenirs from a concert he'd attended with his ex, the vet. The frayed hem reached her midthigh. Besides the shirt, she was nude, and she was being careful not to offer more than her head outside for fear of neighbors seeing. She was as shy about her body as the man was about his thinning hair, though she was effortlessly athletic with thighs so powerful and large they were patterned in tiger-stripe stretchmarks. The man loved to feather his fingers over the ridges, even though that annoyed her maybe as much as when she touched his scalp.

"What are you staring at?" She squirmed her body farther back into the house. "Come back inside and I'll let you touch." She was smiling. She wanted to try again. The man doubted he could, but he longed to wrap his arms around her. He'd need to after he injected the monkey.

"I will soon," the man said.

"If you won't snuggle me," the scientist said, "then, George, want some ice cream?"

56 The Man with the Yellow Hat

The monkey sprang to his feet, but the man caught him once again by the wrist. The monkey acquiesced with limp limbs and somber lips, as if proving his remorse, but the man was decided that genuine guilt belonged to humans exclusively. That's what the article had concluded. The scientist would agree, surely, if she reviewed all the evidence, if she knew all he did, if she could just forget how she'd helped name a monkey George.

"Aren't you being too tough on him?" she said.

"That window washer's still in the hospital. He could've died." The man watched her eyes lower, and the man stashed the syringe behind his back.

"We can't control everything," she said.

The man found that ridiculous, a scientist devaluing control. Wasn't that the basis of every experiment? They'd never prove any hypothesis without control. But, of course, he couldn't say any of this, couldn't tell her about the needle, about the solution he'd figured out with his ex the vet. She would want to talk him out of it, a talk that would start with surrendering the monkey to the zoo or finding a sanctuary, but would end with her convincing him he should keep George, the monkey they'd named, the animal he'd once loved, and who in life had he loved more? If he didn't end it now, they'd be forever trapped in this torturous curiosity cycle.

"Fine then. Guess I'll eat all this chocolate myself. I'm worried I might get too stuffed to make room for the banana and whipped cream." The door breezed shut on her sweet mockery. Her kindness was authentic, unlike his, unlike the monkey's victims, who chuckled in front of the crowds and sued him later. The man wanted a million more years with the scientist, baby or no baby, but his father's death age loomed. Every second mattered, and the monkey he'd named George leeched the man's time with its need for constant supervision.

It took his ex-lover, the vet, to give it to him straight. Kill the monkey. *Should've done that when you found him stowed away on your boat*, she'd told him. She was right.

The Man with the Yellow Hat 57

"George," the man finally said to his monkey. "Monkey," he said when the monkey didn't respond to his name. "I forgive you. I doubt you meant to hurt anyone."

But a man was hospitalized with cracked bones, internal bleeding. He should've known when the monkey kept studying the window washers through his apartment window. The man had been working in his office for only a half hour when he returned to the living room to find the sliding door open. The monkey was across the street, swinging from the window washers' lift. He heard them shouting, swearing, then the screams, the crash. The monkey hadn't killed, but almost. The man could feel his own veins tightening, and at this rate he could pop off a heart attack even younger than his father. This monkey was fatal.

Even the cops said, "Accident" as they patted the monkey's head, but the man had seen the window washer's blood staining the concrete. After, the monkey had clung to the man's shirt, buried his face in the man's neck until the cop finally told them to go home. Up the stairs, all six flights, the monkey's baby-sized fists wrinkled his yellow shirt. The monkey's bony skull and coarse hairs ground into his skin. Before, the man had enjoyed the affection, the attention it brought him from women, from their children, their joy at his monkey and his yellow hat. And he probably loved the monkey—had loved him; he knew he had, but he struggled to recall the warmth in his chest and still hadn't by the time he'd reached the balcony and peeled the monkey free and locked him in the kennel to call the vet.

Holding the monkey he'd named George was what holding his child would be like, he used to think.

The man yanked the monkey into a headlock. It didn't make the chattering baby-talk sounds it often made. Instead, the monkey squirmed. Its animal instincts to break free were taking hold—no such thing as simian remorse—and the man drove the needle into the monkey's arm. It chirped at the sting, and the man winced. He maneuvered his thumb over the plunger, but before he could press, the monkey wormed free. It hopped onto the guardrail, swayed backward, almost falling. It showed teeth, a gesture that meant kindness in humans. In primates, a promise of violence.

A gust knocked the man's yellow hat to the balcony boards. He could feel his combed-over hair flopping up, exposing him. The syringe, still full, dangled by the needle from the monkey's flesh. The man lunged, but it was too quick. The monkey jumped off the rail. The man leaned over to watch it spidering down the fire escape in bold leaps, and in seconds the monkey was out of sight. Gone. Easier than the push of a syringe.

The man waited for the monkey to materialize, loping down the street, for it to become someone else's problem now. Animal control's problem. He'd survive or he wouldn't. The man wouldn't post fliers featuring the monkey's massive eyes. He wouldn't answer calls for a few days. It was better this way, just to imagine he'd never named a monkey George. He dropped back into his lounger, kicked the kennel away. It smeared through the feces pile and collided with his fallen hat. It would be a tedious process to smooth the creases and remove the stains, but he'd worry about that later.

He closed his eyes. He felt the wind on his scalp again, the cold coming on, the night the monkey would find himself lost within. Perhaps the monkey's curiosity would draw it through an apartment window toward a television streaming cartoons. There, the monkey could charm a new family with a brood of children. Or, perhaps, the monkey would dive into a grocery store dumpster, eating rotten fruit until its belly bulged, and then it would curl up and die of exposure in the night. No one would find it, and the dump truck would collect its corpse without ceremony. The man dug his fingernails into the crown of his balding scalp. Now he'd have a new red wound for the hat to hide.

A warmth touched him then, a pressure across his chest. He opened his eyes, and the monkey he'd named George was straddling him. It held the needle like a dagger. The man couldn't read the monkey's face, couldn't tell which emotion this tiny mammal was faking to get the evolutionary jump on him.

The sliding door opened once again.

The Man with the Yellow Hat

59

"I knew it had to happen," the scientist said to his back. Her voice cracked. It would take time, but he could convince her how euthanizing the monkey would free their lives. "I wasn't going to push you," she said. "But I'm so glad you've made up already."

She hadn't seen the syringe, then, only the monkey perched atop his chest. The monkey lowered the needle, as if to hide it from her as the man had before, which was, of course, ridiculous, that they'd share a fear of being perceived as monsters. "Yeah, hon, it's good," he said.

"You lost your hat," she said, and he could hear her walking close behind him, rounding him and the monkey. She tugged his hat from behind the kennel, then leaned over the monkey they'd named George to kiss the crown of the man's bald scalp. Maybe she'd lean in too far and drive the needle into the monkey's chest. And wouldn't that be perfect, for her to pull the proverbial trigger, for her, once again, to make his life simpler when he could do so little for her? When he and his monkey named George mostly drove chaos into her life? He couldn't even give her a baby. She pulled away from the kiss, and the cool air struck him again. She placed his hat on the balcony boards closer to his chair. His head remained bare.

"I'll leave you two alone. Forgiveness is precious," she said, her voice jumping a pitch. And then, from behind him, from the doorway, she said, "Or what do I know?"

Once they were again alone, he met the monkey's massive eyes. It glanced down, away, risking a nanosecond vulnerability, and the man grabbed for the syringe. But the simian reflexes beat his. The monkey leaped from the man's chest.

"George, wait," he said, but he couldn't bring himself to say more. The monkey touched the needle to its own furry thigh, miming what the man had done. Maybe the monkey's curiosity would neatly solve all the problems. The monkey inserted the needle into its flesh and squeaked. Its thumb hovered over the plunger. The monkey he'd named George was holding the thing just as it was designed, as if he'd planned all along to euthanize himself, to fix everything, to give the man back all he'd taken,

60 The Man with the Yellow Hat

all the stress, all the embarrassment, all the time. The monkey would even gift him his own hairy scalp, if it could. This impossible choice, this impeachable kindness, the monkey might commit it. The man closed his eyes again. He was just a monkey. He was just a monkey.

When he opened his eyes, the monkey—George—still held the needle, but was now studying the man's face, as if awaiting directions, and usually if the man said anything, George would do the opposite. *Wait at this bench, George*—and then he'd be dumping a truckload of dirt into the city park pond. *Don't feed the animals, George*—and then he'd be swimming inside the penguinarium. *Stay on the balcony, George*—and then the blood and the limbs bent at surreal angles and George holding a squeegee and hanging from a rope over the massacre. So, here, now, the man said nothing. What could be the opposite of that?

But what if only nothing awaited the man? What if George was it, the man's only shot at progeny.

George lowered his hand, and the man reacted in a knee jerk that had him slapping the needle out of the monkey's fingers. It rolled onto the boards. The man squirted the pentobarbital into a flowerpot. Next to George, his hat lay crumpled and crushed. He must've stepped on it in the scuffle to get the syringe. He picked it up, inspected its crinkles, the deformity, the smears of feces. There would be no salvaging. He flung his ruined hat over the guardrail. It sailed as if designed for floating toward its own demise, and the man and George marveled together at its flight.

George jumped into his arms, as he had many hundreds of times before, but the man returned him to the balcony boards. Instead, the man offered a single finger for George to wrap his hand around. Together, they stepped through the sliding door. The coolness of the night followed him, snuck up his naked scalp, taunting him. The apartment was dark, except for the yellow bedroom light, where he could see the scientist's lovely large thigh through the threshold. George released his finger. This was the man's view from the hallway: yellow lamplight and the thigh he loved most. The breeze was trailing him, tickling his scalp, unrelenting. He unbuttoned his yellow shirt and entered the bedroom.

Later, when she was on top of him, the Sonic Youth T-shirt rumpled in the corner, her eyes closed, her thighs gliding against his, he noticed at the edge of his vision the monkey. He was standing in the threshold. He was watching. He was holding the syringe, emptied. Those giant eyes stared on. And the man thought, All right. That's all right to be a little curious. It was bound to happen sometimes.

The man wrapped his arms around the scientist's lower back, held their torsos tightly together, so there could be nothing between them. This felt like what intimacy might look like. But a baby wouldn't care. An emotion, sincere or fabricated, couldn't produce a child. Evolution, nature, whatever it was, didn't care either. Nature fused cells as simply as it split them into cancer, killed fathers and men whose names it never cared to learn. Nature wasn't curious. Only George, who reached to touch every human hand and asked *Who?* He peered into every cage and asked *Why?* He gazed across every gap and asked *How far?*

George thumbed his earlobe and leaned his head against the doorjamb, watching the man's lips sink into the scientist's neck. And the man, too, was curious to see what might come of this night.

THE WHITES

We wear only white. Sneaker to cap. It's the housepainter way. Except for the day Simon's ass was splotched brown. From midthigh to lower back, he was coated in eggshell-sheen Mocha Morning, looking like he shat himself, like he suffered from unrelenting explosive diarrhea. And if a guy looks like shit, you give him shit. All day we rechristened him: Hershey squirter, the brown geyser, Mount Saint Smellen, shit box, shit slacks, shithead.

Simon tried to ignore us at first, chomped his upper lip and escaped down the stairs to caulk windows in the foyer. But after lunch we lined up, leaning across the balcony to smoke-break while we pontificated on the weakness of his sphincter paired with his quaking bowels. When he refused to give us a rise, Ray chucked a wet roller nap and slashed a brand-new gash of brown across his back. Simon still ignored us, and we wanted the shift to never end.

We knew Simon had just bought those gleamingly bleach-white overalls from Sherwin-Williams yesterday. We knew he was proud. We knew he thought this was his final rite of passage, regalia to celebrate graduating to master craftsman, even though he'd been pushing paint less than a week and most don't last past that. The whites must've costed him three hours of labor, and that's four packs of smokes or a tank of gas or an eighth of midgrade grass or a bottle of bottom-shelf tequila that gets you just as drunk as the top shelf. Those overalls could've been anything worth having, but instead Simon wasted 180 minutes of back-rolling with the eighteen-inch roller behind the sprayer. Would he trade those overalls for 180 minutes of more brutal work: sanding and choking on limestone dust, or scraping maybe-lead-paint at the top of a thirty-foot extension, or, hell, 180 minutes cleaning up a site after us, after we've painted it up perfect but left crumpled McDonald's wrappers and spit-kissed cigarette butts and cups of cold piss in every corner? Any swap of labor for uniform is injustice, yet Simon suited up before anyone forced him. We had too much reason to hate the fool.

The ruinous brown stain had all started with Simon being the kind of dumbass who backed into a freshly sprayed wall. At the beginning of our shift, Ray had let him man the sprayer gun for the first time, and we all saw that shit-eating grin crease his cheeks behind the respirator. Simon was even doing all right, waving the fan smooth enough in the corners not to goop up any drips. But he got proud, and when he stepped back to admire his work, he stamped his ass into the brown wall behind him.

Our cruelty was Simon's own damn fault, yet he wouldn't accept his lumps. He picked up the wet nap Ray had thrown into his back, and he hurled it back at us. We didn't flinch. He missed by miles, and the nap smooched the banister brown. He absentmindedly wiped his nap-throwing hand against the chest of his overalls, and like magic he'd made a brown palm print. When he noticed, he panicked and tried to rag it off, which, of course, spread the smear magnificently larger. We busted up. It was too glorious. Ray couldn't take it, said he was going to pee himself, and ran off to piss out the second-floor bedroom window.

"We'll see who's laughing when you have to do this yourself. I quit," Simon said to our crew who had been just fine before he was hired, who would be just fine through a hundred more hirings and firings. He stormed out the door.

That's how we know when you won't last. Paper-thin skin, short fuse, no sense of pleasure in the harassment. If you require pride on the jobsite, you're a target and soon a goner. Was it easy for Ray when we made him dump our five-gallon piss bucket every day for the first week and we

64   The Whites

kept filling it to the brim with water just to make sure he'd slosh our
diluted urine on himself? Manny was a model of humility when he drove
away, waving like a prom queen after we'd painted a giant cock and balls
on the windshield of his beater pickup. We threw Whitaker's keys onto the
roof eleven times when we found out he didn't like heights. And Kelly still
goes quiet when we talk about what we did to his double cheeseburger.

But we didn't do shit to Simon. He couldn't stand not being the Michael
Jordan of painting. Us, we failed out of welding school and got laid off
from GM and couldn't handle zapping pigs and slitting throats all day and
started a taxi business and then ran over an old lady named Irena's big
toe. Painters must know how to absorb failure. That's why we wear all
white, the most common color. White ceiling, white trim, white primer,
white spackle, white caulk. And then there are the hundred thousand
shades of almost-white every apartment complex chooses, every spec
house, every rental, every indecisive or anal-retentive homeowner—they
go white. We know how to swallow white.

So tough fucking luck that Simon clumsied his ass into a brown wall.
The more we thought about it, the more our amusement fermented into
bitterness. We were caulking the windows Simon was supposed to caulk
and watching his big brown ass out the window as he smoked cigarettes
and swiped at his phone and shook his head at the sky. He lingered like
paint fumes. We pulled our caulk gun triggers in tandem, snapped off
beads, ran wet fingers to smooth the seams.

Simon stomped back inside. "Okay, so I need this job, okay?" He spat
at the floor. "I can't leave, okay? I retract my quitting."

None of us had anything to say because the boss wasn't here and he
had never been here and we probably wouldn't see him today or tomorrow. Working for On-a-Roll Painting was our salvation and our purgatory
because Boss didn't check backgrounds or require references or proof of
citizenship or anything. He paid cash and he paid shit, seven bucks an
hour, worse than any painting business in town, but we had work.

"I stabbed a guy, all right," Simon said. "I stabbed a guy and I don't
know what happened to him. I haven't been anywhere near that town in

The Whites 65

a year. Bunch of people saw me do it, okay. Simon's not even my name," Simon said.

We kept caulking, our eyes trained on the tip of the tubes we'd sliced at perfect forty-five-degree angles. Manny's gun clicked its spring like a shot in the fallen-silent house.

"The guy I stabbed was an asshole," Simon said. "We went to high school together like eight years ago. That night, he told me he always knew I'd never be anything. He said that and walked away from me, pumped a quarter into this old Pac-Man arcade game. And what's so great about him? Maybe he's a goddamn accountant or he plays drums in a shitty bar band or works the plumbing section at Home Depot. Nobody from our town became much more than nothing."

Manny offered Simon a caulk gun. Talk is easier while holding a tool. It makes you feel a little more here, a little less invisible, like the caulk globs we smear on our white Dickies.

Simon stepped up to a window in the middle of us. His brown ass looked like a hole against all the gray Sheetrock. "So I grabbed one of those rolls of silverware off a table, and it happened to have a steak knife inside. Had to be a steak knife and not some worthless butter knife that you usually find in there. I moved in close enough to see Pac-Man's pixels over his shoulder. I remember watching him eat three ghosts and he almost had a fourth and then I buried that knife in his side. People were screaming before I was out the door. I drove all night until I was out of gas."

We finished caulking the downstairs before we knocked off. Best to end when you can let a whole story dry and settle overnight.

Simon stayed silent after his story, because he'd spilled enough. He spread that mess all over us. You can always tell a painter's experience with how he handles paint on the carpet. Some will stress it and make a big fuss with cleaners and cussing. Others will move on and pretend someone else did it. The veteran painter, though, he bows his head low like praying and then dribbles out a stream of spit. There's something magic about saliva that cuts right through. If he doesn't have a rag handy,

66　　The Whites

he wipes with his shirt. Spit, wipe, repeat, until you leave no trace. Only we will always know there's spit in your carpet.

But we'd teach this to Simon later. For that night at quitting time, Ray distributed the Coors cans. We drank from tailgates. We busted open a fresh gallon of ceiling white, and Manny took up the brush. He swiped it over the brown on Simon's new overalls, over his chest, over his ass, up his back. Even under a few coats of paint, even with the brown erased, we couldn't quit imagining a blossom of red blooming through Simon's whites, through Ray's and Manny's whites, through us all.

RETAINER

He was hurling children into the pool. They screamed for their lives, which goaded Ben's throws until he had them sailing a good five feet. They submerged in bubbly plumes, then popped up begging for him to do it again. His back was aching, biceps going rubbery. But when he lowered himself into a lounger, the children whined like air wheezing from a pierced balloon. The spectating parents cheered. If he tried to strike up a conversation, he'd fumble it all as he always did, stuttering and commenting on their socks and asking about their jobs and then how much that paid. But as the silent kid catapult, he was the party's heroic star.

Only three of two dozen were his kids. Ben's youngest had been invited to the party by her best friend, Nevaeh, which was *heaven* spelled backward, his youngest liked to brag. His other kids had been invited out of pity after Nevaeh's mother found out his wife, Chloe, was sick. More the merrier, Nevaeh's mother had said. Now he was earning their invites by heaving partygoers. Other parents might notice how fun he was, might invite him to not just kid parties but gatherings where adults sipped wine and traded life's terrors for tipsy mingling. In a couple months, when Ben's wife was gone, he'd need to commiserate with other adults, need to have some friends who weren't nearly dead. Chloe had said this. She wanted him to have people. But Ben hated new people, and the only person he'd ever needed was her.

68 Retainer

The children lined up in a single-file curve that dripped across the pool deck to Ben's spot at the edge of the deep end, where he stood in dampened khakis. Most of the parents wore shorts or chic bathing suits and cover-ups. He was the only sap dressed like he was going to church. Some of the kids wore neon floaties or pink life vests, and with these buoyant children he'd fake a showy windup and then gentle them into the water. Still they screamed joy. The bigger kids he'd let fly, and they'd contort in the air into cannonballs or horrendous belly flops. The parents hooted their children's splashes. It was a great sport, this kid tossing. Ben had never been popular in school, had zilch for friends in college beyond the teachers who all gave him As so as not to have to interact with him. At work as the IT manager, despite the open-office layout designed to encourage collaboration, his coworkers avoided his desk as if it was a leprous island. Even when he was a teenager, his brother used to report that Ben was the school's weirdo, and his dad had always laughed in agreement. But here, at the pool, he was a champion.

An eight-year-old blond boy donning Spiderman trunks strutted up for his fifth turn and demanded Ben launch him higher. All the other kids were going way higher, and he was fed up with getting wimpy, lame throws. Something about the kid—his missing front teeth that made him spit when he talked, the drip-drip from his trunks that could've been urine—sent volts through Ben. He pitched him with everything he had, and the kid broke the water in a sickening clap.

The kid's body lingered below the water, and Ben readied to dive, inventorying the pocket losses he'd incur—phone, wallet, key fob, and his brother's twenty-year-old orthodontic retainer he carried everywhere like an unlucky talisman. His own two oldest children glared at him from their perches where they dangled ankles in the water. He bent his knees. But that glorious asshole kid surfaced laughing. He gave Ben a thumbs-up and dog-paddled to steal a purple noodle float from a little girl.

And maybe it was the adrenaline-anxiety-anger cocktail bullying his veins that made his muscles overthrow the next kid with uncalibrated strength. As soon as she left his grip, he grasped for the tiny girl's yellow

Retainer 69

life jacket already airborne. But there was no stopping her parabola that arced from euphoric joy to flailing panic. Her shoulder collided against pool edge and then her cheekbone smacked.

The kid wailed. The parents' loungers screeched across the deck. She bobbed in a halo of pinkening water. The other kids backed away, as if poison was leeching into the pool. Ben's mind bleached in blinding white, and his fingers pressed against the wire of his brother's retainer in his pocket.

Other adults were splashing into the pool, phones and wallets surely destroyed. His own children had taken refuge on the deck, staring with shared horror. "Why did you do that to Joselyn?" his daughter Sarah asked. Sarah, his chosen one, the only invited one in his family full of pitiable party crashers.

"It was an accident, idiot," his son said, and Ben was so grateful for his broody preteen that he didn't tell him to hush.

"Is she going to die?" Sarah asked.

"You're so stupid," his son said, but then he touched his dad's shoulder. "Right, Dad?"

The other parents had the poor girl out of the pool now. She was softly blubbering, and the watered-down blood dyed the white towel under her pink. Ben felt the breezy brain of faintness encroaching. A couple parents scooped ice in handfuls from a beer cooler. Nevaeh herself wore a rainbow boa and a pointy birthday hat and posed alone with one hand on her hip. She'd forever despise Ben for stealing her eighth birthday.

"Let's get out of here," Ben's son said. "This is gay."

"You can't say 'gay,' you stupid bigot," his oldest said. He'd been hoping for her fourteen-year-old wisdom. She always knew what to do, how to make his wife smile, what doctor to call, which snacks his wife loved last week but now made her vomit. "And if we left, that would be like a hit-and-run. Dad would be in so much trouble."

"Plus, they haven't even done cake yet," his youngest said.

The wounded girl on the pink-stained towel stared up at the clouds and looked angelic enough to fly right up into heaven and doom the rest of Ben's miserable life. He waited for the other parents to force his head under the pool water while his children watched. He waited until Nevaeh's mom bandaged limbs, checked for a concussion. She announced she was a nurse and all was well under control. The girl sat up, managed a smile when Nevaeh's mom brought her a present wrapped in glittery paper. Nevaeh glowered with perfected hatred.

Nevaeh's mom approached him, tall and lovely and strong, purpose clapping with every flip-flopped footfall. "No one's demanding you stay," she said, slapping Ben's shoulder. "No one blames you."

"Really?"

"Well, no. They blame you, but fuck them."

"We don't get to say 'fuck,'" Ben's boy said.

"Well, I get to." She gazed through her black curls. She was at least six feet tall, and even Ben's son's growth spurt didn't get him near eye level. "My kids know I can say 'fuck' and that if they ever do they'll have sore asses."

Ben wanted to hug this woman for the plug she'd pulled to release pressure. "There has to be something I can do?" Ben said.

"Ease up, Sarah's dad. The kid's not dead. Lotta overreaction, in my opinion, but I see some shit every day at work. Anyway, if anyone's gonna have it out with you, it ain't gonna be on my pool deck."

He herded his children to gather their towels. "Call me if you get updates?"

"Sure, Sarah's dad," she said. "But you gotta give up your number. I might even need your name."

Her hand was hot in Ben's when they shook upon exchanging numbers and names. Hers was Sierra. She was immense enough to fill that name. And he wanted to be small enough to crawl inside the smallness of his own.

Once the night arrived and the kids slept, he told Chloe what had happened. "I wish I could've been there," she said. She was eating a Twinkie, one of the few foods she could stomach. Before all of this, she'd been the type to touch only organic granola, and she'd delight in buying trunk loads of kale from a roadside farmer.

"I think about that poor kid and I want to vomit." He reached toward her back, gentled fingertips over the jutting vertebrae.

"I always want to vomit," she said.

"Send them some flowers. Recycle some of mine. Or maybe a stuffed shark, because of the swimming."

"What if they think I'm making fun of her?"

"Just own it." She opened a second Twinkie, and that meant it was a good night. Ben sometimes worried he'd snap her wrist helping her stand. If he tossed her in the pool, she'd splinter and then float like a pile of twigs. "Kids are made of rubber and steel," she said. "Remember when Marissa fell out the car window?"

"I never imagined a face could bleed so much."

That had been his fault too. Marissa, his oldest, had been four then. He'd left her in the car for two minutes while he went in the store to buy them Slurpees, and he'd returned to screaming. On the way to the ER, she'd nursed the strawberry Slurpee, as red as her blood.

"I feel like I'm made out of glass and moldy peaches right now," he said.

"What I wouldn't give to feel like moldy peaches. Even mold."

"That was a stupid thing for me to say."

Chloe's fingers crinkled a ghostly Twinkie wrapper. "There's no great way to say much of anything. I like noticing that. It's better than Twinkies."

They laid back on the bed together. Only with Chloe could Ben say anything. Soon his wrong words would have nowhere to go. He placed his hand under her shirt, rested it against her belly that sank beneath her ribs. She was sleeping before he could say another stupid thing.

When he awoke, it was to a blast of dark confusion. His house seemed foreign and his body buzzed with the anxiety of leaving a stovetop burner on somewhere in the world. He waited in the dark for his life to resettle, the one where he had three kids and his wife would soon be dead and he'd just broken a kid at a stranger's pool.

He counted Chloe's exhales, wondered how many more she'd get. His breaths tasted like rot, sticky on his dry tongue. He inched closer so he could smell her breath, that mix of sugar and opioids and stomach acid. He'd bottle it if he could. He'd trade one million of his own breaths for one hundred more of hers.

Ben shifted to his side to face Chloe, and sharpness bit his thigh, his brother's retainer still in his pocket, always in his pocket since he'd found it a few months ago, after the doctor had offered up Chloe's expiration date formally, nine months, one year if they got lucky. He slipped out of bed and headed to the attic, where the air was as hot and rotten as his breath. Fluffs of fiberglass insulation bulged from the inside of the attic's sore mouth. It had become his insomniac hobby to return to this museum of his previous life, the boxes full of outgrown baby clothes and paint-smeared crafts no parent could throw away, Chloe's dresses that would fall over her frame if she tried them on now.

Near the back, lodged in the attic's molars, sat the boxes from his childhood where he'd excavated the retainer. He pushed aside cracked boxing gloves, a bucket of battered Titleist golf balls, baseballs from the stadiums where his dad had taken them: Fenway, Turner Field, Tropicana, Shea. Ben despised sports, but his father and brother had breathed them.

He opened another box, and the smell of a past life met him. Nag champa incense, the chemical bitter of hair dye, the whiff of marijuana tar trapped inside a pipe. This box memorialized teenager Ben. He caught himself wondering if he might scrape some ancient resin from his pipe. Chloe had turned down the medical pot prescription, said she didn't need to die paranoid, and Ben had hidden his disappointment. When he was high, at least he felt justification for acting like an awkward weirdo.

These treasures from a past life soothed nothing, though. None were as preciously painful as the retainer, which he lifted to face him, as Hamlet had lifted his buddy's skull. He tried to conjure his brother's face. They chatted on the phone every few months, but he hadn't seen him in two years now, even though he lived only five hours away. Alister, his big brother, knew little about Ben's disintegrating life. He wished he had a question to ask the retainer and Alister's ghostly skull forming around it, but what could he say? Alister was the last adult in Ben's life who should've cared, could've been here. But Ben had ruined his brother's life. After eighteen-year-old Alister showed their dad Ben's pot stash, he'd retaliated. Ben stole his brother's retainer and watched favor in the house shift. For hours the family dug through garbage bags and overturned the house, while their father poured shame on Alister for his complete lack of responsibility. The search ended when their dad thumped Alister's chest, a punch that dumped Alister on the floor. Back then, his father's way had seemed as solid and inevitable as stone. Now, that anger seemed like an amorphous cruelty.

One year after the retainer theft, the contents of Alister's room had also vanished. Nothing remained but a note spray-painted on the wallpaper of his empty room: *fuck off forever*. They'd respected his wishes, like fools. A decade and more passed coldly, and once Ben had kids, his father melted into an affectionate grandfather role, there for every Christmas, every birthday, armed with the same crisp twenty-dollar bill plus a shiny silver dollar for each kid's present. They'd adored their grandfather.

It was like Alister had never existed, an exile in West Virginia, just two states away. But he should've been there, all those years. Ben should've had his brother. Ben could've had someone left now, rather than trying to accrue new friends at his dying wife's urgings. A sociable Ben only led to more disaster.

The retainer glistened pink like a gem. He stowed it back into his pocket, and all night he slept with it poking his thigh, as he listened to his dying wife's breaths.

Nevaeh's mom, Sierra, called with news. Yanny, the brittle girl Ben had hurled, had a fractured elbow and four stitches. Her parents had inquired about Ben, who he was, his job, whether Sierra knew if he'd been drinking. "Like I'd let some motherfucker be tossing around kids at my baby girl's party if he was drunk," she said over the phone.

74   Retainer

"I don't drink. I haven't in months," he said. His wife used to request Moscow mules, but now even a sip of alcohol was a study in nausea.

"I mean, she was there watching. She could've said no to letting her kid get tossed around by some stranger," Sierra went on. "And it's not like you're just some asshole-off-the-street kind of stranger. Your kid was invited."

Ben fingered Alister's retainer, the wire bar digging under his fingernail. "I am so sorry."

"How're you doing? Let's talk about that and not these litigious helicopter parent pricks."

Sierra's ridicule of the parents surprised Ben. But how could he not be grateful for an ally? "You really think they'll sue?"

"Could be bluster, but, shit, probably." Sierra's breaths puffed through the phone, and Ben imagined her long body performing pull-ups while she talked. "Really now, tell me about you."

"I'm okay."

"Yeah?"

"Yes."

"You sound like one glum fucker."

"I'm okay," he said again.

"Meet me at the Starbucks on Bancroft Street tomorrow at four." And before he could forge excuses, she ended the call.

Chloe flicked a hollow Twinkie wrapper into the air, as if Sierra's prediction of a lawsuit meant that much. But when Ben told her she was nice about it, and that he found her foul mouth refreshing from the way others walked on eggshells around them, she told him to go. "You're gonna burst if you don't talk to someone."

"I've got you. I've got the kids." He squeezed the ridged plastic of the retainer in his pocket.

"We don't count. Someone outside is what you need."

"I like it inside." He removed his hand from his pocket and reached for her. The retainer spilled from his pocket and dropped between them.

"What the hell is that?" She inspected the impression of his brother's mouth. "Is this one of the kid's?"

They'd all fostered mouths crammed with crowded teeth, and Sarah would be next, though he doubted they could afford an orthodontist after the final medical bills.

"I found it."

"Tell them to take better care."

She handed the pink plastic back to him, and he squeezed the wires in a fist that stung pleasantly.

"Just go see what that Sierra lady wants, Ben."

And he could deny her nothing.

His car drove itself over the familiarly heat-cracked Carolina roads until he was parked. Rain pounded his car's roof, battered the blacktop, and he sprinted through the downpour. Something was snapping at his heart as the heavy perfume of coffee struck him. He'd almost forgotten he loved it so dearly, and it made his throat a lump.

He ordered a black coffee and asked if they had free refills, hoping. The sweet barista boy wearing a pimple on his nostril like a nose stud said he'd have Ben's back when the time came. Ben surveyed the packed shop for Sierra until he spotted her standing in the back corner. He neared, fidgeting the retainer's wire. It had begun to wobble. Sierra turned and moved toward him sweepingly, snagged his sleeve, and tugged him to a booth. Ben wished she'd pull him farther, out of the shop and through the rain and past their cars and on.

"How's your wife?" she asked.

"We're okay," he said, because that was easier. He'd given details to only one supervisor at work, the one who would need to approve inevitable bereavement leave. His wife had explained to the kids.

"It sucks. Fuck cancer," Sierra said.

He sipped his coffee and let it burn his tongue.

"I have to get real with you," Sierra said. "I shouldn't even be talking to you, but a dude's got a right to know when he's getting fucked."

Retainer

Sierra told him about the plans to sue him, and he was just as unsurprised as when the doctors gave his wife her stage-four timeline. He'd buffered himself for tragedy then and now by anticipating worse. He'd imagined the doctor telling them Chloe would eviscerate into ash in five minutes.

Sierra was still talking. "They tried it on me, of course, and I told them I'd be happy to connect them with my lawyer who loved chewing up my ex-husband in the divorce and spitting his broke-ass into a studio apartment. That scared them off me and onto you, I guess. I'm sorry for that. But I'm sure as shit glad it ain't me."

The rain outside eased. Ben's coffee hit the perfect temperature. In his pocket, his thumb rocked the retainer wire back and forth. What could the parents get out of him anyway? Ben was already going to lose the house. He'd pulled his pension. The little broken girl seemed owed something, and he lamented her being stuck in a sling for the next school year, having to skip out on dance or soccer, being coddled for the next months and maybe forever by her parents. The whiff of chlorine might chill her very soul for a lifetime.

"Maybe you end up fine. Maybe no judge really feels like shitting on a future cancer widower, you know. Use that pity for all it's worth, man."

The wire snapped. Ben's fingertip explored a newly exposed edge. He pressed against its fresh danger. He forced himself to keep eye contact with Sierra while the wire pierced his skin. It was as if Alister's teeth could finally bite back, as Ben deserved.

"I'm sure you got people who can help." She drummed her mint-green fingernails atop her coffee lid. "Call in those favors."

"I might be out of people."

"I hear you. My ex, that dickhead, didn't even show at Nevaeh's party," she said.

"I'm sorry."

"He's the sorry one. He's the sorry sack of shit," she said. "I'm enough for me and Nevaeh. Hell, I'm too much." She downed the last of her coffee in one final, fatal swig, exposing her muscular neck. "But you, you're the

Retainer   77

type that needs backup. You're quiet. You're too nice. You need someone who can play hardball."

Alister—the former high-school athlete who'd once shared an inscrutable love of sports with their father—had been arrested a few times: trespassing, possession, some drug use that outdid the pot Ben's dad had busted him with. Alister had gone to court and knew some lawyers. He'd always been charming and never ended up doing time, despite their dad saying he deserved it after their falling-out. Ben tested the sharpness of his pity on Sierra. "It could be you to help."

"No, man. It couldn't."

Ben was embarrassed enough that his body stood from the booth, and his legs wanted him to run, but Sierra said, "You're bleeding." And they both looked at the blood dotting through his khakis.

After Sierra, he was too electric to return home. The tall woman's gravitational force had flung him onto the freeway, speeding north. He called Marissa from the car, told her he had urgent business, to watch over her mother. He ended the call without saying "I love you," and there was another sting. But the retainer had drawn blood. It rattled atop his dashboard, mocking him, but not for much longer. He drove ceaselessly across the West Virginia border as his bladder bulged with coffee and his eyes went bleary, until he reached Buckhannon. He passed through the downtown of tidy, red-brick storefronts. This was the municipal revitalization that had absorbed so many of America's dwindling downtowns filled with their terminally optimistic businesses. And then in came the grant money, and you ended up with bone-white sidewalks and polished windows, trees springing through wrought-iron squares—all this curated beauty surrounding hope that would soon rot.

Beyond the nostalgic glitz of the downtown from no one's childhood, mossy ranch houses gave way to cornfields interspliced by patchy forests. Among these outskirts, his brother lived.

Alister's house had faded into a green paler than seasickness. Tangled rolls of chain-link fence and rusty husks of a half-dozen car bodies cluttered the yard. Kudzu choked the property's pine trees. Ben parked in front of a stranger's house and walked through their yard. The neighbor's lawn was well kept, recently mowed, tiger lilies strategically planted at the property's edge, an attempt to soften Ben's snarled chain-link. Vines wove through his haggard fence and made a tangle of steel and leaf. He vaulted himself over and stalked the unkempt grass until his back pressed against his brother's peeling siding.

Ben gripped the retainer in his fist, this artifact of ruination commemorating his first worst mistake. Last he knew, Alister was scrapping metal: iron washbasins, fridges and stoves junked at the side of the road—treasures people were too stupid to realize they owned, he'd told Ben during their last three-minute birthday phone call. Before the fateful fight over the retainer with Dad, Ben's brother's trajectory had been solid as carved marble. He'd play football in college, on scholarship, major in mechanical engineering. But the chosen son had long ago swerved his future into a career scavenger hermitting in this ramshackle house, thanks to Ben. Through an open window, a chromium sink faucet gleamed. He pitched the retainer underhand, and the retainer clinked inside the sink.

"Who the hell's out there?" a voice shouted from inside. "Identify yourself. You government? You repo? If it's you, Alvin, I told you I didn't piss on your precious tiger lilies."

Ben remained hugged against the siding. A flake of paint fluttered past his chest. "I got this twelve-gauge full of birdshot that loves to shake hands with intruders," Alister's voice said.

His brother didn't seem capable of shooting a man, but what did Ben really know? He sprinted through Alister's untamed yard and dove into the kudzu wall. The world turned green. His brother hadn't fired a shot, but he might still live up to his threat. Ben flung himself from one tangle to the next, deeper into the kudzu, leaves bleeding their viscous sweetness all over him. He tried to fight through, but he felt his body slowing until he was stopped, knotted in vines.

This could've been Alister's elaborate trap, revenge for all that lost potential from his youth. Once upon a time, Ben had entertained plans of potential. Like his father, he'd known where each of his children would go to college, what they'd study, the scholarships they'd earn. He'd retire at sixty-four, sell the house, buy a condo in Corpus Christi, where he'd fish for crabs and drink Moscow mules with Chloe, the best and only person he needed in his life made unlonely by her presence. And then cancer stormed drunkenly through his glass menagerie of future fantasizing. Now, all he wanted was time, even granules of it, before Chloe was gone and he was alone.

The kudzu behind him rustled. Ben thrashed but his arms were stuck. The leaves shuddered. The dirt seemed to thrum. His big brother, Alister, stepped before him. He wore a black D.A.R.E. T-shirt and held no gun. He'd gone bald mostly, a thin bramble tangling the sides of his head. He needed a haircut. He needed a shave. He looked ten years older than Ben.

"Why'd you run?" Alister asked.

"I stole your retainer," Ben said. "I ruined your life." He determined himself to face his brother's eyes. He couldn't remember the color, and the kudzu was too thick to allow enough light to know. How does one lose his brother's eye color?

"How are the kids? How's that sweet Chloe?" Alister said.

"It was me all along."

Alister smiled, spit. His mouth was a mass of brown teeth begging to be pulled. "What are you talking about?"

"You and Dad, you two were never the same."

"Why'd you throw this through my window?" Alister withdrew the retainer from his jean pockets.

"I'm so sorry," Ben said. "It's your retainer. I stole it. I made Dad hate you."

"Benny Bear, you don't know shit about shit."

So, his brother told him a story. He told him as he used a serrated knife to saw the kudzu vines paralyzing Ben. Alister told him how he'd been in love with a girl. He was sixteen and she was sixteen, and they were too young, but they loved each other like horny rabbits. They were both too embarrassed to buy condoms so they'd hold each other as long as they could when they made love—a torturous game of chicken, flinging apart just before Alister came. She got pregnant, of course, and when Alister went to Dad for help, Dad shut it all up. He drove out to the girl's farm to tell her father they'd be having no part in it. His son had a future, and some hussy wasn't going to screw that up for him. But Alister didn't want Dad's future. He wanted only to love the girl. He wanted to get out of the car and promise the girl's father his devotion, tell everyone, but before he could do anything, their dad was kicking the farmer's ribs, had him fetal on the ground, and just kept kicking and kicking.

"And Dad kicked that man until he soaked the dirt in blood. What could I do then? She wouldn't talk to me after that, and all I had left was hatred for Dad," Alister said. They sat at Alister's kitchen table now, Alister cleaning Ben's wounds with an ancient brown bottle of peroxide. The table was made of a massive slice of maple tree trunk. Between the brothers sat a thousand years of a tree's life, centuries told in concentric stripes. It seemed a beautiful, exposed thing. Ben wondered how he could've afforded it on scrapping money. The whole house was decorated in elaborate wooden furniture, a lovely interior, the opposite of the outside.

"I always just wanted what you and Chloe have, and our old man robbed me of that," Alister said. "So, it had nothing to do with you stealing the retainer." Alister pressed it against the roof of his mouth, behind his brown teeth, but the broken bar stabbed him and he quit, wincing. "That retainer was just another excuse for him to slap me around."

"Still, I'm sorry for it," Ben said to his brother's back. Alister reached into a drawer to produce a pair of needle-nose pliers and superglue. He pinched at the retainer's broken wire.

"Just wish you'd been around. Few minutes on the phone a few times a year don't make brothers."

"You weren't at Dad's funeral," Ben said.

"Now you know why." The retainer made a cracking sound, but Alister kept fiddling.

"He was nice to my kids. Always. Only person I ever saw him hit was you," Ben said.

"You probably got me to thank for getting all that out of his system."

The brothers looked each other in the eye, long enough that it stung. What he wanted most was to tell Alister all about Chloe's dying and how it wasn't fucking fair. That injustice shot down to the deep depths of a pit of accidents Ben had stumbled into—stealing a retainer, being so awkward no one could stand him, overthrowing that poor girl in the pool. Then, finally, at the very bottom: being loved by a girl who gave him three beautiful children and then got herself some terminal cancer.

How could he say it to a stranger? They'd spent most of their lives barely knowing each other, and Alister could've been anybody now. Alister, this stranger, rested the pliers against the tabletop, the hundred lifetimes of tree spirals. He wrestled the retainer inside his mouth until it clicked into place.

"Hot damn! That's why you don't throw away nothing," Alister said. He flashed his brown teeth again, and blood was filling in the cracks, collecting in his gum line, provoked by the cobbled-together retainer. But he kept showing his brother those hideous teeth, battered enough to chew cancer and scare off lawyers. Ben bit the inside of his own mouth until he tasted blood too. The brothers bled together to celebrate this reunion of mouth and wire.

SMOKE AT THE END
OF THE WORLD

We smoked the houses out before they even existed. We smoked when they dug foundation, smoked when they poured concrete. We inhaled when they tossed up the studs and struts and cripples, held it in when the crane dropped the prefabbed A-frame rafters, and we exhaled, finally, only, when the last nail landed. We smoked from rough plumb to toilet seat, circuit box to light switch, Sheetrock to primer to topcoat of eggshell Candlewick white.

We smoked until they caught us dropping ash onto the brand-new carpet. That was the first sign, and we should've read the tobacco leaves that leaked from our flicked butts congregating in the street curbs. Not that knowing would've stopped anything. But at least we could've quit hoping, could've packed up and cut out.

In September all was normal, all of us clutching a tool handle or a ladder rung or a roll of insulation, while our teeth clenched a cigarette butt. By October, as Michigan began its cold cruelties, there was Mark, the newly hired construction manager, standing on the freshly set bone-white driveway wearing a white polo, fists against his hips and chest puffed, blond as a Hitler Youth. He said, "Hello, fellas. Grand to meet you, fellas. We'll be slamming out so many houses as we move this subdivision from phase two to phase three, and then we'll tackle a thousand more of these mothers together until the lumberyard runs out of two-by-fours and we retire fat and rich."

Smoke at the End of the World

Nobody nodded to Mark. We kept on working and smoking and maybe dreaming a little about this new concept of ever having enough money to stop working.

Then his smile dropped when he broke the news: "But, fellas, sorry to say, no more smoking in the houses. At least not after the carpet's down. Homeowners want it smelling fresh, and so do the bosses, our bosses the builders."

We consented, minimally, by some of us flicking our butts out the window. Sure, we supposed we could imagine how some wouldn't want their babies crawling through brand-new Berber that smelled like second-hand contractor smoke. We tolerated the decree, save for the carpet crew, who, later that evening, filled Mark the Construction Manager's shiny white Silverado to the brim with piss-soaked padding scraps. It was a sight to see, him opening his cab door to a deluge of blue pad springing forth. The rest of us still smoked most of the time, and most of the time was what mattered most.

Few weeks later, Mark sneaked a secret meeting with the housepainters to ask why their touch-ups weren't blending. Perfect is impossible if you know how to look at a wall, they told him. "But couldn't it be the smoking," Mark asked, "the tar tinting the walls just enough to mismatch the paint?" And, yeah, there'd been that old guy's house stacked with books and bedbugs and cockroaches, and he sat chain-smoking on his leather armchair like the king of pestilence while they painted around him. The walls had gone from white to brown. But that had been thirteen years of exhaling smoke. Couple days of smoking in these new houses—no issue.

"See, but maybe," Mark said. "I just want to help you boys do your job better. I'm here for you," he said. And then, poof, no more smoking after primer.

Our doom should've been clear as the windowpane that Mark inspected with the tip of his index finger. Just outside the window, the excavator boys and their yellow backhoes were missing. No exhaust. No new foundation holes. Just the same trees spilling their dead-red leaves. Our crews dropped from seven days per week to six. We were so relieved to finally

84 Smoke at the End of the World

have a day to drink our pay, to fuck our wives and boyfriends, maybe even go to church if one could find time for God.

Too comfortable to notice what we should've feared: one day off meant less need for us. But six twelve-hour days still filled the gutters and curbs and front lawns with cigarette butts. So many that Mark hired his teen-age cousin to sweep the street, a black-haired boy forever bent at our butts, from sunup to dusk, just like us. Inevitably, he started smoking, too, and he'd be puffing and broom-pushing and every twenty minutes spitting his own butt into the shuffling pile. When Mark rolled up in that white Silverado and spotted his cousin-boy smoking, he slapped the smoke out of his mouth. Mark marched into the nearest house, his face creased and ruddy. A wormy vein under his right eye pulsed. He promised us the next one caught smoking in a house after Sheetrock was hung wouldn't see another contract.

We couldn't resist goading him, asked him about the insulation, about how maybe that pink fluffy fiberglass might absorb the smoke, too, stink up the house from inside.

"Goddamn right," he said. "No smoking after insulation either."

Might even be seeping into the copper and the PVC, we joked, into the dark knots in the pine studs.

Which meant no smoking once frame went up.

What if it all started at the concrete, the very foundation corrupted from the start? we asked.

"No fucking smoking anywhere," Mark shouted and stormed out of the house and into his truck and down the subdivision road.

We reverted to our natural wild state of smoking and worse. We ashed in the new carpets, floated butts in the toilets, ground them in the garbage disposals. We stashed butts atop doorjambs and between studs and inside circuit boxes. We challenged Mark's black-haired cousin-boy to a smoke-off to see who could suck down a Camel Wide Filter fastest, and he beat a mason and a roofer before a painter set the subdivision record with a fifty-four-second smoke. Mark's cousin-boy went pale from all the nicotine, slept it off in a dumpster full of carpet scraps.

Smoke at the End of the World

For the next few days, as the early snow flurries began, Mark's truck idled by on patrol, but he didn't stop. And no one told us where our next contracts would take us now that this sub was nearly complete. Every hour of continued silence punched us in the lungs.

After a week went by with no Mark, all we had left were finished houses full of carpet and most of us leaning against our trucks waiting. Inside, no one smoked, as if our goodwill gesture might conjure Mark with a fistful of contracts. Pristine houses surrounded us, ready for market, built on spec. For the last four years, families herded in before a Realtor could even show them. Our new job was watching the snow mounds build atop the doorsteps. The ground would freeze soon, and no more digging would happen. Somewhere, we prayed, awaited a hundred holes for us.

Finally, Mark's Silverado showed and slowed to a stop. He blew a plume of smoke out his window. He was suckling a fat cigar. "Congratulations," he said. "You've finished. You've built a house for every single person in America. In fact, maybe you've built two for each."

Someone flicked a butt at his chrome rims. Mark puffed, and his cigar cherry was splitting down the side.

"So, thanks for fucking me over, boys, by building all the houses Michigan will ever need," Mark said. "What the fuck am I going to do with a construction management degree and no more construction?" Then Mark puked out his window. It was red and laced with bright noodles, probably spaghetti or all his viscera.

"Biggest assholes in America, you boys with your hammers and brushes," he said. "And we'll all remember who's to blame."

Mark gunned it, peeling rubber against the fresh blacktop. Only the burnt smell lingered with us as we waited another week for Mark to deliver another contract. The builders ignored our calls. The black-haired cousin-boy kept sweeping though, sweeping and waving. Paid by whom, we had no clue. The trade of cleaning up our mess was the last one left, and we hated him.

December hit and Christmas loomed, and we smoked outside the spec houses no one was buying. We smoked when the Realtor showed up in

86 Smoke at the End of the World

her red skirt and green blazer to check on the houses and Windex her FOR SALE sign. She ignored our collective exhales when no one showed for the first open house or the seventh.

We smoked while the first FORECLOSURE sign went up. We smoked and watched that first family pack every possession into brown boxes and stash them in a U-Haul. A man in a wrinkled suit scraped PETER-SONS off the mailbox. Then the Gomez family left. The Piazzas hugged each other in the yard and cried, and we smoked and smoked. FORE-CLOSURE signs lined the street, every house we built now homes for ghosts.

We broke into the bank-owned homes. Mark's head would've exploded. We smoked inside each one. Whether saying goodbye or saying fuck you, it was a thing to do, better than waiting for work that wouldn't come. Better than listening to the news talk about bubbles and subprimes and bailouts that wouldn't bail us out.

After we couldn't buy Christmas presents, after we missed our own first mortgage payments, Mark's cousin still swept. Black-haired cousin-boy remained long after Mark's truck had swerved away. He looked to us with his pleading five-gallon bucket full of our cigarette butts. His work would last as long as we smoked, and we'd smoke for forever. We flicked still-flaming cherries at the cousin-boy, the orange embers fire-working against his body. He tried to swat them off with his broom, but we were too many. We flicked into his arms and hands and face and hair. He shouted, and we lit more. We circled him, lighting and smoking and flicking, the cousin-boy cursing us to hell, until one of us landed a butt into the neckline of his shirt. He wailed like a wild baby, swatted at an invisible burning. And then his black T-shirt began to dissolve in a slow smolder. He slapped at the bright hole of his pale chest, and our own bared lungs felt the new cold with him.

EAT FIRE

We've always hated Christmas and the mountains of trash that trail it. But this year is a special kind of hell. Hottest ever and the trees are bursting into pine-scented fire pillars. I ask Bossman Duckworth if we'll be getting hazard pay. He says yeah right. I ask if we can maybe get some gear like the firefighters. He says to give him a fucking break, says he wonders why now we suddenly want to play dress-up when we never even wear the gloves and goggles sanitation engineers are supposed to wear anyway. How about fire extinguishers? He budgets a rusty garbage can we hook to the outside of the truck and fill with water.

On this worst day of our year, this first trash day after Christmas, it's a record-high 119 in New Mexico, no rain for three weeks, and the rich bastards in Whistling Cactus subdivision are all hiding in their houses after dragging their Douglas firs to the curb. The trees are a rusty brown color. It's rare to see green anymore. But if you have the big bucks, you can still get yourself a live one, a real tree. Seems that's always how it goes—a bank account buffered in a heap of zeros means access to the impossible. For us, for me and Cherry and baby Zart, we strung rainbow lights around the same emaciated plastic thing we've been using for twenty-two years, inherited from my parents, a droopy white tragedy that sheds plastic needles and has turned a yellowish tint from Dad's lifetime of smoking and then ours, until we quit twenty-seven months and fourteen days ago. We couldn't toss Dad's tree even if we wanted. Nine-hundred-dollar fine

88 Eat Fire

for discarding plastic, about the price of one of those once-green Douglas firs. We've already heaved forty-five into the hopper today. I tried to do the math in my head, but settled on: a fuck ton more money than I want to think about not having.

I'm riding the step outside the truck, and Enrique's driving, same as usual, when we pull up to our fifth burner of the day.

"How about you get this one, buddy?" Enrique says, because I always get all of them.

"Sure, sure. Don't strain yourself behind the wheel." I waltz up to his window and pat his hairy arm. "Gotta baby those hemorrhoids."

"Merry Christmas on fire, my friend," he says to my back and revs the engine.

Everyone always wants to hear about the weirdest things we find, about body parts and such, and, yeah, sure, I've seen some of those. Plenty weirder: a trash can brimming with curdled milk, a can full of mannequin hands, scores of living pets and one living baby, AK-47s and AR-15s and handguns galore stuffed into mattresses and rotted-black pumpkins and recliners and broken TVs, and once, a grown man playing hide-and-seek from the night before who got stuck in his can. But spontaneously combusting Christmas trees I've never seen. I'm not a scientist, but it's hotter than balls, so fire seems logical. Tack on the water rationing, even though Albuquerque played nice for Christmas and said folks could have 1.75 gallons total for Christmas-tree watering. Maybe the sun refracting off these giant windows is igniting them. Maybe a burning Christmas is our new tradition.

I douse this burner with the last slosh of water we brought, and it makes little difference. The tree sizzles mockingly. I notice the homeowner standing in the shade of his garage, wearing tighty-whities and a sapphire-colored kimono. A dragon's head tangles through the silk's wrinkles and against the dude's bare protruding belly. He's sipping coffee, and when he sees me seeing him, he shrugs his hands up like: What the fuck? As if I'm the one who should mind my own business. As if I haven't seen his Twinkie binge boxes and his *Chubby Nubiles* porn mags. I know

Eat Fire

208 Cholla Lane like I know every house number's trash can. So I holler to him: "Mind me using your spigot to cool off your tree, Herman?"

Me using his name spasms a jiggly jolt through his body that gets him to pull that kimono over the orbit of his belly. I watch him watching me some more, a standoff he finally breaks by scratching his ass, dumping his coffee on the driveway, and turning to go inside his air-conditioned cave, where he resumes watching me from his giant front window, as if the glass is one-way, as if I'm not still forced to suffer a staredown with that black-eyed belly button.

"Screw it," Enrique yells from the truck. "Just go use his hose. What's he gonna do?"

"No, man." I try to spit on his driveway to match his coffee tantrum, but I'm all dried out from sweating, and a foamy dribble clings to my lip. "He can deal with it on his own." I give it a weak kick with my steel toe, and the flames blaze higher. Letting it burn won't do any real damage, of course. There's nothing to burn near the curb. New Mexico outlawed watering grass three years ago, and the whole country followed this year. Law-abiding lawns are dirt and sand. The fancy ones, like Herman here, sprinkle pea stones or quartz crumbles, as artificial as Bossman Duckworth's toupee. This tree will merely stain an ugly char across his driveway.

Onward we go, swiping up trash cans full of toilet-paper-thin biodegradable wrapping paper. Used to be so thick and shiny when I was a kid—bows big as my head wrapped around paper wrapped around boxes full of the plastic Walmart wonders we'd break and toss into the garbage within the year. Most of that nostalgia would mean misdemeanor now. Zart and Cherry and me had a perfectly legal Christmas since we couldn't afford nothing, since I convinced Cherry to quit her gig, since I figured my job would be enough but turns out I'm shit at math, and baby Zart ended up getting two sock puppets fashioned out of my holey wool socks. Thank Christ Enrique gag-gifted me a stuffed Santa that pulls down his pants and poops brown plastic when you squeeze it. Cherry was able to superglue up his pants, and Zart hugs it all day long.

Duckworth radios in, blares through the radio about how he just got a call from some Herman Hancock who said we skipped his trash. I tell Duckworth about the stingy water situation, and what are we supposed to do? Piss on it? He says we can pick up all the goddamn trash, which he says is our exact goddamn job, or we can go the heck home. He asks if we want that. Do we like the prospect of unemployment? I think about how it would be nice to tickle baby Zart's belly in the morning, and then try to imagine having less money than we do now. I tell Bossman Duckworth sorry. He says swell, and to hurry up about it so we don't milk the city's tit completely dry. Enrique revs the engine again, and I latch onto the grab handle as he lurches pointlessly, peeling rubber for the next fifty yards. Cherry's breasts flash into my head, how they were last Christmas, torn to hell, scabbed in black clumps, bruised purple by that devilish baby that we love more than anything. Zart tore her up breastfeeding. I wonder if the mothers in these houses have such war-torn breasts, or if they've found a way to pay to avoid that pain. My guess is on yes. No scabbed nipples on this block.

Enrique pumps the brakes and slaps the outside of his door in a way that means we must be coming up on another burner. He pulls me up so close flames nip at my boots and I have to jump for it. Jackoff thinks it's funny. I trudge to the side of the house with my empty watering trash can to tap their spigot. Enrique's hooting an impression of fire truck sirens from the cab. But when I go to fill my can, the spigot handle is padlocked. Water bills are high, but they're not murderous. Nothing compared to what it costs to get a couple hearts of romaine these days, a bag of oranges, a single banana. I haven't had a jalapeno in two and a half years. Sometimes I'll buy three McDonald's dollar burgers just for the pickles, but lately they're sliced thin as paper.

Cherry and I don't lock up our spigot, even though we have nothing to spare. If someone needed to steal some water—dying of thirst or putting out a trash fire—we'd allow them that. The penny-pinched-tight buttholes of these rich fuckers get my neck burning, and I really don't need any more heat when I'm already drenched in sweat.

Eat Fire

91

I slip on my heavy gloves, reach through the flames for the tree trunk, and I hammer-throw that flaming mother up into their driveway. Screw Duckworth.

"Gooooooo-aaaaaaaaal," Enrique draws out.

I strike a pectoral flex at him before I dump their trash into the hopper and jump back onto the truck. I'm still dumb-headed and full of adrenaline, and I'm already regretting my insubordination. I watch the driveway blaze as I ride the step for the next five houses. Eventually, it'll smolder into coals and seep a soot pool into the driveway, and then we can circle back, and technically I'll still be doing my job all the way. That's the beauty of hindsight that comes from riding the step. I get to contemplate the world in reverse while I propel forward. I wish I would've been planning smarter when I told Cherry to quit her stripping job at Ogley Pete's, when I told her a sanitation engineer would bring home enough money. From the current vantage of my rear-facing view, I see how obvious it was, us getting evicted from the house last month, and the playmat with the purple tiger and the yellow giraffe spread across the lawn, all dew soaked and tromped over by a little trail of ants. Turned out Cherry needed to keep flashing her baby-battered breasts. Turned out we all needed those crinkly dollar bills stinking of cologne and penned up with phone numbers and squirting dicks.

I swipe sweat from my stinging eyes. These days every day is the hottest day. Cherry and I watch the news in the morning and we used to laugh when they brought up record temps. Those tan-faced, besuited news anchors always act surprised, act like it's earth-shattering news every time they mention breaking a record that got broken just last year and the year before that.

This next house's tree, like the last two, is blazing like God's blowing commandments through it, and, at this house, the spigots turn but the water's off. They must've seen us coming and tossed the shutoff. We can't keep doing nothing or Duckworth will get more calls, will preach about how people line up at his office every morning to apply for jobs that don't exist. They're crossing fingers that we'll screw up and be fired,

92 Eat Fire

and they'd work for half my wage. But these homeowners get to hide in vinyl-sided air-conditioning streaming world news, shaking heads at some foreign famine and then clicking over to some charitable PayPal write-off. Cherry would've kept her job if we needed it, and I guess she should've. She was good at it. But after baby Zart, it became a cycle of feeding and flashing and feeding and bleeding and patching up to flash some more. She was embarrassed of customers seeing the baby bites, and I was embarrassed of her being embarrassed. I never minded her dancing, but I minded those drooling assholes seeing inside our home from those scabs. I minded them making her feel something realer than her fake eyelashes and red vinyl knee-high boots. I told her to just quit. Just say fuck it. We'll get by. But we didn't. We didn't. And the only constant is more trash.

So, fine, I'll be the one to fix this. I slip on the heavy gloves again and hurl that sparking, spitting, burning motherfucker into the hopper, followed by a garbage can full of thin wrappings that stoke the flames, and now the back of our truck is a flaming mouth, nice and angry. I slap the side, shout, "Hit it," to Enrique, who's squinting into the mirror, and maybe he winks, but he's no longer hooting.

This is how we'll do our job. We'll eat fire like nothing's wrong, like it's nothing special. Every few houses we find a burner and I hurl it into the hopper, pound the packer panel button, and all the flaming trash huffs into black smoke. Our truck is a door-to-door smokestack. We're a five-mile-per-hour pollution felony. Good thing we work for the city, and it'll fall on Duckworth's lazy lap before ours. I hope. Or maybe everyone will just pretend not to notice.

Before the end of the block, I can hardly keep hold of the grab handle for the heat surging through the metal. Enrique's hairy arm is silent in the rearview, so I guess we're not so funny now. I laughed the first time Cherry screamed, "Ouch, little asshole slut fucker," into the face of our suckling babe, who just smirked up at her, doe-eyed and pleased with his new teeth's trick. I laughed until she tried pumping and suddenly the

Eat Fire 93

tubes were sucking blood, red spattering the translucent cups, red clouding into the milk like a horror movie.

I start singing "O Christmas Tree" while I sling trees and cans, and when I realize I barely know the words, it's on to "Grandma Got Run Over by a Reindeer." I make sure to toss a bag right as I answer the gravesite quandary of whether we should keep her gifts. "Send them back," I shout and slam another burner into the hopper. Enrique drives away before I'm back on the truck. He must be thinking I've gone bonkers.

Enrique finally stops. I'm pouring sweat, my lungs squeezed. An old woman is hunched over a crackling log of fire. She's showering it on a mist setting through a fancy hose attachment. The mist casts rainbows over the fire, just over where the molecular spritz of water is evaporating into nothing. The urge to crush her in a hug pulses through my gloves. Her futility is sweet. Enrique whistles a quiet version of his sirens. I cross my arms and grip my ribs. The old woman keeps sprinkling the flames as if they were petunias. Watering flowers is a misdemeanor, but that doesn't keep Cherry from nursing an orchid. Such needy assholes, those orchids, but she's kept it alive since eviction.

"That thing got a jet setting?" I say, but she doesn't hear me. Enrique's sirens louden. She drags a pink-painted fingernail across rivulets of wrinkles, but doesn't look up.

"Any other setting?" I say, though she's making progress. The fire at her feet sputters, weakening, yet still burning enough to roast marshmallows. That's me—a roasting marshmallow puff of flesh, holding off combustion as long as I can.

Behind my back, the truck groans, its steel belly rumbling with flaming ulcer. When I look back, Enrique's slapping the outside of the door, rushing me. And I spot the mailbox number, 516 Prickly Pear. This is Mrs. Happ, then. Last month, her bin was full of uneaten casseroles, all gone to rot by the time we got to them. Two pickups of staring into broccoli tops and carrot slices swimming in mildew, and I hated her. Third week in a row, I couldn't stand it anymore and went digging for celery. I

94   Eat Fire

ended up finding a stack of funeral programs, dearly departed Mr. Happ's wrinkly face smeared with cream cheese.

I lean forward, duck into her field of vision. I wave the heavy glove, which has taken on a tarry sheen of soot. She startles, hops back, and I envision heart attack or stroke, me reuniting her with Mr. Happ. "Our truck could use some of that," I say, soft as I can. She aims toward the truck, but we're forty feet away. The water falls uselessly, coating me in a mist so fine it might as well be nothing.

Droplets tangle into the black hairs on my forearms. Her jaw clenches. It seems too hot for so little water to make any difference. But then, yes, yes, there it is. I feel it. The infinitesimal sprinkling of water touches my skin. It's not enough to cool me. It's so thin, like the Presbyterian baptism we took Zart to get, and after I wondered how God could possibly notice a tiny water flick. I didn't put the twenty I'd planned to give in the offering plate.

Mrs. Happ's tree is still burning, and the truck now booms a steel-bending belch loud enough that Enrique flails out the door and scuttles down the street. Flames spit out the hopper. The heat surges. I pull off my shirt. I think of Cherry's dancing. Maybe this widow will go full blast with the hose if I dance well enough. Maybe God will even notice. Maybe the skies will split and drench another record-breaking December heat wave. If there was even a chance I could earn that, I'd dance my ass off, never stop, through the heat, through the record books, until baby Zart replaces me and there's nothing left to burn.

ORVILLE KILLEN: LIFETIME STATS

ORVILLE SOLOMON KILLEN

Height: 6'2"   Weight: 170

Born: September 4, 1934

CARD NUMBER 247

Bats: Left   Throws: Right

Home: Paynesville, West Virginia

Bouncing back from a stint in the pokey after a car chase with Johnny Law last winter, Orville shot up from the minors to the bigs on June 25. After only two seasons shortstopping for the Single-A Lancaster Roses, Orville was ready to roar as a Detroit Tiger. His quick hands at the bat and at scooping grounders assured him a place. If his lead foot with the boys in blue forecasts anything, you can expect to see him heap up the stolen bases.

Fun Fact: Orville collects costume jewelry. He stashes chunky ruby rings and emerald brooches and amethyst pins in a cleat shoebox under his bed. He secretes the box under every hotel bed in every city his team travels to. His favorite: the silkiness of the pearl bracelet. Orville rubs the pearls against his front teeth. They grit and grind and make him wince, and that's how he knows they're real. The only real thing he owns. He rubs and imagines a Bermuda beach while his teammate and roommate Bobby Haney snores and flatulates.

Year	Team	LEA.	G	AB	R	H	2B	3B	HR	RBI	AVG.
1959	Detroit	A.L.	38	142	16	36	7	2	0	12	.254

Orville Killen: Lifetime Stats

ORVILLE SOLOMON KILLEN   CARD NUMBER: N/A

Position: Off-Season Laggard
Height: 6'2"   Weight: 165   Bats: Skunk Skulls   Throws: Rifle Casings
Born: September 4, 1934   Home: Paynesville, West Virginia

One week after the season ends, Orville meets his cousins on his family's property, a hunting cabin off Panther Creek. They meet at 5:30 p.m. every day for two weeks to shoot deer. His cousins work the coal mines by day, hunt until nightfall. By day, in his hotel an hour away, Orville browses department store circulars, fingers glossy pages, fantasizes stealing the whole glittery city and stowing it in his pocket. He doesn't think about his mother, won't let himself imagine her happy and wearing that burgundy Chanel dress on page 117 or that felt toque on 66. She'd hate their extravagance anyway. He naps, does push-ups, masturbates, does pull-ups, naps, then returns to the cabin. Later, while sighting a twelve-point buck, his cousin Ethan says, "You should go see your mama. She's not for much longer," and Ethan's brother Don says, "Give him a break. He's a baseball star." Ethan says, "That ain't an excuse. Ain't like it's work." They all miss the buck. They don't kill any bucks all season, but they shoot all the small game that crosses them. Orville leaves Ethan and Don the work of stretching pelts across the cabin their grandfather built.

Shots fired	Kills	Squirrels	Skunks	Possums	Deer	Avg.
107	71	43	22	6	0	.664

Orville Killen: Lifetime Stats 97

ORVILLE SOLOMON KILLEN   CARD NUMBER: 129

Team: Detroit Tigers   Position: Infield

Height: 6'2"   Weight: 170   Bats: Left   Throws: Right

Born: September 4, 1934   Home: Paynesville, West Virginia

Orville blazed the base paths, stealing forty-one bags and gambling for two or three every knock of the bat. He ranked third in the league for triples, fourth for steals. Too bad his loafers couldn't speed like his cleats, though. Macy's security busted Orville stealing two pairs of silk women's underpants over winter break. Says his third-base coach, Billy Hitchcock, "I guess I know what to buy that sly fox's girlfriend for Christmas."

Year	Games	At Bat	Runs	Hits	2B	3B	HR	RBI	Avg
1960	121	476	72	133	28	8	0	37	.279

Orville Killen: Lifetime Stats

ORVILLE SOLOMON KILLEN   CARD NUMBER: N/A

Position: Fire Tender
Height: 6'2"   Weight: 180   Bats: Not now   Throws: Rocks mostly
Born: September 4, 1934   Home: Paynesville, West Virginia

The stretched pelts from last year's hunting still cover the cabin that
leaks rain and bleeds cold all winter. He chooses to stay here over
another hotel. This is closer to his mother, even if he doesn't go to her.
Instead, he runs trails, splits wood, watches his skin goosebump. His
cousins are too busy in the mines to hunt this year. Real jobs don't gift
big fat cushy chunks of nothing time, they inform him. Orville keeps the
fireplace burning all hours. He dreams about razing the mountains.
He dreams about his mother's house burning up fast instead of this
forever-long death that she's doing. Orville tells himself he won't let the
fire die until someone from his family finds him, forces him to face her.
No one comes. They're all busy working. When he leaves for spring
training, he tears every pelt from the wall, stuffs them under the car
seats until they're spilling tails and hollow eye sockets. He stacks extra
wood on the fire and drives away. He chucks a pelt out the car window
every few dozen miles.

Days of Fire	Lbs. Wood Burned	Times Imagined Touching Skeleton Mom
68	4,791	4,799

Orville Killen: Lifetime Stats

ORVILLE SOLOMON KILLEN   CARD NUMBER: 71

Team: Detroit Tigers   Position: 2B
Height: 6'2"   Weight: 169   Bats: Left   Throws: Right
Born: September 4, 1934   Home: Paynesville, West Virginia

Anyone following this rising star knows Orville loves to steal. However, turnabout isn't fair play with Orville. At second base, Orville won't tolerate stealing and has tagged out over fifty would-be base thieves. When a White Sox sprinter aimed his cleats at Orville in a dirty slide, Orville still nailed him—despite the cleats stabbing. With blood welling through his sock, he led the Tigers to their tenth straight win. Postgame, his teammates stripped the browning blood-soaked sock off Orville. They celebrated their win streak by swinging it over their heads and draping it around their necks. Orville smiled, curling the toes of his one bare foot, thinking how fine it was to share blood.

Tip for boys: Love is a many-splendored thing, but no fleeting romance can match the camaraderie of brothers-in-bats. Team morale is the secret ingredient in any winning lineup. Don't be afraid to hug your teammate, to slap his buttocks, to smooch his cheek and then slug his bicep. Don't worry about what your dad would've thought before he coughed himself to death, or about that time your uncle guzzled half a fifth of bourbon and then talked about stomping queers. No one will question your love for another man if it occurs atop the diamond's red dirt.

Year	Games	AB	R	H	2B	3B	HR	RBI	Avg
1961	135	492	85	140	32	7	2	68	.285

Orville Killen: Lifetime Stats

ORVILLE SOLOMON KILLEN   JACKET SIZE: 46R

Position: Pallbearer

Height: 6'2"   Weight: 159   Casket Position: Left-center

Born: September 4, 1934   Home: Paynesville, West Virginia

His mother looks shriveled and waxen in the casket, a golden raisin, worse than Orville imagined. Her bony hands clutch a foxtail. That orange-brown tail had draped her neck every special occasion he could remember. Everyone knows the story: she claimed she shot the fox with a Colt revolver when it was trying to sneak into her kitchen one night. Orville slips the tail from her hands and into his pocket just before they close the box. Mother weighs ninety-three pounds at death. Due to his dedication to the bench press and deadlift this off-season, Orville could nearly heft his mother's casket by himself. But Uncle Rory is there, sucking a tobacco wad, spitting brown into a dirty handkerchief he keeps in his breast pocket. Rory's sons Ethan and Don are there. Ethan's missing an eye, some accident at the mine with the dragline. Rory's progeny of hardworking boys are behind in the count, and Orville has never been stronger—until his shin throbs where that bastard from the Sox cleated him. Once the casket has sunk down its hole, Orville rubs the offending muscle. Rory kicks dirt Orville's way, dirt that will cover his mother. He hisses, "Big-city baller Orville is all tuckered out. Can't handle a little manual labor." Rory's boys snicker. After the preacher belts out his best lines, *dust to dust*, Uncle Rory takes them out for beers. He tells a story of how when Orville's mom—Rory's sister—was a girl, she used to run naked in the holler and howl at the goddamn moon. He tells them how she didn't stop her wild until a man put baby Orville in her loony womb. Orville's face burns. He vows to himself to cut ties for good. He's never coming back. Mom has joined Dad in the dirt. The hunting cabin by the creek is ashes and char, as is most the forest around it. But Orville's on the rise. Orville won't be stopped. A better life in Detroit awaits.

Lbs. Earth atop Casket	Killen Eyes Left	Times Fist Clenched Under Bar
7,692	7	31

Orville Killen: Lifetime Stats

ORVILLE SOLOMON KILLEN

Team: Detroit Tigers

HT: 6′2″ Weight: 155

Born: September 4, 1934

CARD NUMBER: 527

Position: 2B-SS

Bats: Left Throws: Right

Home: Paynesville, West Virginia

Despite a flare-up of last year's cleat injury, Orville made the most of the season. Great in a pinch, he snapped a dozen doubles from the pine. Not every player can hop off the bench and inspire a rally in the eighth, but that's what Orville did the last game of the year against the Yanks, when he sailed a liner over the right-field wall, only his third career home run. In the locker room, his manager gripped his shoulder, scruffed his hair, said, "We'll get you back to starting soon as we can, you skinny bastard." Later that night, his manager struck while the iron was hot and traded Orville to the White Sox.

Year	Games	At Bat	Runs	Hits	2B	3B	HR	RBI	Avg
1962	67	186	24	41	12	0	1	18	.220

ORVILLE SOLOMON KILLEN

LICENSE PLATE: S86 6591

Position: Driver

HT: 6'2" Weight: 165

Hits: Lampposts Throws: Bottles

Born: September 4, 1934

Home (almost): North Corktown neighborhood

Orville's last winter in Detroit is a rip-roaring riot. He paints the town, spending every night drinking with GM workers or with the stadium groundskeepers who live in Black Bottom. They trade stories about lost fathers, lost mothers, growing up poorer than mud, but then they talk about "real work" and Orville quiets. After the bar, he drives them over icy roads in his giant baby-blue '59 Cadillac on whiskey runs down Woodward. One morning he wakes with his head lolling out the driver's side window. He's in the Detroit Institute of Art parking lot with two flat tires. He buys admittance so he can take a piss and call a tow, but then he stumbles into the Diego Rivera mural room. He gazes up, dizzies at the chrome maze of pistons and cranks and belt pulleys and men working. Above that, so high his sore neck burns, Diego's bare bodies bruise him—those soft skins floating over brown knots of fists. Heaven is naked and soft. Orville vomits splendidly on the marble floor.

Oz. Alcohol	Detroit Miles	Collisions	Passengers	Percent Remembered
961	3,129	17	32	.245

Orville Killen: Lifetime Stats

ORVILLE SOLOMON KILLEN   CARD NUMBER: 330
Team: Chicago White Sox   Position: SS
HT: 6'2"   Weight: 170   Bats: Left   Throws: Right
Born: September 4, 1934   Home: Paynesville, West Virginia

A professional ballplayer knows how to bury the hatchet, or bury the cleat spike in Orville's case. The young gun assisted thirty-one twin-killing double plays over to Herman Fingers's mitt. Two years ago, Herman spiked Orville in a dirty slide, but Orville shows there's no place for grudges in the Elysian business world. Orville throws so hard nosebleed spectators hear Herman's leather pop. No base runner stands a chance, and Herman's palm throbs bright as blood after every game.

TRIVIA-TASTIC QUIZ: Who was the last player to *start* wearing a baseball glove?

ANSWER: Bid McPhee, Cincinnati Red Stockings second basemen, held out until 1896. He'd brine his bare hands in salt water before games to leather-toughen his skin. On wearing gloves, he claimed simply not to see the need.

Year	Team	LEA.	G	AB	R	H	2B	3B	HR	RBI	AVG.
1963	Chicago	A. L.	135	460	57	112	21	4	2	45	.243

Orville Killen: Lifetime Stats

ALIAS: ALLEN JAMES JOHNSON   FAKE ID NUMBER: M187155822310

Real Estate Agent   Illinois Association of Realtors

HT: 6'2"   Weight: 165   Steals: Left   Stashes: Down
                                                       Crotch of Underwear

Born: October 30, 1931   Home: Mooseheart, Illinois

Tip to young athletes: if your skin is as white as Orville's, the chances of getting arrested for shoplifting decrease exponentially every year, quickly becoming lower than Bill Bergen's record for worst batting average at .170. In one off-season, Orville successfully snatched from Chicago stores: three silk ties, six pairs of women's underpants (two lace, four satin), one lilac cashmere sweater, one thread-thin gold chain soft as water, one knobby purple brooch, thirty-seven Italian silk neckties. If you maintain your wits—as Orville has learned by saving his drinking until after the rush of petty theft has stung his chest—great gains are well within reach. Anyone can do this with practice and strategy. That is, any white man who has the money to look like he doesn't need to steal can do this. This kind of man can easily disguise an aching desire to own enough soft and shiny things to make up for a childhood of bark and rust and mold and soot and threat.

Steals	Caught	Fake ID Uses	Theft Heartbeats
49	0	0	11,847 but fewer each time

Orville Killen: Lifetime Stats

ORVILLE SOLOMON KILLEN

CARD NUMBER: 384

Team: Chicago White Sox

Position: 2B

HT: 6'2"   Weight: 170

Bats: Left   Throws: Right

Born: September 4, 1934

Home: Paynesville, West Virginia

Rising star Orville was ready to leap into the retiring Nellie Fox's long shadow with his quick step, rocket right arm, and a .984 fielding percentage. First baseman Herman hated to exchange his hall-bound partner for a country bumpkin, white-trash hick, inbred backwoods imbecile—but here comes Orville! He split the season starting second, matching his predecessor's precision. During the postseason run, an ecstatic Orville broke into every teammate's locker and hung a $12.59 silk necktie on a tiny gold-painted hanger as a gift. When he got to Herman's locker, he adorned a golden hanger with the socks he'd been wearing for a five-game winning streak. He then peeled off his underwear and jockstrap and hung those as well.

—What is Orville's favorite way to imagine Herman's death?
—Rub edge of nickel or dime over blank box for magic answer ©:
Pickaxe through the eye.

Year	Team	LEA.	G	AB	R	H	2B	3B	HR	RBI	AVG.
1964	Chicago	A. L.	81	276	47	74	14	2	2	24	.268

Orville Killen: Lifetime Stats

ORVILLE SOLOMON KILLEN   CARD NUMBER: N/A

Position: Killer

HT: 6′2″   Weight: 170   Drives: Left   Smokes: Right

Born: September 4, 1934   Home: Paynesville, West Virginia

Driving outside DeKalb, Illinois, Orville is lulled into memory by the endless winter wheat whipping past his windshield. Uncle Rory was slapping his scalp because Orville was nine and couldn't pull the hook from a trout. He was afraid of the suffocating body, the death flops, the gnashing, crunching sound the pliers made as he yanked the swallowed hook through viscera. "Pull harder," Rory said. "Worthless soft hands." His mom appeared from nowhere sprinting and punched the back of Rory's head. They fell on each other, wrestled into the creek. Orville stood on the shore alone, a gasping fish at his feet. The Buick thumps twice. Orville slams the brakes, swerves, finally halts with the hood buried in wheat. He hopes the thumps weren't human. He finds the corpse up the road, a large yellow dog, steaming red entrails spilling from its anus. Until noon, Orville knocks on farmhouse doors. Until dusk, Orville digs a grave under a birch tree. He slides his favorite string of pearls over the dog's neck. He lifts his mom's foxtail necklace from under his shirt and considers giving this to the dog, too, but he can't seem to unlock his fingers. He lowers the dog into a hole in the earth. He weeps and throws dirt. Weeps and throws. Dirt and dirt and dirt.

Kills	Door Knocks	Grave Depth	Earth Moved	Memories Worth Keeping
1	27	4′7″	2,138.8 lbs.	0

Orville Killen: Lifetime Stats

ORVILLE SOLOMON KILLEN   CARD NUMBER: 146

HT: 6'2"   Weight: 175   Bats: Left   Throws: Right
Born: September 4, 1934   Home: Paynesville, West Virginia

Orville spent the season stopping stealers, stomping his cleats onto sliding thighs, shoulders, guts, faces, then getting beaned by retaliating pitchers thirty-seven times to lead the league in taking lumps. On a fateful September afternoon, he rubbed elbows with greatness when he decked Mickey Mantle. Mantle was limp-sprinting for a rare double despite his failing knees. Orville expected a slide, but Mantle didn't drop, and Orville rammed his elbow into the Mick's eye. Mantle dropped, clutching his weeping socket. After being attended by a small swarm of medics, Mantle stood, hobbled off the diamond, arms slung over his teammates. The crowd cheered. As soon as the Mick ducked into the dugout, the crowd hissed. They chucked a hot dog and beer cup maelstrom, and three shoes and a toilet plunger. Accidents happen on the field, but Orville sucker-punched baseball's sacred son. Herman strutted to Orville, patted his back, hoisted Orville's elbow to the crowd. He then proceeded to pretend Orville's elbow hit him in the eye, too, and rolled in the red dirt. The crowd broke into laughs, ate their hot dogs again, decided against throwing shoes. Later, to the press, Herman dubbed him Orville "McKiller."

Year	Team	LEA.	G	AB	R	H	2B	3B	HR	RBI	AVG.
1965	Chicago	A. L.	121	418	53	117	27	5	10	51	.280

Orville Killen: Lifetime Stats

ORVILLE SOLOMON KILLEN

HT: 6'2"   Weight: 170

Born: September 4, 1934

PHONE NUMBER: 309-319-6659

Holds Phone: Left   Throws Phone into Wall: Right

Home: N/A

December 27, Uncle Rory's voice crackles through hundreds of miles of phone line, all the way from West Virginia. He and Orville's yuletide salutation exchange is as subdued as reading tax forms. "Don has cancer," Rory says, "of the lungs. Stage three, they say." Orville says nothing. "Don's the one with both eyes, the one of my sons is what I'm saying." Orville knows which one Don is. He waits, phone pinched between ear and shoulder. He laces a silk necktie through his fingers, knots, pulls tight. The receiver hisses. Orville waits for Rory to ask for money. He's been waiting for this, for the family to realize his resources, the star of the Killens, his name, his plays, his stats broadcast over thousands of radios from mountains to farmhouses to city apartments. Orville the star. Orville the one who escaped the mines and the poverty and the family fists. "Thought you'd want to know," Rory says and hangs up.

Calls Received	Calls Made	Intact Killen Lungs	Dial-Tone Beeps
1	0	7	39

ORVILLE KILLEN

CARD NUMBER: 261

Team: Chicago White Sox
HT: 6'2"   Weight: 180
Born: September 4, 1934

Position: 2B
Bats: Left   Throws: Right
Home: Paynesville, West Virginia

Orville cranked out an average year. In 162 games per year, there's always a new thrill, a record broken, an unfathomable feat defeated. But in this year, for this man, he did his job without event. Workmanlike batting and fielding marked him steady as a coal miner. A lack of record, however, might also be considered a personal record for Orville.

Year	Team	LEA.	G	AB	R	H	2B	3B	HR	RBI	AVG.
1966	Chicago	A. L.	162	590	60	148	28	3	4	63	.250

Orville Killen: Lifetime Stats

ORVILLE KILLEN

Team: Chicago White Sox
HT: 6'2"   Weight: 170
Born: September 4, 1934

CARD NUMBER: N/A

Position: Thief / Almost Lover
Holds First-date Lilies: Left   Shakes: Right
Home: He tells them Orlando,
San Francisco, Bermuda, Oklahoma,
New York

"What you need," Herman says after their last game of the season, "is a good woman. Like mine. Fix you right up so you're not such an asshole." Orville gives him the finger, tells him good luck not getting traded in the off-season. As Chicago cools into its bitter freeze, Orville feels his cracks ache, the fissures in his skin, his tissue, deeper, in his skull, his kidneys, his pancreas maybe. His body stings every time the wind belts between skyscrapers, and maybe another body's hot flesh could restore him. He makes love to twenty-two women that winter and one man. None of them repair anything. After the damp sheets and during the bathroom wipe-ups, Orville steals their underthings, balls them between the mattress, and then pretends to help them search the floor until they give up and leave. He wonders if the fixing might be done in marrying. His parents' marriage lasted only three years before his dad died. At work, the docs prescribe rehab for most aches and pains. Out here, the cracks refuse to cure, so he sticks with what works. He steals.

Steal Success	Lover's Underwear	Orgasms	Snow Globes	Gas Lighters	Buicks
1.000	23	12	66	21	2

Orville Killen: Lifetime Stats

ORVILLE KILLEN
Team: Chicago White Sox
HT: 6'2"   Weight: 175
Born: September 4, 1934

CARD NUMBER: 556
Position: 2B
Bats: Left   Throws: Right
Home: Paynesville, West Virginia

Detroit burned while Orville swung the bat like murder. In Detroit, they killed forty-three humans near Twelfth Street, and Orville struck out 137 times. Thirty-two black men dead and one four-year-old girl, Tanya Blanding, mostly by bullets, one by downed power line. Orville wanted to split seams with every swing, knock it over the nosebleeds. He succeeded twenty-seven times, a career high and good for twentieth in all of baseball this year. But only hitting twenty-seven home runs dug into his ribs like failure. Herman would wrestle Orville to the clubhouse carpet after home run games, strip a sock, and nail it to the clubhouse wall. Smoke choked the Detroit skyline like storms by day, like blood-sun apocalypse by night. Orville swung like he hoped to shatter Chicago's summer-blue sky. Detroit is no longer his, never was. Neither is Chicago. Neither is anywhere.

Year	Team	LEA.	G	AB	R	H	2B	3B	HR	RBI	AVG.
1967	Chicago	A. L.	159	574	57	108	20	4	27	62	.188

Orville Killen: Lifetime Stats

ORVILLE KILLEN	STETSON SIZE: 24.5 INCHES
Team: Average White Man	Position: Employed, Obviously
HT: 6'2" Weight: 175	Looks: Left Looks: Right
Born: September 4, 1934	Home: N/A

Mechanics' garages are easy to slip into. Under cover of hydraulic drill zips and the lifts whining and the grunts of coveralled men, Orville slides into the office door, finds the key begging to ignite the black Ford Falcon parked out back. It's easy to be invisible. An expensive overcoat, a Stetson hat, starched collar and necktie peeking, a pair of sunglasses wide enough to hide his eyes but not too much of his white skin. He's in camouflage better than wearing woodland pattern in the forest near Panther Creek. He looks like someone's customer. And what will he do with this Ford Falcon? Drive it all the way down US 33 and crash it into a West Virginia quarry? Or farther south to his grandparents' land that he now co-owns with Uncle Rory and set the rest of the forest on fire? He cruises Wacker Drive until dusk, stalking the Chicago River's turquoise water chipped by white shocks of ice. At dusk, he speeds the Falcon toward the docks. He jumps just before the car crashes into Lake Michigan. The car submerges and disappears in silence. No one notices. The only evidence is a palm-sized kneecap contusion that lingers for weeks.

Stolen Miles	Suspicions Raised	Lake Michigan Gals.	Gals. of Water in Orville
206	0	1,299,318,233,875,360	13.4

Orville Killen: Lifetime Stats

ORVILLE KILLEN

HT: 6'2"   Weight: 180

Born: September 4, 1934

CARD NUMBER: 70

Bats: Left   Throws: Right

Home: Paynesville, West Virginia

On July 4, while green and red stardust burst over your head, Orville was jetting off to Cincinnati, where he'd been traded and would land with a splash. In his first game for the Reds, he nearly hit for the cycle, getting a double, triple, and home run, but no single. Most players who near this feat miss the ever-elusive triple. Orville hit two of them, the last one in the ninth. He could have just stopped at first, but his horse legs and stubborn heart spoiled it all. Why wouldn't he stop? Who doesn't want the cycle? What player ignores history? The record books hold a grudge, spin a curse; Orville wouldn't leg out another triple all season, or ever again.

—What was Orville's last meal in Chicago?

—Rub edge of nickel or dime over blank box for magic answer ©:

Herman's wedding band.

Year	Team	LEA.	G	AB	R	H	2B	3B	HR	RBI	AVG.
1968	Chicago	A. L.	55	217	39	68	14	2	8	30	.313
1968	Cincinnati	N. L.	71	250	22	43	5	2	1	17	.172

114 Orville Killen: Lifetime Stats

MR. KILLEN   ADDRESS: FOX RUN LANE, 1B

HT: 6'2"   Weight: 185   Shoots: Left   Loads: Left

Born: September 4, 1934   Home: Anywhere but Paynesville, West Virginia

Orville is too close to home. He feels the coal soot and the hop clover pollen gritting into his sinuses. He has still not shat Herman's wedding band, which he stole and swallowed in July, but that must be coming, or else something is very wrong. Three days before Christmas, a plain brown box arrives at the door of the duplex he's renting. "Mr. Killen" is scratched in heavy pencil across the brown paper. Inside the paper, Orville uncovers a steel-toed-boots box. Inside this, he finds himself. Baseball cards. Dozens of 2.5-by-3.5-inch Orville Killens, the same few images repeated over and over. Some are creased, pin-holed from hanging, sun faded, dog eared, sooty fingerprints stamping his shoulder. Near the bottom of the box, a note:

> We've been collecting you. Good to have you back near home. Come visit.
> Always rooting for you,
> Uncle Rory

Many dozens of Orvilles squint and stare up at him. He drives into the country and sets up a sawhorse on a dirt two-track. He points the car's high beams. After loading the pistol he stole from Woolworth's, he aims between cardboard eyes and fires. Christmas Eve, Orville sucks from a bottle of bourbon until the newspaper rental listings blur into inky waves.

Shots Fired	Forehead Hits	AVG.	Cards Showing Eye Color Same as Mother
37	15	.405	Every single one

Orville Killen: Lifetime Stats

ORVILLE SOLOMON KILLEN   CARD NUMBER: 159

HT: 6'2"   Weight: 185   Bats: Left   Throws: Right
Born: September 4, 1934   Home: Paynesville, West Virginia

Despite a decline in his bat speed at the plate, Orville's eying the ball
like a hawk. He finished thirty-first in his division for bases on balls.
While old injuries hamper base stealing, he still knows how to turn two
and assisted in three double plays in one game on July 30 against the
Pirates . . . But, look, every player is not a legend. If they're lucky, they'll
hit a decent peak, and then begins the inevitable decline of age. They get
slower, weaker, meeker, sensing that ninth-inning grim reaper barreling
down the third-base line. Despite what we want to tell every child eagerly
fingering this card and flipping to the back for more than the front-side
thrill of a uniform-clad visage, there are times when unswerving
optimism runs out of steam. Better to say nothing than to elaborate on
spent, aging bodies. So we won't recall Orville's demotion to triple-A,
his refusal of reassignment, his swollen left leg, the wince he tries to
hide with every stride. We won't reveal that he quit instead of admitting
he could no longer steal bases and stop stealers. We will simply say,
zowie! What a sight to see those halide lights transforming nights to
days, men to giants, summer evenings to everlasting.

Year	Team	LEA.	G	AB	R	H	2B	3B	HR	RBI	AVG.
1969	Chicago	A. L.	81	259	19	53	8	0	2	22	.205
MLB Totals 12 Yrs.			1226	3999	570	1073	216	39	59	449	.268

Orville Killen: Lifetime Stats

ORVILLE SOLOMON KILLEN   HOUSE NUMBER: 129, SAME AS
                                     ALWAYS

HT: 6'2"   Weight: 180   Knocks: Left   Signs: Right
Born: Here, Long Ago   Home: Here, Finally

For four hours driving on the freeway, Orville strokes the foxtail he stole from his mother's casket years ago. It is not as soft as stolen undergarments or silk ties, not as beautiful, not as rare. This same foxtail brushed his shoulder when he was six and his mother first positioned his body into a proper batter's stance. He remembers the exact words she'd whispered into his ear as she choked his hand up on the bat: "Folks has got it wrong about the fox. He don't steal. What he does is take everything he's good enough to take. So you be the fox, and you'll never have to cough up a lung in those mines like your daddy."

Orville drives his Buick all the way to the address from the boots box full of his cards. It is an address he knows, a house number he's been trying to forget for a decade. He parks in front of the ranch-style clapboard house. Someone has recently painted it blue. It was a yellowing white before. When he knocks, a boy answers the door, around ten years old, and his eyes widen. "Holy shit," he says, and Uncle Rory is immediately behind him, swatting his head for swearing at the guest. As soon as he recognizes Orville, he repeats, "Holy goddamn shit."

Orville imagined this differently. He wanted throats sore from yelling. He planned on fists splitting red and raw against cheekbone and jaw, his and theirs. The shame he's avoided for so long should be dripping down his spine. *You should've seen your mother die, you selfish prick,* Uncle Rory should be saying. But he does not. Instead, they drink cans of beer and sit on the boy's bed while Dead Don's son shows off his baseball card collection. In polyurethane pages, rows of pristine Orville Killen cards flash by. Orville's already seen the images, but never cards this bright and new and perfectly kept. Don's boy picks one of each year to have Orville sign with a black marker. Dead Don's boy looks so happy.

Orville Killen: Lifetime Stats

He blows on the marker ink to dry it, then slips each card back into a transparent pocket. Before he goes outside to play, the boy displays the binder of cards on the coffee table for all to see, for anyone to take, unconcerned that someone might steal his treasure.

Foxtail hairs	Mother's Pitches	Killen Survivors	Complete Orville Collections
577,158,063	238,209	4	1

MISTINT

Paint the Town was having a going-out-of-business sale. The mistinted paints were 50 percent off. By noon, they dropped to seven dollars a gallon, four dollars a quart. Harbro's store had distinguished itself for its customer service, the color consultations, the satisfaction guarantee that cursed him with this ocean of mistinted cans. He set up shelves of Tortoise green, Battleship gray, Sunburst orange. The pinks alone absorbed a whole table. No one ever stuck with pink. It always pained him to mix it for customers, knowing they'd return displeased. Hot pink, Bubblegum, Posy, Petunia, Rose Petal, Cotton Candy—fill a wall and face your mistake as raw as an open wound. And any pink could be yours for deep discount.

He had three gallons of Briar Rose pink alone, a tint he custom-matched to Princess Aurora's dress from *Sleeping Beauty* for Jason Gwynn's nine-year-old, and she'd already grown out of that phase before he could dip roller to pan. Sweet old Harbro had replaced the cans at no extra charge. He ate the loss, ate all the town's mistakes. That was what you got for putting the customer first.

When Harbro's kids were young, he'd tell them they could pick any mistint they wanted to paint their rooms. They'd loiter in the shop after school, a daily half-hour ritual where they could admire their old man in his element. He'd buy them Cokes and describe the new colors they could take. But they buried their noses in books, finished their homework,

Mistint   119

awaited their mother's pickup, never once perusing the mistint shelf, their technicolor birthright.

Harbro lined up the wheats and mints and sky blues, the hues home-owners imagined would spice up their two-stories, until they witnessed a whole room too far from the off-white they'd always known. One color Harbro had none of: whites. Whites and blacks. He possessed no Alabaster, no Candlestick, no Ivory or Coastal Sand or Pearl, no Sugar Cookie or Cream or Vanilla, names sweet enough to eat. Black was just black, and he had none of that. Few fancy names for black. No hundreds of hues named by creatives back at corporate. When you wanted black, you were sure.

Purple, hell yeah, he had that. Violet to plum to mauve, he had you covered.

Turquoise, of course. Palmetto, you bet. He was swimming in red: burgundy and maroon and crimson, salmon and fire engine. When the septuagenarian Parkers wanted cardinal for an accent wall to surround their picture window where they bird-watched, he matched it better than God painted a feather. But once they dabbed a brushstroke to wall, they got to thinking Redwood red would better match their trees out back. He took pity on their social security budget, even when they returned to exchange the gallon of Redwood for Merino Wool white, the indecisive featherbrains.

Every color must go because Harbro was done getting kicked around by the impetuous populace of cheapskate Gladwin. Harbro's shop had been on the rocks for the last three years, scraping profit in the summers, only to dip into the red during aching Michigan winters. So Harbro's little store—that his wife, Lena, long ago named Paint the Town—had to shutter. He'd already sold everything else, all those off-the-shelf bases, every last brush and roller arm and nap. Once he found walls desperate enough for these ridiculous colors, he could call it quits for good.

A customer pulled up in his truck—a yellow pickup accessorized by a bullet hole in the tailgate. "I'm here to gander your wares, Shopkeep," the man said, his elbow swung over the window frame. "Name's Dom.

120   Mistint

Not Don. Dom. Like *doom* missing an *o*." His truck's tires squished over the curb and climbed onto the sidewalk, two feet from Harbro's stock, from Harbro's face. Dom could've reached out and pinched his nose.

"I got a parking lot. Most people shop on foot," Harbro said.

"I'm not most people." He let his truck slow-roll as he ogled the cans. "Suppose I got a use? What price could you name?"

Harbro pointed to the sign behind him: seven bucks a gallon, four for a quart.

"What I mean is how much for the whole lot?"

Harbro guessed he had three hundred gallons, enough to fill a Jacuzzi. He was going to lose his ass any way this panned. Paint the Town was already kaput, his family moved out, the nests all empty.

"Make me an offer."

"I got cash." Dom flapped a fan of green bills from below the window.

The only customer in the last three hours was that old man who'd haggled him down to $3.27 for a gallon of Hazard yellow. His lease on the store lasted another twelve days, but did he want to babysit the mistints and prolong this? "I'll take a thousand."

Dom whistled to his steering wheel. "Say another number," Dom said.

"That one's already in the basement," Harbro said.

"Let's see what's beneath that." Dom eased his foot off the brake and rolled back a few feet to eyeball the pinks again. He hummed like dinner was being served.

"Nine fifty."

"Closer," Dom said to Harbro's reflection in the sideview mirror. The man's brown broom mustache wiggled under his red nose.

"Eight seventy-five, but that guts me."

"The correct number happens to be seven forty, which happens to be exactly what I have in my lap."

"Damn it. Fine," Harbro said and reached for the bills.

"All right, partner," Dom said, "you may proceed to load my truck bed."

Mistint

Harbro suffered this final humiliation. One more couldn't hurt. Cash was a better roommate than mistint cans moving into the garage. He had plenty of space, of course, since Lena had left him. She was the one who'd first thought they could become the town's paint supplier, and he'd chased her optimism until Walmart showed up, then Lowe's. Turned out people didn't love mom-and-pops as much as they thought, as incongruous as a gallon of periwinkle blue. They wanted the predictability of white rafters, wanted workers as scared of you as you were of them. This town gave zero rats' asses about color theory; they wanted their off-the-shelf eggshell white one-stop-shopped alongside their wrenches, nails, Christmas decorations, and zero-point-turn-radius, self-mulching, riding mowers. They wanted to be confronted by an array of stunning hammers that reinvented what they thought a hammer could be. New handles coated in space-age grip materials, innovative claws, pink chromium, so that customers could surprise their beloved family handypeople with another duplicate tool they'd never use. Hammers and hammers and hammers, an infinity of hammers.

The town needed him as much as his kids needed a can of satin-sheen vermillion.

By the time Harbro had loaded the last can into Dom's truck, he'd worked up a sweaty hatred for this fool who couldn't be bothered to exit his truck and help. Just another customer who felt owed servitude after squeezing Harbro for a deal.

And when Dom said, "Wanna see what I'm up to?" Harbro wished he still held a quart to pitch through Dom's windshield.

"I don't do consultations anymore. This here's a going-out-of-business sale, if you couldn't guess."

"You wanna see what your colors can really do, you should hop in the back." Dom hooked a thumb toward his bed.

The final mistint sold meant closing time for good. Who would care if he wasn't behind the counter at Paint the Town? And Harbro would be going home to nurture his fresh loneliness. Microwave lasagna and

Mistint

Family Feud reruns awaited. He hadn't shared a moment with another human outside of work in months.

Harbro stuck his keys in the shop door and locked up. The truck's engine revved at his back. His stomach fluttered in a way it hadn't since Lena showed him two lines on the pregnancy test, or when he opened Paint the Town's doors for the first time. Life had been mostly gallon cans of beige since.

He climbed into the truck bed, set his buttocks atop two can lids, and off they went.

They passed the other sagging downtown businesses, all that brick-and-mortar idealism that would fold within a year or two, if not months. If you made it to Christmas, maybe you'd last until summer on the barbed gifts of holiday hopes. Lucile's Biscotti Paradise had a two-for-one sale going for three weeks, and Deep Cuts record store advertised a blowout sale that had started a week after the store's grand opening. Purple Treasures thrift shop and Stately Ladies consignment opened only on Saturdays now. Even what should've been bulletproof—Merwin's Newsstand, which sold porn mags, cigarettes, and liquor—had shuttered last month. Harbro knew all the anguished owners. Weeks after opening shop, everyone lost faith that the American consumer might get off their ass and stop online-ordering two-day shipping wonders.

They drove past Dale the Auto Doc, who'd closed up last May. Even car repair had been outsourced to the YouTube do-it-yourselfers. The truck rolled past the downtown's main street, through the tidy houses painted in off-the-shelf tans and whites and blues.

Harbro remained squatting atop paint cans as they turned onto a dirt road skirting the corn grown to be pulverized and bagged into hog feed. Here, the driver sped up, and Harbro clutched a wire can handle, though it would do nothing to secure him. The truck whizzed by a forest, whizzed by a creek, whizzed by a gray barn poking over a crop of rotten pumpkins that the good-for-nothing people of Gladwin couldn't be bothered to purchase on a discount. Even with the free hayrides, Walmart sold plumper ones for half the price.

Mistint   123

The truck sharp-turned onto a narrow two-track. Harbro bopped up
and down over the pitted path. "You're going to get the biggest kick out
this," Dom called out the window, and Harbro wished his scramble to
avoid an empty house hadn't spawned this joyride to nowheresville. Copper dust plumed up from the road, and he choked. Dom slid the back
window open.

"Almost there," he said, the mantra of the incomplete and inconsolable.
Harbro had thought that himself—*almost there*—when his kids both left
home four years ago. Life, he'd assumed, was nearing successful com-
pletion with the child-rearing accomplished. He could lean back into
another couple decades of work and a laissez-faire marriage with Lena,
who he never anticipated had been despising him the whole time. Almost
there and soon enough he could be dead without being to blame for any
great sins. But Lena left, and his kids busied themselves with careers.
They had yet to even ask how he was holding up after their mother left
him. What failing had he committed? He'd been searching for his own
Mauve Mistake, his Princess Pink, his Dayglo Orange. He'd gotten rid of
their cocker spaniel when it had drawn blood on his youngest, dropped
it off at a shelter and lied about it running away. He'd never hit anyone,
and when his daughter was five and drew with crayon all over her walls,
he'd bottled his temper, even though nothing was harder to paint over
than crayon. He'd never slept around outside the marriage. When his son
came out, he hadn't been disappointed. He'd said that was fine. Harbro
had never bothered anyone, had spent his evenings like his own father
had, watching TV, one beer every other evening. He'd been dependable as
Ceiling White. So where was the big sin? Why had everyone abandoned
Harbro?

At a void in the dense trees, the truck turned a tight loop and backed
to a clearing of raw dirt. As the truck reversed toward it, Harbro noticed
a darkening of the ground, shadows, a concavity. It was a pit, wide and
deep, a mouth yawning its earthy gullet. The truck kept backing to the
edge. From Harbro's vantage, the tires seemed to be levitating. He was
going to be dumped. He'd accidentally stumbled into the truck bed of

Dom's suicide. Just over the tailgate, the pit beckoned, stretching deeper the closer Harbro neared. Flashes marked the chasm's walls, white refrigerators and pale couches and ovens and tires and countless trash bags. And Harbro would now be dumped alongside all the paint he'd ever mistinted, though, damn it, the colors had never been his fault. Not once. He'd always given the customer exactly what they'd ordered. They'd been the fools who hadn't known what they wanted. So few knew. Lena hadn't known. Their marriage was her mistake, not his. If Harbro was such a pain in the ass, then shame on her for prolonging it.

The truck halted. Harbro clenched his fingers into fists. The tailgate floated over an endless pit.

"Don't fall in," Dom called from beside the truck bed. He offered a hand gloved in tulip print. Harbro grasped the hand and held his breath until his feet found dirt.

"Folks come out here to dump all sorts of junk. Been doing it decades." Dom raised to his tiptoes, chin stretching for a better abyss view. "It's a sinkhole. God's free landfill space." Dom started lifting paint cans and arranging them at his feet. Harbro studied this stranger as he handled a can of Pelican orange. He'd mixed this orange for Mrs. Dunfee's front door, and she brought it back claiming it wasn't autumnal enough.

Adrenaline still throbbed in his throat, but he couldn't find words for the questions he should've had. His body urged him to burn off this buzzed energy, so he busied his body with the instinctual motions of customer service. Harbro worked steadily, handing cans to Dom until he was encircled by silver lids.

"Time to pop these suckers open." Dom wielded a beer bottle opener, slow going. Harbro patted his pockets, and sure enough he still carried paint-can openers. They came complimentary with purchase, and they might as well have grown like fingernails from Harbro's extremities. He dropped one atop the lid Dom wrestled with. Dom switched tools and popped faster. He whistled to himself and then chucked the beer bottle opener into the pit. It clanged deep inside.

Once they had most of the cans opened and looking like a rainbow had vomited polka dots, Dom asked, "You sure got a lot of colors wrong, my friend. Is your tinting computer on the fritz?"

Harbro felt his face go hot as the red can he was opening. "I tint manually. Never used a computer. Supposedly, a customer could bring in their baby's favorite blankie and the computer's eye could match the color. Bring in a picture of your beloved Corvette or dead grandma's brooch or favorite team color—boom, perfect match, right? But there's a lot more to it. That computer can't account for how a person will really perceive color. I always got it right, when anyone cared to ask. The customers, they're the problem. They don't know what they really want. I'd warn them, but no one listens."

"Hot damn, I knew it." Dom cranked a lid so exuberantly that it sailed into the pit. "I snagged me an artist."

"I didn't say that."

"Preach more about how you beat the machine, how you're the John Henry of the paints."

"Well, you see, the computer eye can't account for the saturation in a photo, for sheen or glare. It's an eye with no brain. It misses the real color, the essence, the idea, what the customer really has in mind, and, as you can see"—Harbro fanned fingers over the opened cans—"they might as well all be colorblind."

His business had survived against the box stores so long because of his forgiveness, because he'd let the customers retry until they found the perfect match. Harbro could read people. He was a clairvoyant uniformed in a paint-splotched apron. Yet, at home, his kids' preferred hues remained inscrutable. His marriage had soured into a sun-bleached shade of yellow, impossible to color-match.

"Yet everyone loves color," Dom said.

"But which color, that's what no one knows," Harbro said.

"Man, can't nobody know what anyone wants. And all I know is I need a shit ton of color." Dom raised a quart of midnight blue to his

126   Mistint

chin, and Harbro wondered if he might take a sip to toast. "Ever seen color fly?"

Dom hurled the can into the pit. In the late afternoon-ing sun, a fin of dark blue flared. "You have now!" Dom said, laughing. Then Dom catapulted a gallon of red that slapped against dirt like a knife dragged raggedly. Red striped its bloody hue across the pit's long throat. Next he tossed a can of yellow that splattered against the door of an old refrigerator, smacking with a gong. He heaved a screaming orange and an auburn quart, one in each hand. Down into the pit they went, followed by pinks and turquoise and the liver purple. Dom spun a gunmetal gray, and it spiraled its dismal tint through the technicolor tunnel. And more and more. Reds polka-dotted mocha stripes swiped over sky blues.

Harbro watched in awe, until the colors ceased. Dom balked with can in hand. Staring, staring. "Aren't you going to help, Mr. John Henry of the tints?" he asked.

Harbro leaned down to an opened gallon of some garish amalgamation of yellow and green. That baby-puke tint had been for Molly Case's teenage son, who'd picked the color for his room just to piss off his parents. Molly had nearly been in tears when she returned the paint. *My son's an asshole. And it just happened one day, like he woke up a cockroach. You ever read Kafka? Except a cockroach would be an improvement, in my case.* He'd wondered if his kids were cockroaches. He couldn't tell what they were, these kids talking laconically about their days at dinnertime. Harbro had touched Molly Case's hand and then mixed up a new can of Buttermilk topcoat for her at no cost. Harbro's son's room had remained the same shade of beige his whole childhood. His kids had been careful of walls, clean and conscientious, all through their adolescence. To this day, in Harbro's empty house, the walls remained the same neutral color.

To forsake Molly Case's insectile son, Harbro could chuck this can. For Molly. He wanted to. Dom threw a half-dozen more cans while Harbro stood mulling, his brain a single gallon full of shelf white. His impartial, unreadable children. His beige life now glared against an accent wall of blazing, lonely numbness.

Dom paused tossing cans to climb into his truck bed. He leaned his torso through the back window. While he rummaged through his cab, his back legs flailed out the window, and Harbro thought how foolish he looked, how vulnerable. Why hadn't Lena just told Harbro how much he bored her, how much she resented him? Why hadn't she just told him what was so unpalatable about a life with him? Just say it. Just speak. Dom's legs flopped, edging his body deeper into the cab until he started cussing, stuck.

"Little help, man?" Dom cried.

Harbro's wife had left nothing behind, not a single pair of shoes, not a threadbare T-shirt or sock hidden behind the bureau. Traceless. On the Monday she'd left, he hadn't opened the shop. He'd brewed a French press, enough for two, and watched talk shows until he'd drunk both of their coffees. He should've smashed something.

"I said I need a spot, paint man."

He should've taken an axe to their mattress.

"I believe I am completely stuck."

He should've thrown her portion of coffee against their untouched beige walls, then emptied the fridge, mustard and soy sauce and ketchup bright as blood. Should've decorated each wall in travesty. Wiped his own shit on them. Still not enough.

Harbro whipped the can he'd been holding at the truck, at the wriggling ankles attached to the ridiculous man. The can erupted inside the cab, a yellow-green vomit bomb. A scream gurgled through all that color.

Next move was to make a run for it, but when Harbro turned, the pit gaped its reminder that the earth was an endless hunger. He couldn't jump the chasm. If he retreated down the road, Dom would catch up. Harbro shuffled, accidentally kicked a can into the pit. It dribbled a noncommittal line, the paint oozing slower than the can's descent, as if it didn't want to let go. He kicked another can, this time on purpose, a canary yellow that spilled like a sun god's spirit.

Before he knew it, he was punting cans. Intoxicating catharsis swept through his limbs. No more refunds. No more remixes. Not for Dom.

128 Mistint

Not for his wife. Not the kids. No one was getting anything back. No do-overs. No better versions for anyone in this life. Harbro was gasping. The armpits of his T-shirt clung to his skin.

Clicks sounded behind him. Harbro pivoted to find Dom, smeared in yellow-green, snapping photographs from the truck bed. Dom aimed the camera toward Harbro, its long snout of a black lens and gleaming glass eye. "Don't stop now, paint man."

"What the hell are you doing?" Harbro asked.

"I'm capturing you, man! Beautiful, enchanting, glorious you. It's even better than I'd hoped."

Click click clickity click went the camera's shutter. But Harbro was just standing, just breathing. Just a static life. Just work routine followed by sedentary domesticity. Open, close, go home to eat and sleep then do it again. He'd never risked doing anything worth photographing. Wasn't that enough to fill a decent person's time? The pit before him answered back, no. It taunted Harbro with its kaleidoscopic larynx.

"How far down does it go?" Harbro neared the edge, lifted himself to see all he could, and still no discernible bottom.

"All the way," Dom said through his clicking camera.

"All the way where?"

"Find out, paint man. What a picture that'd make," Dom said. *Click click click* went Dom's shutter. "They'd put you in galleries. You'd live forever."

Harbro lifted a leg, extended a toe. He was a ballerina with a paint-speckled sneaker.

Do it do it do it do it do it, the clickety clicking camera coaxed at his back. His ears bounced. What was the point of sticking around his empty house, empty nest, emptied paint shop?

"Best use for a life is art," Dom said. "To art! To life!"

Of course he couldn't. That would be as crazy as this final customer. His kids would hate him forever. That would require loving him, though. If he fell into a paint pit, maybe they'd grieve. Maybe that would shake them enough to paint a wall heliotrope, or garnet, or indigo as deep as

Mistint 129

nightmare. Someone he loved could show him some goddamn color preference.

Harbro shot off, sprinting toward the pit. Just before he neared the edge, he had a sensation of what he must look like through the camera lens. The peachy flesh of the back of his forearms, the pinkish ovals of his always-tender elbows, the sweat shadow tracing a gray cruciform across his back, the flaxen bald spot winking through his sparse silver-pepper hair. As his feet found the rim, Dom would be mashing the shutter. So much light an expensive camera could absorb, sucking it from the sun. As his body left the earth's moorings, he tried to bicycle-kick dramatically, for the camera, for Dom, for art, for some reaction from anyone, for the purity of paint, for every abandoned hue.

Then it was gravity's decision. Harbro's body lurched, dropped. He hit hard, hip and knee and brutalized shoulder. He'd crashed sooner than expected for an endless pit. He gazed up through a tie-dyed funnel. Through the pit's throat, sun-struck trees raked the blue sky. This hole was hardly endless. His body had landed on a washing machine. If the pit had ever been endless, there were always enough appliances going obsolete to fill a chasm of any size. Filling pits with junk was the American life cycle, the excretory system of capitalism. And Harbro the failed small-business owner, failed father and husband, had finally found his rightful place at the end of that system.

A shadow above him poked through the tunnel's sky-blue circumference. *Click click clicking* resonated down. Dom was documenting. But Harbro was out of interesting moves. One per life was what you got.

There didn't seem a way out. So this was it. This was Harbro's retirement, and he still had $740 in his pocket and probably a dislocated shoulder and maybe a broken rib. Dom clicked and circled the pit, and that was fine. Just fine. Dom was the only one in Harbro's world of quiet disappointment to embrace color, any and every tint.

Then Dom's head disappeared. A dropped rope slapped next to Harbro. It dangled before him, and prickles sharp as the whitest bright-white poked at his veins. A noose, Harbro thought at first. He touched the braided rope. But at the end swung a knot too small for his head.

"Put your foot in." Dom's voice echoed down. "I'll pull you up with the truck. What a ride it shall be!"

Above, the truck engine cleared its throat. A wisp of gray exhaust floated across the blue sky. Not much up there. A week and a few days on the store's lease. He owned their beige house outright, and he needed little to keep it running, to keep himself going until social security kicked in. The rope began to crawl upward.

Or he could sell the house. Wouldn't even need to repaint, not a single mark of evidence to touch-up. Sell and go somewhere bright. Anywhere. His granddad had grown up in Nova Scotia. That name carried a ring, as tinny as an empty gallon can. Nova Scotia Nova Scotia Nova Scotia. It sounded better than any name the paint companies marketed. Nova Scotia was spectral, a lightning force occurring in the great black din of outer space. A burst of light, a gaseous brilliance of sparkle. Or, no, that was a supernova, but close enough. Close enough.

And the rope crept up his shin. Harbro's options were stay here or return to empty stasis. Or third option: go and go and keep going until you find nova. He grappled the rope, clung even as the effort stabbed into his shoulder. But never mind that. Couldn't mind that. He struggled his toes through the knot and he was rising, lifting, his body mashing against the dirt, smearing through that earthy throat soaked in every mistake Harbro had made. By the time he reached the lip, he'd be wearing every color. He'd make quite a picture for the shutter waiting to witness him.

If his kids could see him now, his grown kids, adults who minded their own business, worked all day, paid taxes on time, and didn't feel compelled to worry about their own lonely father. If his self-exiled wife could see him. Maybe this coat of colors was what they'd needed him to be. He should've risked this, should've painted himself blue as the sky, bright as a blood moon, the deepest magenta of the freshest bruise. His whole life he'd been the primer forever waiting for its topcoat. Now he'd wear every color that had ever gone unwanted.

GOD CHOOSES THE WHEELBARROW

God and I are playing Monopoly again. He's chosen the iron as his game piece. It is forever the iron and only occasionally the wheelbarrow. When I ask why, he claims to enjoy the novelty of the design, so simple and useful. So, pride in humanity, I assume. No, not exactly, he says. And then he puts a hotel on the yellows, and I'm staring down the barrel of an exorbitant Marvin Gardens visit.

"You knew I'd land there," I say.

"Eventually," God says.

"Seems unfair, your knowing everything."

"I don't need to cheat," he says. "Show a little faith." He then licks a five-hundred-dollar bill and sticks it to his forehead. I don't feel like laughing.

It's hard to guess how many games we've played. Hundreds maybe. Thousands. Monopoly does that to you, its long yawn of capitalism stretching on for days, the cogs of profit churning, win some lose some, the ebbs and flows of the free marketplace. At least it beats my work back in life. Who knew how many hours I'd spent painting houses?

"71,629," God said.

"Is that a lot?"

"You spread 16,480 gallons on the walls."

"That seems like a lot."

God realigns the hotel on Marvin Gardens until it's exactly straight. "Municipal development goes so smoothly when there are no contractors on the board to overcharge and push back deadlines." God smiles, and the five-hundred-dollar bill flutters down from his face.

"Hey, don't blame me," I say. "Uncle Pennybags sure isn't innocent."

"Maybe the proletariat are implied. They're busy building green houses and cherry-red hotels."

"After work, they're all getting drinks at Baltic."

"Ha. Yes!"

"And where are they now, the proletariats, the real ones?"

God pinches the wheelbarrow up from the board, holds it between us. "Nothing much is cleverer than this." And then I land on Marvin Gardens and mortgage everything.

God always requests another game. He's always up for more. When I tell him I need a break, he suggests we walk.

God conjures red wooden bridges over koi ponds. Each koi throbs up to the surface flashing a different pastel color. God tells me I can snatch one and eat it raw, tells me they taste like marshmallows. I once again do not take God up on his offer. We sit on benches carved out of pink quartz.

I'm ready to ask again what I've been wondering since the first Monopoly game. In life, I couldn't even bring myself to ask for a fifty-cent raise. Monopoly has been teaching me to roll the dice. So I ask: "Where is everyone?"

"How do you mean?" God picks at a toenail with a fish bone that he then transmutes into a chopstick, then a dentist's pick.

"Everyone, I mean. Anyone."

"Well, people are busy, you know."

"Are they in hell?" I ask.

"Dave, come on." He ceases picking to look up at me. "You know that's not my thing."

"How about my mom then? My sisters?"

"Oh, they're resting," he says and stands. Leather sandals materialize on his feet. He walks a few steps, stops, and changes them to some black Harley boots. I follow him because I hate to be left alone here. I have the

God Chooses the Wheelbarrow

sense that God is instilling this dread of loneliness in me, though I have no way to prove it and no one to prove it to. We traverse a few more bridges and he switches to some of those old Reeboks with the basketball tongue pumps, then some mink-lined slippers, and finally he settles into a pair of pink Crocs.

"Can we go see them?" I ask, tagging behind God, in my own pair of Crocs, powder blue, shockingly comfortable.

"See who?"

"My mom. My sisters."

"Or is it 'whom'?"

"If not them, we could see someone else? Your choice."

"How about another game of Monopoly?" God says. He walks over the Milky Way, the rings of Saturn, a river of cats, Astroturf, an ocean, eleven YMCA swimming pools.

"Sure, God," I say.

"I call the iron."

No hunger, no tiring, no dips of that familiar melancholy—all that makes it pretty damn difficult to gauge the length of time we've played Monopoly. God keeps clocks. He finds them almost as amusingly designed as the wheelbarrow. But they all read different times and seem to tick at different speeds. God assures me that knowing wouldn't make a difference. Despite no urges, no earthly needs, I struggle to shake wanting to know what time it is.

And when I ask, God replies, "Time to get a watch!"

So, I have three houses on Boardwalk and Park Place and hotels on the greens. The bougie side of the board promises certain financial death, but God has Baltic to New York Avenue strung up in hotels. Plus, he owns the utilities, which I land upon with a greater frequency than seems mathematically probable. Every time I shake the dice to decide what I'll have to pay him, he bellows, "Let there be light. Let there be water."

I land on a St. Charles hotel and give God all my cash but a pale twenty-dollar bill. I take another stab. "I know my mom and my sisters are a big ask. They're a lot. Believe me, I know. But I was thinking maybe someone like Winston. Winston's the easiest guy in the world. He'd love you. How about we hang with him?"

Everyone loved Winston, a guy I'd painted houses with in my twenties. He was always a little stoned, always hugging everyone, complimenting their posture, asking after the health of everyone's grandparents, recommending they go on cruises. I never ran into him again throughout the rest of my life, but he'd been so sweet when we'd existed together. God can't deny Winston.

"Take a ride on Reading," God says to himself and hands me a corn-yellow hundred.

"Monopoly is even better with three."

God rolls doubles, ends up just visiting. "Would he want to be the iron?"

"No way. Winston is a cannon man, or maybe the car. A real man's man," I say, and when God tucks his beard into his chest, I scramble. "But not in a creepy way. Respectful guy. And funny. Nice. You'll love him."

God buys a set of hotels for the reds, assuring my doom. "Your turn," he says.

I land on Indiana, just as he knew I would, and that's game.

God outstretches a palm and aligns three hotels and five houses upon it. His palmistry lines weave through the red and green domiciles like suburban streets. "Play again?"

"How about we play for him? I win and you invite Winston to join us for a game?" I say.

God closes his hand into a fist. "Let me think about it."

We stroll the statue garden, which looks a bit to me like a junkyard of human ingenuity: a steam engine, a cotton-candy machine, blow-dryer as big as the Chevy Silverado it leans on, jackhammer, wood chipper, box of deck screws, mannequin wearing a pastel blue leotard with headband

God Chooses the Wheelbarrow

and leg warmers, and his newest additions: a row of 3,003 different kinds of irons across from a row of 1,001 wheelbarrows. We count them together. God seems very pleased with himself.

"Any additions you'd like to see?" God asks me.

"How about Jesus?"

God's smile sags. "I think you're missing a key point here. See, this is a statue garden."

"I mean, can I meet Jesus?"

God's smile has one deep dimple on his right cheek. He ruffles his robe skirts in his fists. "Ready?"

"Yes."

"Wanna close your eyes?"

"Do I have to?"

"It would be more fun."

When I open my eyes, there is the same God who's always been there, grinning wide, his dimple dark as a hole.

"Where's Jesus?"

"He's me. I'm him."

Most my life, I was working during church time, the sabbath, I suppose. But as a kid I'd learned the Sunday school fundamentals—the holy trinity: son, father, and holy ghost, all three for the price of one. I never got how that worked when I was a kid. Like claims of paint and primer all in one can. Now I see that it's all just God and more God.

I buckle down. I razor-edge my focus. I buy every property I land on and bolster my liquid assets by mortgaging everything until I've erected a line of hotels on the oranges, then the reds, then the purples. If I win, God will have to grant me someone. He seems reasonable. He's been considering it. He must be getting bored with just me. I've written a list on a papyrus scroll: my first-grade teacher, Mrs. Lamott; Mom again; my third cousin Trevor, who lost a nostril to a dog and never stopped talking about it; my uncle Bobby; my car mechanic, Walt; Lucinda at Sherwin-Williams,

136 God Chooses the Wheelbarrow

who mixed the paint and always called me "darling." We play games back-to-back until my eyes should be bleeding, but I feel no pain. I never will or can again.

I win for the first time since our terms. God tosses down his properties with a playful smack. He says, "Winner picks up." He hovers while I reorganize the dollar amounts and stack the properties and gather my hotels. My head buzzes with that thrill I used to get when rehearsing the compliment I'd give Lucinda for matching that last gallon so perfectly.

"Rematch?" God asks, balancing the top hat on his fashionable pinky.

I can't feel disappointment, of course. Instead, I think of more names to add to the scroll. I repeat Lucinda. I rewrite Mom. I write down every soul I ever pushed a brush beside, except that claptrap Yancy. Then I write down Yancy anyway. When I run out of names, I write down the 1987 Detroit Tigers roster. I repeat the list. I repeat again.

God praises my skill, once I'm rolling sixes on command. A few million throws and anyone can figure it out. God's game steps up, too, a perfectly balanced competition, enough for me to think I could win each match, though I almost always lose.

"Winner picks up," I tell God.

We walk through the Gobi Desert, through the Mall of America, across the bottom of the Bering Sea, through the center of the earth, through a black hole, through my childhood neighborhood. No one else is ever anywhere. But I can tell God is making a gesture, letting me revisit where I grew up. He is God. He knows, of course, what I truly want, even though it is an odd kind of want that I'm not really able to feel in any kind of disparaging way, so that it isn't really discouraging but only slightly less blissful.

Yet I ask: "Why me?"

"All my children are special," God says, as we walk-float over a flooded golf course.

"I never had any," I say.

God Chooses the Wheelbarrow

"You kept busy working."

"Did I do it wrong?"

"You were rolling those dice, passing Go." God dips down to pluck a purple jellyfish.

"And where would I be if I wasn't here now?"

"Oh, you've still got the wrong idea." God lifts his robe as we wade across a stream. Radioactively glowing trout navigate between our legs. "Now doesn't matter. It still doesn't."

But I start keeping ticks inside the Monopoly box, hidden under the instructions. I use the cannon to scratch little plowlines. God doesn't seem to notice. Maybe he doesn't care.

"What would my kid have been like, if I did have one?" I ask. "Is that a thing you know?"

God rolls doubles, passes Go, rolls eleven. He's going for speed, stacking cash piles. "I know everything," he says, and then rolls twelve, then twelve, then eleven, and buys Tennessee. Unless one of us screws up a roll, we can tell how this one will end.

I imagine a girl, green eyes, left-handed and decent at guitar, like her old man. She'd do shitty in school, except for science class. She'd love chemistry, do too many drugs for too many years, and then go to graduate school before she engineered polymers for DuPont. She'd call every Friday at six, stop by when she could, and we'd drink two beers together on those precious nights. I'd get only 183 of them, if she would've existed.

"Is that right?" I ask God.

He rolls another twelve and twelve and eleven.

"What I imagined just now—is that how it would've been?"

God doesn't pass Go. "I'm not so sure I see the point in this anymore."

We try Battleship, Risk, chess, Stratego, but God grows weary of war. Connect Four follows, then Bagh-chal then mahjong then Mystery Date and Mouse Trap and Life. Next come the card games, but God has no

138 God Chooses the Wheelbarrow

imagination for cards, can't get interested in a game held in a single hand. He prefers elaborately designed boards, humankind's most absurd and inexplicable ideas.

I return to the Monopoly box to make my secret scratches. When I fill every inch, I celebrate the occasion by swallowing a green house. Next, a hotel, then three more houses. I pass God walking and pop one like a mint. He shakes his head, lowers his vision to his pink Crocs, and hustles away. After the houses and hotels, I eat the race car, then the dog, next the top hat. I make sure to brush God's shoulder over the koi pond bridge the day I pop the iron, his iron. His mouth opens, yet he says nothing.

They don't come out the other end. No digestion in heaven. But they have to be somewhere.

God and I don't cross paths for what may be one thousand days. I've given up keeping track, and I haven't seen the Monopoly board in however long it has been. So, there is no way to know, but somewhere in my gut that has become a subdivision for plastic green houses and red hotels I sense time passed.

I linger at my childhood house. It's the only home where, in life, I didn't pay rent. The only place of any permanence in my lifetime of working on other people's houses while I lived inside leases. So, I repaint every room red and then yellow and then black. I paint the outside green, and that feels productive. That feels like a labor God might find clever. I mow the lawn, which doesn't need it, but the grass grows long just as the mower approaches so I always feel satisfied. I tear up the carpets and find hardwoods, which I refinish and then also paint black, and then I tear up the hardwoods to find more carpet, luxurious red shag. I smash all the windows and make the flooring sparkle. I reshingle the roof with pots and pans and stainless-steel kitchen appliances.

I sneak into God's sculpture garden and steal all his irons. I deposit them down my chimney. But then I decide I don't like that God won't see. I excavate them and build an iron tower God could spot from the koi ponds.

God Chooses the Wheelbarrow

I forget about the green houses populating my gut, forget about the ticks inside the Monopoly box. Time—or whatever its heavenly equivalent is—passes lethargically but still with enough energy for erasure. I try to forget about him, but it's all just God and more God.

When I spot God from the shiny roof of my childhood home, nostalgia shoots through my toes. I want to ask him everything. I have better questions now. I think I now know how I could've made him prouder, spent my time better—fewer gallons of paint on the walls, fewer times passing Go, and I could've adopted a dog named Trick. I want to tell him, but I trip over a skillet, ram my chin into a saucepan. God passes down the street.

He isn't alone.

Which means I'm not alone.

I squint at God's new guest. They seem shorter, my sister's height perhaps, but they wear cutoff sleeves, like Winston wore to work every shift. The flash of tan flesh swings back and forth at God's side. Their strides match God's robe skirts. The guest wears skirts too. No face appears. God obstructs my view until they turn and only the back of God's guest's head remains.

I yell my sister's name, then Winston, then Jesus, then Lucinda, then the name of my never-born, imagined daughter. Clarice, I shout again, from my pots-and-pans roof and into the heavens. They stop walking, and she seems as if she's going to turn. But God puts a hand on her shoulder, reassuring, warm and generous, and they turn the corner.

I return to work shining up my roof. I climb the tower to place a few more irons at the top so that on their next walk through my neighborhood they'll have to stop and marvel at my labor. They'll have to notice. They'll have no choice. And then I'll claim a job well done.

PRIVY

Bill's nose kissed the toilet, his cheek pressing against the cold tiles of God's house. He wrestled with the closet bolts, but the porcelain base refused to align. He was the only one bowing in this church on a Tuesday. The Second Presbyterian Church of Saginaw, Michigan, required a new shitter for the women's bathroom, and thus begot Bill. Certainly not the only man for the job, but the cheapest, credited with passing quality and a polite demeanor according to his few Angie's List reviews. Bill's company, Up and Up Plumbing, had made their bread on undercutting the competition. The company was really only just Bill. Bill and his sister Rita, who answered calls and booked appointments while running an unregistered day care out of the double-wide she'd won in her divorce with that dickhead husband of hers that Bill had been forced to slap around a half-dozen times after said dickhead had slapped around his big sister.

A knot hardened in Bill's lower back, and he had to stand to stretch his spine. He gave the bowl a useless kick, knowing nothing would give. That's what cheap got you; this replacement the preacher had selected was even chintzier than the ancient one he was replacing. But Bill was the king of cheap. This was his terrain. He prostrated himself again to squint under the base at decades of churchgoer gunk and the remnants of an ancient wax ring. The bolts were maybe a quarter inch off, just off standard, probably some weird metric shit manufactured in Cambodia

Privy   141

due to, again, that preacher's cheap-assedness, which was, after all, how Bill had lucked into this job. He rattled the bowl with a grip as cruel as he'd used on Rita's ex that time after he'd bloodied her nose. The porcelain still refused to settle home.

The women's bathroom door scooped open, hinges whining, needing WD-40. He wondered if it was that preacher, Dwight, come to check on him. He waited for that bearded crone to loom behind him, dentures gleaming, making another joke about the "crapper being crapped out," and then snickering like a schoolboy. Bill turned to discover stubby black heels planting themselves before a toilet two stalls down. Dread oozed down his forearms, viscid and vile as a forty-year-old wax ring. The moment the door squeaked, he should've yelled *Occupado, hombre*. But it was too late. A skirt dropped to sheathe the ankles, followed by the cloudlike collapse of white panties. Urine hissed. All sound echoed off the omniscient tiles: the toilet paper roll shrieking, a sniffle, the folding of paper even, the wipe against pubic hair he tried not to imagine. His breaths rioted out his whistling nostrils. All too loud not to be noticed.

Bill had passed the moment when he could've identified himself—a plumber in the women's bathroom. Since his work was mostly residential, he'd never found himself trapped in this awkward limbo. Now each passing second made his silent presence more painful. He hadn't prayed in years, ever since his prayers had been answered and then turned against him after his wife came out of surgery, clumps of metastasized tissue lighter. All had gone better than expected, and against odds she'd recovered, rock-starred remission, and then after her one-year cancer-free checkup, she didn't return home, never again. That had been five years ago. And just last month, his teenage son, August, had driven away on the license he'd freshly earned. He left home without a word. Bill had recently been considering praying again. But what if God held grudges, annoyed that Bill only ever begged God as a last resort, as if the boss of the universe were some emergency hotline hack? Bill hated those midnight emergency calls when someone's water heater blew out its ass, and he couldn't blame God for delivering shoddy miracles under

142 Privy

such circumstances. What Bill *had* blamed God for was his wife's cancer when it looked like it might swallow her. He'd blamed and despised and damned, before the inevitable God-groveling.

Being so close to God now, crammed against His new throne, praying overflowed easily enough: *Please let this woman finish pissing and never know I was here.* He feared for a moment that maybe even his prayer's words could echo off the cruel tiles of God's bathroom and alert the woman.

Buzzing answered his prayers. Bill strained his ears to make sense of God's incoherent pulsing response. It didn't make sense, just as a customer couldn't understand the clogs in the P traps and gully traps and U-bends. They'd gladly shell out his emergency-call hourly rate for Bill to translate their house's cosmic mysteries of plumbing.

God's buzzing was cut off, finally, by a woman's voice. "We're done talking," she said, snapping at God from her stall. Not even a hello. But, of course, it wasn't God. It had only been her cell phone on vibrate.

"Fuck you is what I think about it," she said, thundering inside her stall.

Bill raised himself from the tile, slowly, slowly. Even the rustling of his denim seemed to scream. His traitorous flannel shirt and jeans—he'd strip and flush them all down the church's toilet if he could.

"I'm not giving up my kids when it's convenient for your work schedule. You and your lawyer's joint-custody offer can both go straight to hell."

As she damned souls on the other end of the phone, Bill calculated escape. Run or hide. He decided on the latter and stepped up to perch on the toilet seat. He'd secured its cheap plastic locknuts—thank Christ—though who knew how long the Cambodian-molded plastic might withstand his weight.

"And I'm not selling the house either, which is my house now, so you just better get comfortable in your one-bedroom fuck pad, Lloyd."

If Bill rose to his toes, he could probably see a portion of her face over the stall walls, but that might risk exposing himself. "The kids love

Privy 143

that house, so they get it, so I get it, and I get them. You can move on to destroying other people's lives."

Bill couldn't imagine ever talking like this to his wife. But maybe if he had, August wouldn't be gone, joining his mother in a family exodus, as if Bill didn't even exist. And he hoped he could remain invisible here, hoped the cheap toilet held, hoped the porcelain base didn't crack from its teetering atop nonstandard-size bolt housings. Partition walls were God's gift to bathroom privacy, and he thanked the lord for manifesting the man who decided no one needed to see each other while shitting. He'd once read that the Romans used to share a single bench, all lined in a row, conversing while they shat into a communal trench. Modern plumbing allowed everyone to embrace their private shame in peace.

She cleared her throat a few times, an anger clogging in her throat as this wicked Lloyd on the other end of the call murmured on. Bill could get back to work soon. Be done and finish safe and sound and unaccused of church-lady-peeping perversion. But then he noticed his toolbox, bright yellow and squatting near the door. She'd certainly spot it in the mirror when washing her hands. His wife had gifted him this toolbox, remarking that the usual gray and black were so boring, and he could leave an impression on customers with a banana-yellow toolbox.

"No, Lloyd," she finally said. "That's not how it's going to be. I'm clean, and you know that, and I'll piss in any cup to prove it. I'm keeping my kids and keeping it all and that's how it's always going to be. And I'll teach the kids to hate you if I feel like it. That's that free speech you're always bitching about, Lloyd. How do you like it?"

Bill eased back onto the tile. He lifted his toolbox, careful not to rustle a single socket wrench. He cradled the loud yellow in his arms and raised his boot to return to hiding, but her words stopped him. "I don't give a shit if you're recording this. I'm their mother. And you won't get a goddamn anything. Have a horrible fucking day, Lloyd." And then silence draped its heavy curtain back over the bathroom.

Everyone shat. Everyone pissed. Everyone conducted deeply personal, life-changing moments while sitting on a toilet. Bill's livelihood involved the facilitation of such constants. The trouble here was Bill had pushed too far into the private. His extended silence had frozen him into a porcelain statue cradling a yellow toolbox. He might never move again, might never catch up to his far-flung wife and son.

The toilet flushed. The stall door squeaked on its hinges. The toolbox in Bill's arms was heavier than he remembered. Her heels clicked tile, five, six, seven steps. The sink sounded its aerated rush, punctuated by the crank of the soap dispenser. A corner of his yellow toolbox was stabbing into his forearm. He burned to readjust.

The water stopped. Only a dripping followed that he could fix with a quick quarter turn of the wrench. The heels should've been clicking again. The hand dryer should've picked up its roar. Yet only the unchecked drip-drip-dripping panged so hard it felt like the energy could bend each wrench in his box.

"You know I know you're in here, right?" her terrifying voice said. "I think they say, 'Shit or get off the pot,' no?"

He tried out a few responses in his head, and they all seemed calamitous. There was no exit strategy here. His bowels shuddered, and he suddenly felt as if he may literally need to abide her ultimatum.

"Well, big guy? What you got to say for yourself," she said, and he shifted to see her face reflected in the mirror through a slim crack in the stall's door. She was wiping at a dark streak under her eye. Maybe she'd been crying, though she'd sounded tougher than steel pipe. She wore a purple coat that looked bright and new against her mousy brown hair.

"Bet you think I'm a bitch after spying on my phone call? Men love spotting a bitch, right?"

"None of my business, ma'am. Just doing my job," he said through the crack in the door. "But you sure swear better than any church lady I've ever met."

"What's a church lady usually say?"

"Sorry, ma'am. I didn't mean nothing."

"What a sad language we'd speak if I couldn't say 'fuck,' even in the bathroom." She was re-penciling her eyes in black outlines now. He decided he could set down his toolbox. The box clanged a metallic shudder like a car crash. When his wife gifted the toolbox, he'd resented it, a sure sign she didn't know him, what he liked, what he wanted, as if a plumber was all he was. Now, though, he treasured it, this unsolved clue hinting at why she left him.

"So what's so wrong with the men's bathroom that you had to dump out in here?" she said, beginning to wash her hands again. The water rushed through the aerator. "Or maybe you're some pervert?" Her skin squished with lathering soap. "You get off on the smell? That seems an inconvenient fetish, Mr. Big Boots."

"I told you I was working. Your airhead preacher should've put up the dang sign."

"People come to church for signs, yeah?" she said, drying her hands. The blowers bellowed for far too long. "But I never found one, especially outside this bathroom."

"I'm the plumber. I should've said that first."

"How am I supposed to know that's legit?"

He kicked his yellow toolbox forward, under the stall door. "That ain't no average pervert's toolbox."

She kneeled to the box, opened it. Through that emaciated strip between stall door and wall, her hands grazed the chamfer cones and pipe cutters and vinyl tape rolls. "My husband, my ex, that asshole, only had a hammer, some screwdrivers, a set of socket wrenches he never removed from the store packaging. I'm keeping his toolbox too. He sure as hell won't ever use it."

"Well, I use all that stuff in there. I'm using it now. That's the only reason I'm here. Ain't no pervert."

"It seems possible you could be both."

This woman's words felt like the tightening nut of his pipe wrench. Bill was now serving as proxy for the fire of her husband hatred. He was a sacrificial lamb, he supposed. But how much shit would he have to take, when he'd probably have to also eat the cost of this cheap-ass toilet that didn't fit?

146   Privy

"Push my box back," Bill said. "I got work to finish."

"Which one, do you think, is your most important tool?" she asked. "Or, no, wait. Which one is the most expensive?"

"Just push them back." He sensed they were going deep down some subterranean passage he had no desire to inspect.

"My money's on this one." Through the sliver, she was holding his DEWALT pipe expander, a splurge once it was clear every cheap customer was going to choose PEX pipe, and Bill was the cheapest plumber for the cheap people. But the expander sure as hell wasn't cheap, and even someone who knew nothing about plumbing would recognize its value against his sea of dingy wrenches.

She scooted the box back to him. The PEX expander was missing. She was taking all she could from her husband, and Bill's expander would become her newest trophy.

"I need that," he said through the stall door, fingering the lock.

"I bet you do. Looks pricey."

"Shit," he let slip. Then, "Shoot."

"What will God think of your foul mouth now?"

She disappeared off the side of the mirror, and by the time he'd opened the door, her clicking heels had silenced behind the creak of door hinges.

He should've stopped her sooner, but what could he do—tackle some stranger woman in the women's bathroom? Then say what to the preacher? Thou shalt not steal PEX pipe expanders, or ye shall be chased and walloped by thy plumber. And now he was lumbering down the empty church hallways floored with dreary brown linoleum, brick walls decorated with tapestries made to look like the stained glass of a nicer church. Bill was now wondering if they'd even have enough alms to pay the cheapest plumber in town. He wasn't earning a mint here, but this job combined with his meager savings could earn him enough to take the next week off and go driving down the country to look for his missing son. He imagined August and his mother reunited at one of America's most estranged geographic tips, Key West maybe, which she'd mentioned wanting to visit a few times when the opiates had her dreamy enough to forget

Privy 147

she was dying. Key West sounded like a lovely exile Bill would navigate toward.

Now, though, this terrifying woman would force the money he'd been saving to go into replacing the PEX expander. He tried not to hate her, not in a church.

She was nowhere to be seen, and Bill stopped to sip from the bubbler, a poorly aging Elkay model probably installed thirty years ago. The water dribbled at such a low pressure that to sip he would've had to touch his lips where hundreds of parched churchgoers had suckled over the years. With still no sign of the lady, he popped the few screws on the housing to expose the Elkay's rusting innards. He tightened up the regulator screw, tried the water again, and smiled at its new proud arc. If nothing else, Bill had saved the thirsty multitude from lapping at each other's saliva.

Bill continued through the narthex and into the nave congregated by smoothly sloped oaken pews, all empty. Probably not much different on Sundays these days, when no one seemed so interested in going to church, unless they were going to those rock-concert versions of service. August had begged Bill to go to one of those once, when the chemo was strangling August's Mom's body into a shrivel. The kid had hoped one of these healthy churches could share their survival secret, that overly enthusiastic species of grace. The music had been as loud as the Rush concerts Bill used to attend, but he didn't appreciate the hearing damage it was inevitably causing, damage he'd welcome from Geddy Lee at the mike. The church had doled out free T-shirts and fancy-ass cappuccinos to them after, everyone bubbling and giddy, and then they'd driven home with ringing ears. This, though—this silence of an empty nave populated by carved pews—this felt like true church, one so quiet God had to hear your every stirring thought. He wished he'd taken August somewhere like this back then. Bill sat and closed his eyes. He tried to imagine what a real prayer might sound like. But he kept stalling after the first part. *Dear God—Dear God—Dear God—*

Bill bet no one could hear themselves praying at those rock-concert churches. And those churches were hiring the expensive plumbers when

148   Privy

their toilets quit, those Roto-Rooter boys, a place he'd never work for, no matter how many times crazy women stole his most expensive tools, which was, okay, just once, just this one time.

"Wrap up already?" a melty voice said from behind him, and then a warm hand dropped onto his shoulder. "I hope progress flowed smoothly, regarding the crapper that is." The preacher chuckled through his brown teeth. He was missing one way back there. So was Bill, and it made him like the man a molar-size more.

"Almost done," Bill said. "Just fighting a few last fits."

"Take a load off. This is a nice place for that."

"I can hear myself think."

"Oh yeah? What does that sound like?"

"Nothing all that useful going on up here." Bill knocked knuckles against his skull.

The preacher laughed too loudly, like a bang. He was embarrassed for both of them, probably God too.

"There was a woman," Bill said.

"Oh, we're doing that, huh? We can talk about that, I suppose." The preacher sat beside him. "This woman, she wasn't your wife?"

"What? No, not that. My wife's gone." He'd twisted up the preacher, he realized, made him think he was going to put him to work doing confessing labor. "I mean, I'm talking about a woman here, in the church. I'm trying to find her."

"I'm truly sorry about your wife, Bill. That pain is an unimaginable burden, only matched by the gift of love shared."

"It's not about that. And she's not dead. It's okay. It's fine," Bill said, even though it wasn't and it never would be and preachers were full of lines like this to mop up after their boss's cruelties. "The woman I'm talking about was just here. Did you see her?"

"It's just me, and I'm here for you." The preacher's hand on Bill's shoulder was hot now, and it felt like steam was building up under Bill's T-shirt. "Oh, and the narcotics folks."

"The what?"

Privy   149

"We lend our space. You know, the Narcotics Anonymous."

"Right. Yeah. Where do they meet?"

The preacher was gazing into his phone, distracted just like everyone these days, his eyes lost to a tidal scrolling. That meant, then, no more help from man or God. Bill stood from the pew. The hard, wooden pew had set off his hemorrhoids to aching, and he could only imagine the hell of sitting on these finely carved torture devices for an entire Sunday service. He stepped past the preacher, bumping his phone.

"Where you off to?" the preacher said, still screen-staring.

"It's fine. I can see you're busy."

"I was just looking it up, their meeting." The preacher pointed at his phone. "They wrapped up half hour ago, says here."

"Your phone says that?"

"I keep everything on it. Surprised a young business owner like you doesn't do all that."

How much of an age difference could there have been? That there were still souls to declare Bill youthful made him appreciate the preacher once again, forgive him the slight of ignoring Bill for the phone, which he'd only imagined. Perhaps that woman, too, was trying to commit some kind of high-tech good Samaritanism that he wasn't technologically equipped to comprehend. His sister Rita handled the computers for him. She'd even tracked all of August's social media accounts only to report that the last thing he posted was a photograph of a plate of quiche. That was his mom's favorite meal.

Bill lied to the preacher that he was getting back to work and then walked down the center aisle, flanked by pews. He kept hoping for a misunderstanding between himself and the woman as he reentered the hallway, its cracked brown linoleum, its smudgy windows, the peeling cream-colored paint on the bricks. Just because he didn't understand, didn't mean cruelty. His wife, too, her leaving—maybe there was a hidden kindness somewhere in it. Maybe she was dying again and wished to spare him and August. Though this seemed worse than her leaving him to get drunk for decades in Key West. He tried to pray again: *Dear*

God, Dear God, Dear God. How've you been? You know, I guess, I'm not great. But okay in the scheme of things. Okay, I guess, is what I'm officially reporting, so you can count me as one not to worry about. Not all too much. Except for the expander, which was expensive, as you know. And I need that money to find August. I'm sure you got a hell of a lot more to worry about, though.

He winced for thinking *hell* directly at God. He bowed to take a drink from the repaired bubbler. When he rose, he looked through the window and spotted a purple coat, the skirt, those stubby heels, out in the parking lot. She was opening the trunk of a '90-something Mustang. He rushed out the door after her, his feet light with a tingle like God's breath. The trunk slammed. He was close enough to feel the smack of the sound, and he was probably hustling too quickly, nearing the woman, who, he realized now, was shouting. He must've looked a bit intimidating in his barreling, but it was too late to stop his momentum. And then she wasn't shouting anymore, but instead bending, fiddling at her foot. Her shoe smacked into his chin, wet and cruel.

"You get the left next," she said.

"Wait, just wait. This is all wrong. You've got me wrong." He rubbed at the fresh sting, tasted blood. He knelt to the cracked blacktop, picked up her shoe, and offered it to her.

"Okay, yeah, thanks, creepy plumber guy." She lifted her leg into a triangle to replace the shoe standing up, flamingo-like.

"I'm not creepy."

"Spy on a gal pissing and then chase her down in the parking lot."

"It's out of context."

"Put it in context then."

"You stole my fricking expander." Bill looked down at his boots and imagined throwing one at her in retaliation. Both at his cancer-defeating wife. He worried, then, that God was still on the line, listening in after the prayer. "Can I please just have it back?"

Her hands disappeared into the front pockets of her purple coat. "You'll have to earn it."

Privy 151

"Look, lady, I just wanna finish my job and go home. I got stuff I gotta do."

"Look, guy," she leaned toward him, "I don't want to keep you from your precious stuff. I'll only ask something real easy." He anticipated her asking him about scoring some pills, some dope. He'd long ago flushed all his wife's extra opiates. He'd be forced to have an awkward conversation with Rita, who'd have to call up that wife-beating dickhead ex of hers. So much shit rolling downhill.

"My husband, my ex, was Catholic. I wasn't," she said. "When it was time for communion, he kneeled up there by the priest all lonesome and haughty, and I just had to watch. Like a heathen. Like I was less than."

"So?"

"So I want the preacher's communion wafers. Go get them for me, and you get your expander thingie-whatever back."

"I'm not stealing from a church."

"It's to save a soul, plus your tools. God could appreciate a bargain like that."

"I'll call the cops."

"Call them. You can explain to them your pervert-peeping context." She opened her Mustang's door, sat down inside, said, "You have eight minutes, and then I'm out of here. I got stuff to do too." The door closed.

Bill stared at the Mustang's hood, a shade of green that, like her purple coat, seemed too bright for this faded woman grasping for eccentric revenge or whatever this was. The woman wrapped her fingers around the wheel inside, pretending not to see him. And once again, he wasn't trying to see her, trying to see anything. He just happened to be here, stuck sharing this private space with her.

His legs carried him back into the church and past the bathroom where he hadn't finished his job of bullying the cheap toilet into place. First, he'd have to go to the kitchen. That seemed like where one would keep the body of Christ, which, when you got down to it, was still flour-based, a bit of yeast, dash of salt.

Privy

The kitchen smelled of fresh baking. He was about to give up when the preacher appeared, smiling brownly, as if he thought his terrible teeth some kind of prize. "Forget your lunch at home, friend?"

"No, I'm just, I guess, trying to find something."

"To eat? Or, oh, you're probably following water lines. I'm sorry. I'm sure you know what's best. I have complete faith in you. I'll leave you to it." The preacher turned on the squeaky heel of his cheap rubber Walmart shoes.

"Where do you keep the communion wafers?" Bill asked the preacher's back, because he had five minutes left by now, maybe.

"For that," the preacher turned back around, a look of pleasure broadening over that busted brown smile, "we bake bread. Two loaves feed a congregation these days, and you're in luck." The preacher turned to the counter, to two stained dishrags. He lifted them to reveal a pair of loaves, golden on top. The lifted rags released the heady smell of baked bread, and Bill remembered when his wife used to make it. It wasn't anything special, she'd say, just some frozen dough. But it was Bill's favorite thing, the bread soft as cotton candy. He'd never found out what not-special frozen dough she'd used, so there had been no bread since the cancer had left.

"I need these," Bill said. "I'll cut you a break on the toilet install."

"That's kind of you, but you're already the best price in town."

"What can I give you?"

"You're a good man, Bill. Take them. They'll make a fine lunch."

Bill reached for the loaves. Only two or three minutes left before the Mustang rumbled off carrying his expander. The woman would probably chuck it out her window, not even knowing what the thing cost. She'd never know how this would delay looking for August, which, sure, okay, he should've started earlier. But he'd lined up jobs. He had to work, didn't he? He had to show up for what he'd promised. He couldn't bail on people depending on him.

The preacher touched his palms over the loaves Bill cradled. The preacher bowed his head, said to the floor, "Will you let me say grace over them?"

Privy   153

And then the preacher blessed them, right there in front of Bill. Their
fingers touched over the bread, and Bill's hands felt electric. Christ's being
corkscrewed through the bread's pores. Who could ever eat anything so
alive? Bill set one loaf on the counter. But the preacher pushed it back into
Bill's arms. He said, "I'm sure you're hungry, and I've got lots of flour.
I've got lots of blessings. I'm rich with these things."

The preacher finished and showed Bill those brown teeth once again.
He wanted to properly thank him. God was probably still listening. But
Bill had only a minute left, so he booked it, hustling toward the parking lot.

The cartoon-green Mustang still waited—a miracle, or he'd called her
bluff. He'd made it in time and done just as she asked. She cracked the
tinted glass, not much more than an inch.

"I got what you wanted."

"Hand it over," she said. "Slide the wafers through the window, right
into my mouth. I bet a creepo like you could get off on that."

Bill lifted the two loaves, uncovered them from their old dishrag shroud.

"What do I want with some bread?"

"It's Christ's body," Bill said.

"I know what communion looks like and it isn't that," she said.

"I watched the preacher bless it."

She peered at him through the crack, one eye lined in black piercing
back at his. Her irises were green, or maybe brown. She wore so much
eyeliner it made her eye seem unsure of its own existence, as if it required
demarcation. They had a good long look at each other's eyes through a
slit in the world, like the bathroom stall before. She rolled the window all
the way down.

"That old preacher's a fool. Doubt he could bless a crucifix." Still she
took the bread from his hands and propped the loaves on the Mustang's
dashboard. Her head dipped, like she was falling asleep, like a sleepy
saint, like his wife the last time they'd gone to church together, when the
prayers didn't seem to be working, when she was wearing the fentanyl
patches, when she nodded off midsermon and there seemed no point, no
hope, not a drop of faith left in the world. Even when the congregation

stood to sing, she was still sleeping, deeply out, and people sneaked glowers but Bill didn't care. Her head had rested against his shoulder and he could finally be of some practical use, amidst the rising praise, the choir, the organ, the loudest and the meekest voices in church converging. Nothing could wake his wife slumbering against him.

This woman in her purple coat possessed no peace, and he envied her. Her anger stoked a vital grudge against the person she'd once cherished. He'd recognized that active, intimate fire since he first heard her maiming her husband over the phone. Her children—however old they were, whatever their names, however many their number—they were slipping like August. But she refused to let them slip. This woman battled to preserve. At least Bill had witnessed her say words he'd never dare speak to his wife the survivor. What he couldn't ever say.

The woman's chin rose, her jaw opening. She bit into the body of Christ, a great gnashing bite that filled her cheeks. As she chewed, she offered the marred loaf back to Bill.

Could he? Yes. He drew the sweet dough and flaking crust of Christ into his lips to break between molars. He bit, gaping and feral like her. And then he savored the body as long as he could atop his muted tongue, before it softened, before it fell apart and away.

BICUSPID

She met him at Waffle House to tell him how much she hated him. He agreed to feeling the same. She spit in his scrambled eggs. He knocked over her mug of lukewarm coffee, and it dribbled into her purse. When she wasn't looking, he pocketed the tip she'd left so the waitress would hate her too.

Inside the handicap stall of the women's bathroom, they pressed their backs and palms against the cool, dirty tiles. There, they reached inside each other's mouths. Their fingers clenched the other's molar. They raked at their raw gums for long minutes. They rocked the molars back and forth on thorny pivots. Blood ringed their wrists once they plucked them free. The roots stretched long as nightmares with sharp, cruel claws. They each pressed the other's tooth into their own throbbing sockets.

He called to say she'd ruined his life. "What life?" she replied. His body's best years. He could've had any woman. He was beautiful then, and now his hair was thinning and his stomach soft. She preferred the ways in which his body had thinned and softened, but she didn't tell him this. Thinking about his skin, the pale stretch marks of his ass and the mole on his shoulder, made her gums pulse. She crushed the phone against her ear, so hard it burned. She told him he was pathetic. She told him he was a child. She told him to fuck off and grow up and grow a pair and to stop calling. They licked their teeth in shared silence. Neither ended the call for many more breaths.

156 · Bicuspid

She taxied him to buy a new pickup truck. His died at work on Friday. While she drove, she told him what a miserable bastard he must be to not have a single friend willing to do him a favor. Everyone disliked him.

The seller advertised the truck as a twenty-year-old Ford Ranger, reliable enough despite its age, though marred in rust and dents.

"Sounds like you," he said when they'd reached the seller's gravel driveway, the stones grinding like snapping bones underneath her tires.

"At least I don't look as old as you," she said.

Splotches covered his skin, a smattering of dots on his forehead and a brutally tanned back of the neck. He indeed looked ten years older than thirty. He worked as a roofer, had subjected his skin to sun without wearing sunblock. He smoked two packs of Winstons per day. His teeth had gone yellow. His mouth always tasted like smoke. No one told him to stop smoking because he'd worked hard to own his own tiny roofing company, two employees from Guatemala and two saddle toolboxes full of hammers and pry bars and blades and saws, though no working truck to house them. "I'm younger than you by six years," he said, "and that will always be the case. You'll die first. I'll walk over your grave and just keep walking. Just like you're a stranger."

"Keep smoking. Keep working all day in the sun," she said. "Then we'll see."

His arm quivered as he yanked at his own front tooth. To make sure he didn't finish first, she wrested hers too. They slid them out alone together, the maxillary incisor, like a tiny tombstone barbed with a dagger. They stabbed them inside each other's scarlet sneers, much more stubborn going in than out.

He drove a stepladder to her house two weeks before Christmas and held the ladder for her while she strung blue lights along her gutters. He didn't mention how pointless it was. He knew the importance of this ceremony. If she climbed ladders every day, perhaps it would be unremarkable. But she worked from home, writing how-to articles for the internet. He read them all: how to fix a flat, how to reset smoke alarms, how to meditate, how to poach an egg, how to set up your printer, how

Bicuspid

to organize family photos, how to reorganize a closet, how to convert a bedroom to a home office, how to arrange for cremation. They'd buried their son, embalming fluid pumped through him, makeup applied, open casket. He'd looked like a doll. Completely untouchable. It had been useful to see him this way, he told himself, to know he was really gone.

They'd never talked about this. They never would.

She strung lights swiftly because she knew the best way to hang Christmas lights, the best hooks to use. She'd written a how-to article about it. That and their son had loved Christmas best. Even though he'd grown skeptical of Santa at age six, he'd still clamored for every ritual: the big trees, the fireplace and stockings, the hot chocolates and caroling, the drives to ogle lights. They'd gotten ten Christmases with him.

They didn't talk about those Christmases, either, though they were both remembering them.

He held the ladder. She hung the lights. The house turned blue.

She got too drunk. She punched another woman at the bar. They took it to the parking lot where she fought this same woman to the ground, where she kicked until the woman stopped moving, only moaned. Her victim spit out a tooth, and she took it, then ran into a cornfield where the husks shushed her heart beating like thrown rocks. There she called him. He came. They drove in the new-old Ranger out into the dark-quiet of endless night. They parked and he let her punch his face. She squeezed the woman's broken tooth in her fist while she swung, and it bit her skin. He welcomed the throbbing, the purple and green that would become a pain he could watch darken. She told him he should apply ice soon, later heat to hasten lymphatic drainage. Also, he should eat pineapple. She'd written about how to treat bruises, of course. She'd researched how to make them disappear.

She texted to tell him he was a drunk. And that his mom was a bitch.

He emailed to tell her she was a hypocrite. And she was a classist. She'd learned it from her father, who was also a racist.

158   Bicuspid

They met in the parking lot of the Chuck E. Cheese where they used to go. There, they agreed to stop writing to each other, to stop all communication. He called her hysterical, called her fat, called her cruel and selfish and ignorant of anyone living a life less privileged than her. She told him he didn't know how to think for himself, an automaton, only able to ape the liberal blather spewed from the NPR he listened to all day while working on the roof. He was ugly. He was lazy. He was a doormat, a dumbass, and exploitative of his two Guatemalan workers he paid only twelve dollars an hour on a 1099.

They traded cruelties until the parking lot emptied. Their tongues tasted raw. He wanted to bite hers. She wanted to punch him again, so badly, but he liked that too much. Instead, they climbed into the new-old truck bed, where they tugged each other's cuspids. They traded, and his yellow tobacco stain now winked through her scowl. Her mouth tasted like pennies and stone.

They didn't talk for weeks after the cuspids. For two years, they hadn't said their son's name. Sometimes, she expected divorce papers to show up, but she knew he was too disorganized. Sometimes, he expected to see new posts on her social media, pictures of her grinning teeth, toasting drinks, arm around a new man. But she never posted. And even stalking her accounts led to anxious terror that made her teeth inside his jaws sting, because the last posts were still there. The ones from before, from the time they shared when there was a third person they shared.

They didn't talk about this.

She sent him a postcard, a cute yellow dog sleeping on the porch of a wooden shack backgrounded by mountains. "Thinking of you," the picture side claimed. On the back, she'd written *Fuck you.*

They met and pressed bodies inside the bathroom of a Walgreens. They locked hips while they fished into each other's mouths, prying at slippery lateral incisors. It took longer than either expected for such a small tooth

Bicuspid

that was anchored by a monstrous root. Between their feet, a pool of saliva and blood formed an oval like a third tortured mouth. Her shoes tracked red prints across the white tile. She left the bathroom first, hair wetted in sweat. She zippered her jacket over her spattered shirt. She bought cough drops, menthol flavored, because she'd feel bad if she didn't purchase something after leaving such a mess in the bathroom. He walked out without even glancing around the store. The cashier's mouth clicked and she shook her head.

"Some people are so rude," she said to the cashier.

"They're all like that," the cashier said.

Everyone? she wondered. Or did she mean all men? Or did she mean her husband's skin color? Or did it have to do with his torn, asphalt-pocked jeans and cutoff sleeves on his A+ Roofing T-shirt?

She didn't ask.

She sucked on the tobacco coating her new tooth.

She ran her key along the red car she guessed belonged to the cashier.

"Most people don't know how to properly floss," she told him. They sat in his truck's cab, watching his two-man roofing crew at work. The truck was off, windows rolled mostly up, and she felt she might choke on his secondhand smoke.

"People floss?" he said, flicking ash out the crack in the window.

"The few who do don't know how."

She couldn't remember their son flossing. Only the dentist demanded it. He'd still had five baby teeth.

"Would you like me to floss?" he asked. "Would that make this easier?"

She didn't respond to his stupid questions.

She wanted him to slap her. It wasn't fair that this went only one way. It was sexist, misogynist, to think a woman couldn't take it, to lean on the flimsy crutch of male chivalry or some bullshit like that, while simultaneously despising and degrading her.

160   Bicuspid

"I do despise you," he said, but he would never hit her. He lorded this above her, and he knew it hurt worse than his hands could.

She pulled his carton of Winstons from the glovebox and chucked packs out the window as he drove. She ripped the last pack from his breast pocket and crumbled each cigarette into tobacco confetti that sheeted his upholstery. She plucked the last lit cigarette from his lips and smothered the cherry between them on the seat.

He still wouldn't hit her.

Instead, he parked the truck on a dirt road, so deep into the cornfields they couldn't even see a house. He took the keys and walked away from her. He walked for miles, his lungs burning for another cigarette. Hours later, when he returned, she was gone. He needed a cigarette so bad he scooped shredded tobacco from the floor and tucked it beside his gums. He nursed this slow drip all the way to the nearest gas station.

They didn't talk.
They didn't talk.
They didn't talk.

They met outside an adult toy shop and sat in their own vehicles. They agreed they hated each other too much to share his truck cab again. Also, it was easier not to talk here where they could focus on the patrons hunched in shame and desperation or those few so giddy to find sex still existing in the world and not just on computer screens. They met outside a liquor store. They met outside an auto parts store. They met outside a pot shop. They met outside a vaping store where he blew real smoke out his window at these fools lying to themselves.

It was easier not to talk in these parking lots where only adults ever roamed.

They'd slip bloody napkins through the cracks of each other's side windows. They'd unfold these reddened gifts and find teeth to replace their newly weeping sockets.

Bicuspid 161

She wrote a how-to article on roofing using common asphalt shingles. She made it seem so simple anyone could do it, only seventeen steps. Starting a compost garden required twenty-one steps. She knew he'd hate the article. She savored his imagined anger the whole time she was writing it. She ran her tongue over her mouth filled with mostly yellow teeth, all but five replaced now. Her breath tasted like an ashtray. It made no one want to talk with her, which was fine, which was preferred.

Shortly after she published the roofing how-to, he left dozens of comments, critiquing most of her steps. He'd gone deep into the back-and-forth threads with a user named handy_hank79. Their debate over metal roof superiority had devolved into promises to beat the shit out of each other in real life. He even left a date and time for them to meet in a bowling alley parking lot.

She drove to the bowling alley at his proposed date and time, but as far as she could tell, handy_hank79 never showed, nor did the Ford Ranger.

He didn't say the truth, that he missed their son so much more than he hated her. She didn't say it, either. They shared this, the missing being stronger than the hating. Saying so was redundant. Saying this aloud would solve nothing.

He didn't show up the next Christmas to help her with the ladder and the blue lights. Instead, his two Guatemalan workers arrived smiling. She couldn't be cruel to them when they worked so quickly and were so polite. She wanted to tell them that she preferred to climb the ladder, to string the lights, to feel too high up, high enough that she could fall and die. He knew she preferred this, craved that part of the ritual. This was why he'd sent his workers. They finished before she could even offer them water.

As they were leaving, they gave her a small box. "From the boss," they said, smiling, probably imagining some lovely gift from their employer. She opened it in front of them, the back molar, yellow as a corn kernel. She told them to wait while she ran inside to fetch pliers and pry the

162 Bicuspid

tooth from her jaw. She put her own tooth in the same box and sent it back with the now unsmiling men.

A stranger claiming to be her neighbor stopped her outside when she was getting the mail. The stranger told her a man had knocked on his door. The stranger told her the man had shoved this note into his hand. The stranger passed her a thin slice of yellow paper, folded once. The stranger asked if she was in danger, if the man was dangerous, if he himself was in danger. He could call the cops. He kept a pistol near his bed. "Everyone should," the stranger said, "just in case."

She'd written about how to safely store guns at home. She'd written about how to clean both revolvers and semiautomatic pistols. She hoped this stranger hadn't read anything about gun safety.

She navigated to the address listed on his yellow note. She drove in growing darkness. She arrived at an old house, a tall one, sprawling, beautiful, and ornate. Out front, one ladder sliced across a row of windows all the way to the roof. She climbed carelessly, losing a shoe on the thirteenth rung. He sat upon the roof peak and blew smoke into the moon. She crawled up the roof pitch and sat beside him.

"What?" she said.

"Wait."

So they waited for him to chain-smoke three cigarettes. She thought of things to say to him, to ask, but she'd grown skilled at suffocating words within her sealed mouth. And he'd learned to blow his words into smoke and tar.

A glowing red flashed on around them. She'd never seen a roof strung in so many Christmas lights, and to stand amongst the gaudy display was to feel one's body turned illumination. The colors were hideous. Instead of the blue she loved, that her son had loved, this house was decked out in a rainbow of colors. Still, her son would've begged her to slow down driving past here, so they could all ooh and aah together. She could feel her body casting a dark silhouette against the display.

Bicuspid   163

He didn't say anything. He remained seated until she rejoined him on the peak. He handed her pliers. Together they tugged the last tooth. Together they pressed the pierce of foreign roots into raw sockets. This would be the last time their mouths would fill with blood, the last time they'd trade. They knew each estranged tooth better than any other ever would. And when they spoke, if they spoke, the words would pass through someone else's teeth, through the only other teeth that could ever know such rabid hurt. They could say it. They could name it. They could. All he had to do was open his mouth. All she had to do was part those tainted teeth and speak.

THE FIRST WOMAN

Winona was as rare to us as a sober roofer, rare as a knotless twenty-foot two-by-four. Other women existed onsite: the cleaning ladies hustling their brooms and guilting blue booties on our shoes, the Realtors in their pencil skirts and blazers, the occasional carpenter's wife or painter's sister popping in to help finish a rush job. But Winona was the first woman.

Her feet were the first to touch a new jobsite, and it had been three weeks now since she'd graced us with a sign of contracts to come. She was Eve slashing through the wilds, tugging out our ribs. She worked excavation, dug foundation, so she never interacted with the rest of us contractors, always ahead of us. We filled her holes with concrete, then framing, then siding and insulation and wires and PVC and shingles and Sheetrock. She was the entirety of the skeleton crew left after most of the excavation boys went extinct with the recession. Most of us did. Those few of us who survived famine, we returned to her, and we'd existed these last fresh-wound years as a consequence of her earth-dug spirit.

She was gorgeous as a fever dream, of course, but that wasn't why we watched so desperately. Since she was first, her work meant more work. Her work meant the bubble wasn't busting again, like it did in 2008, when we turned into unemployed men curating useless tool collections. Only the hardiest and most superstitious of us stubborned onward into this thin future where we worked again for exactly God knows how long. This week, when we switched the radios to NPR, it was terror, crashing

The First Woman 165

NASDAQ and Dow Jones, which none of us had nothing in, but that dying might've meant our second and final death, so we spun the dials back to classic rock and rubbed the logo on our Carhartts for luck while we whispered a mantra into our respirators: *Winona, Winona, Winona.*

By Thursday, none of us could hardly sink a nail, paint a straight line, angle a neat miter. The framing rose on the last contracted house in the subdivision, and still we hadn't seen Winona carving us out some new land. The massive maple across the street had bled red autumn into its leaves, so there was little time before Michigan froze its earth to us. If we didn't have holes dug now, the winter would be horror. We'd asked around, and no one knew about the digging crew. The builders were avoiding patrolling the sub in their shiny Silverados, and their scarcity scared the shit out of us. The only construction manager who hadn't been let go pressed his lips when we asked what was next.

Pike was sick of waiting. He brought binoculars that dangled on his chest on a leather strap. He proclaimed today as the day he'd discover our missing woman. He chain-smoked, a dirty Camel butt clenched in his canines while he installed double-panes on a twenty-foot extension ladder. All morning, his binocular lenses caught morning sun, flashes that fooled us into thinking he was signaling. We kept at our walls, our floors, our ceilings. But the sooner we wrapped these houses, the sooner we'd find our fate—another burst-bubble recession. We could only hope Winona was cutting earth in some next-place protoplasmic suburb, bull-dozing God's ground to smooth it all perfect for the coming of our vinyl and gypsum and brass and pine.

Lunchtime, there was still no word from Pike. He remained sentry atop his ladder that he'd propped against the roof ridge. He was eating his usual bologna and pickle sandwich with one hand while he clutched binoculars with the other. His head pivoted on that greasy neck, scouting. We held our breaths.

After weeks without her, our sore eyes hungered for the sight of her sun-bleached denim stretched over her birch-tree-trunk thighs. We needed to spot that ponytail curling her spine like a question mark, spilling out

166 The First Woman

of her cowboy hat that might've been a color once but was now just white. Even from afar, we would estimate the number of buttons popped open, cleavage exposed to sun that would singe her skin tanner than Black Mike's, but not quite as dark as Cut-It-Twice Lou. We imagined her eyes, which we'd never seen, forever shielded under those oversized aviators that reflected brown earth or blue sky.

Was she a beauty? Pike claimed every time he saw her his missing pinky finger stung like he'd jammed it in an electrical box before Dexter had pigtailed the wires.

Was she a beauty? The houses facing her excavation site always crowded with us, brimming with tool belts, each window immediately requiring caulking and trimming.

Was she a beauty? See Winona and know your family will eat for another month. Your chest pockets will bulge with packs of smokes. Your gas tank will fill. You'll make rent and sleep so soundly you'll forget all the dreams where Winona breaks down your door, pins your arms, and straddles your hips.

Pike flung his bologna sandwich. Pink meat and Wonder Bread sailed through the sky. He glided down the ladder rungs faster than a firefighter.

He was possessed, and the only thing he said was, "It's fate," just before he crossed the road to the bramble bushes and pines and that towering blood-red maple, at least sixty feet, tallest thing for miles.

We hollered after him, begged him to ask Winona how many acres she'd been contracted, how many foundations to excavate. We pleaded then whined then growled, but Pike waved us off with his four-fingered hand and disappeared into the woods.

Whenever we gave him shit about the missing finger, he just wiggled his nub and winked, but wouldn't volunteer his story like Dexter did about the lawnmower that ate three of his toes but he found one that had ricocheted into a plumber's truck bed and the docs sewed it back on, though he was pretty sure they reattached it in the wrong spot. What we did know about Pike was that last week his wife left him at gunpoint. He'd been watching reruns of *The Simpsons* on the couch, and she'd shoved a pistol

The First Woman

in his face and told him she was leaving and he couldn't stop her. Why would I stop a miracle? Pike had said. Now, he claimed, he was free to find true love.

So Pike would be the first man to meet our first woman. If democratized, no way would we have voted such an unworthy emissary. But his foresight with the binoculars had paid off, so we lit cigarettes and resigned ourselves to waiting, and that was when Mark Clark spotted Pike's binoculars twinkling atop his ladder, abandoned. We nominated Mark Clark the watcher, and each tinging of his boots against aluminum rung made us shiver.

"I see her," Mark Clark said. "She's in the backhoe. Wearing a yellow tank top. No, green." We nodded in appreciation of this detail. "Now she's out. Bending over. My God. Holy shit, I'm gonna faint off the ladder, boys." We cheered for relief, for confirmation, for longevity and love. We shook the ladder legs and clanged Mark Clark twenty feet up there. If he fell, we'd catch him. We'd hoist him on our shoulders and parade the subdivision. "Oh, wait. She's got something. She's lifting it. An axe. And here comes Pike now."

Mark Clark recreated the scene from up there like only a drywall finisher could. Jericho the housepainter was offended he wasn't nominated for the job, but housepainters are prone to exaggeration—they chose a life of color and cover-up. We needed raw truth, and that was what you got out of a finisher like Mark Clark, the smoothed-out, clear-as-mud truth.

He described it from the top of the ladder in sentences like long swipes of his trowel knife. We closed our eyes so Mark Clark's words could smother us, and we envisioned Pike strutting across that newly barren earth. His boot prints stamped the first steps of man in this fresh earth where Winona had eviscerated the garden, scraped it bare, and then zeroed the grade. We saw Pike raise that four-fingered hand, cigarette dangling out of an orange-tooth smile. He was saying hello, maybe offering a compliment to her perfect dirt leveling. And then, as he noticed the axe still raised, he stepped back, probably reintroduced himself with a pleading twang: *I'm Pike, from across the street, window installer, admirer—*

168 The First Woman

now slow down—a friend, a friend on your team, a friend who knows how hard this job can be, especially when we don't know what comes next, and if you'd just put that down we could be friends because you know what comes next, and I know how beautiful our future could be. She stalked closer and this was the moment he'd waited for, now that he was finally single, and he'd been dreaming about this day, minus the axe, and it was sweet fate, and they were meant to be in truest love, but her tan knuckles two-handed the axe handle, the red blade-head bouncing over her shoulder, bobbing with her steps, and even though Pike wanted to glance at the clay-dust clinging to the sweat in her cleavage, he didn't dare take his gaze off her eyes and the blade as she—his Eve, our Eve—edged closer, within swinging range, and Pike's full-fingered hand raised to ward off evil but might soon be less fingered, mangled and maybe left wriggling in the churned earth, and because she raised that axe, what else could Pike do but collide through the brush, hurtling and tripping and breathing so hard he nearly choked on the cigarette that burned his tongue and filled his mouth with the bitter ash he was still spitting up by the time he made it back to us, panting and puking strings of bile.

We laughed at his gasps, found comfort in his torture, though we still hadn't checked the pulse of our working lives, didn't know how many acres Winona had been contracted to level, how many more paychecks would bubble out of how many holes. Only Winona knew. Maybe a dozen new sites, a few months of promise for a thin winter. Maybe just this last plot, a pity spec build to string us along. Or maybe an entire subdivision, a year of feast and security, vanloads of lovely Winonas spilling across the land.

We sobered and told Pike to go back. The color had drained from his skin. His ridiculous romance fantasy with Winona had been amputated. He refused to return.

Until Cut-It-Twice Lou offered his sister's number. She was newly single, too, and just had one eight-year-old baby named Cina, and he pulled up a grainy photo on his flip phone that Pike studied like a blueprint. He was calculating billable board feet, the payoff on his labor—the way we'd all learned to look at this world through estimate and bid.

The First Woman

He admitted she was pretty, sure, but with no guarantee Pike couldn't risk eating any more loss. His heart had gone tender as a rookie roofer's sunburn. So we chipped in. Mark Clark offered three cigarettes. Dexter pulled a half-burned joint from behind his ear. Black Mike swished his hands in his jingling pockets, said Pike could have it all. White Mike promised to finally return the Stanley tape measurer Pike lent him last year. Pike bolstered amidst the din of offered beers, crinkled dollars, and lucky nails. We knew he'd go back, knew he had to. Pike couldn't quit dreaming—Winona's thighs pincering him after a day of lugging windowpanes, Winona's breath steaming the windows of the bungalow they'd renovate. He'd dreamed it so hard his old lady had smelled its stink.

Pike crossed the street like we knew he would, and we scrambled for the ladder. Black Mike kicked up those ladder rungs first, and Mark Clark tossed him the binoculars. Once he hit the top, Mike crossed himself, and we knew what he was seeing was good. We closed our eyes again and hoped he'd describe as well as Mark Clark, even though a frame carpenter cares more about bones than the smooth finish.

"Back in the backhoe again," he reported. "She's tearing up ground like the dirt did her wrong," he told us. "And, yep, here comes Pike. He's flagging his arms. He's shouting something. And, yep, oh boy, she's driving straight at him. Top speed. But, nope, I guess it goes faster, and I can't guess why that poor son of a gun ain't running yet. Gotta give him credit for standing ground. But I already gave him my change. Yep, I guess we already paid up, didn't we? Oh, there he goes. He's running now, and she's giving chase, and he's back into the brambles, and she's driving on like he was never there."

This time, Pike returned to us hatless. We'd never seen the top of his head, never seen the baldness spreading with cruelty from his part. His elbow was bleeding, and a red rivulet snaked down his forearm and dripped to the ground from his pinky stump. "She didn't even see me," he said and palmed the bald patch on top of his head, as if it was sore. "She'd've plowed right over me."

The First Woman

Now we were fed up. No more niceties and offerings and rubbing of the shoulders. We needed to know how much bounty in Winona's new garden and if we were invited. All we had was pathetic Pike. We pushed him, punched his back, swung our boots to his ass, but he wouldn't budge. We called him a pussy, of course, called him a dickless baby-balls crotch lump, our mantra of genitalia-deriding coercion that never really convinced any of us to do anything. If we all counted the times we'd had our pecker's existence questioned, we'd be a crew of eunuchs.

Finally, we broke into his truck. We'd become ravenous. We snapped his CDs in half, blew snot rockets on his upholstery, pissed into his truck bed. Idiotic and unstoppable animals.

And then the tree fell. That massive maple that had silhouetted our sunsets for the last year was absent from the sky. Its final crash silenced us all. Jericho, that romanticizing painter, claimed to have seen its fainting swoop from the sky. Jericho had found the binoculars and volunteered to climb the ladder and scout this time, but none of us trusted him.

Still feral, we herded across the street to witness with our own eyes. We didn't know what we'd find, and communal dread seeped down our spines, wetted our armpits. The sixty-foot red maple seemed too big for one woman, one Winona, one anybody. One miscalculation of that wedge she cut or a nudge of Midwest wind or, hell, a big enough crow shit dropped on the right leaf—she'd be crushed. We prophesized an unspeakable sight: her sun-bleached cowboy hat ringed in blood to match those crimson leaves. An image like that must be witnessed firsthand, certainly not narrated by some goddamn gasbag housepainter.

We crossed two lanes of concrete, humped through the ditch. We pressed through the untamed brush deliberating each step, just like we stretched out finishing our jobs, the subdivision, the last stop before months on the couch half-heartedly searching for work between watching reruns of *Judge Judy* and *General Hospital*. Oh no. Dear God. We did not rush.

When we hit the tree line, just before Winona's raw desert, our eyes rewarded us; Winona perched atop her tree stump, gloating over her kill.

The First Woman 171

She was peeling an orange, and we smelled the sting of those rinds zesting under her dirt-dragged nails. We waited for someone to act, to ask what love-dumb Pike couldn't manage, but how could we break that spell? How could we spoil this portrait that Mark Clark was already snapping with his phone's camera? She was the perfect pinup model for our world—this handful of feasting atop a destroyed giant.

Then Pike, lonely lost loser Pike, was striding across the torn earth, doomed to fail once more. His balding head glared nakedly in the evening sun's deepening glow. His four-fingered hand hung at his side, arm striped with dried blood, and we doubted he'd installed a window all day. Of course, we hated him, wanted to trip him, but he acted first among us, so all we could do with our judgment was spit it at our frozen feet.

She spotted him, and the orange in her palm bled against her squeeze, dripping down her knuckles. She'd rejected him twice today, and maybe they'd been doing it since the dawn of time, the way she tensed, repulsed, furious. We expected her to flinch toward the chain saw as Pike neared, chin tucked to his chest, baldness glinting luridly. We admit we wanted Winona to yank the pull cord and bring those oscillating metal teeth to life. We admit we wanted to see Pike's other fingers severed. Perhaps his flesh sacrifice would bring us weeks more of work.

Pike approached the precipice of Winona's foundation hole. With his boot toes dangling the edge, he stared down, clasped his hands together like a prayer, and, without chancing a look her way or our way, he stepped into the hole and disappeared.

We knew how deep it had to be. In the old days, before that first recession, it was forty-two inches to the frost line. These days—five feet, six feet, seven, deeper than a casket—no way to tell how brutal our summers, how deep you'd have to go to avoid the crush of winter's freeze. There was no such thing as playing it safe enough. Maybe Winona had made that hole plummet right down to the center of the world's hot heart.

Sure, we should've retreated to the jobsite for extension ladders and extension poles and extension cords so we could fish out our fallen man. Truth was none of us had ever been good at rescue. When the contracts

172   The First Woman

evaporated from that first burst bubble, and the frame carpenters disappeared, and then the insulation guys and the vinyl siders, followed by the plumbers and the drywallers and the trim carpenters, the last crew didn't ask where the others went. Those goddamn, godawful, selfish-as-shit painters, they didn't ask after our shadows when they were the final ones to touch up a house. None of us did and none of us would. We're all guilty. We're all satisfied to say nothing about apocalypse, about domino extinction, so long as we have a few more board feet bid out to finish.

Within the shade of a pair of browning pine trees, we waited for our minds to erase the memory of that four-fingered man so we could get back to our last houses and our hoping. But Winona stood from her stump. She lifted her chin and rocked up onto her boot toes. She seemed satisfied enough with whatever she was seeing in the hole to bite an orange slice, and then she stalked the perimeter of her finely carved foundation hole. As she walked, she chucked her rinds into the hole, aiming at something.

Still we hesitated against the itch of our collective question: How long did we have left? How many more holes? How many more homes? Will we survive? Even just one of us?

Winona chucked more scraps into the hole until a solitary orange wedge remained pinched in her fingers. She dipped to one knee and lowered the orange, single and glistening and slick. She reached, stretched, lower and as low as she could go. Finally that four-fingered hand arose, dirt smeared, quavering, open palmed, and she dropped the slice into the hand. We imagined the fruit's sweetness and salivated. The back of our throats stung.

After that, she rumbled up the backhoe. A mound of fresh, dark dirt squatted like a buried elephant on the south side of the hole, and that's where Winona navigated the backhoe's bucket. She plunged and scooped and pushed, and the earth fell back to where it belonged. She was refilling her hole, burying our hopes, burying our man.

We guessed this was revenge for his foolish heart. This was recompense for his ogling, for all our ogling. This must've been Winona's violence to answer our gaze that weighed like shingles stacked on her

The First Woman 173

shoulder. So we watched in fascination as one of ours, the first of us—this time, that is, because we'd seen extinction before—was swallowed up by Winona's earth.

But Winona stopped. From the cab of the backhoe, she peered into the hole, into the depth where we'd all end one day, and out of that dank inevitability climbed Pike. He trudged up the ramp of dirt she'd constructed for him, behatted, for somewhere in the hole he'd found his hat to cover his naked scalp. He slapped the dust out of his jeans, which swirled up brown clouds like a magic trick at his hips. The backhoe still rumbled, and he moved toward it. Pike stopped short of the cab and plopped into the backhoe bucket. Winona slapped at the console, raised him up to the sky like an offering. He rode in the bucket and she drove. We crouched to hide behind the trees that would soon be plucked to clear the way for precious weeks of work. Or the trees would remain to wilt and molder and we would scratch red pens at classified sections and stare into the glow of online job ads and curse ourselves for never learning to do more on a computer besides order a pizza and find elaborately fetishized pornography.

But that torture was for after we'd been cast out of the suburban fantasy, back to our apartments where we'd calculate if we could renew another year's lease. For now, all we had was a partially obstructed view of Pike cradled in the raised bucket of the backhoe as it wheeled across the land Winona had razed, and then they set out for farther, thumping over rows of soybeans, a powder-coated yellow machine dotting that sea of green, the last harvest, and tangled up within that dot, four fingers and a bleached cowboy hat reached toward each other but couldn't touch for the distance from cab to bucket, from man to woman, from Pike to Winona and back again until kingdom come.

WORK FROM HOME

Through the peephole, Neighbor Bob's bald head gleamed under the porch light, magnified and pale, filling all I could see. This would be the first neighbor to visit since we'd started renting here two months ago, since construction of our new house in Portage forever fell apart and we plan B-ed renting this bungalow in Kalamazoo. At least someone cared, but I wished it wasn't Bob, anyone but Bob, my next-door neighbor who constantly trapped me in yammering front-lawn conversations. My rental neighbor, my consolation prize. No house-warming baskets full of cheeses and brownies like would've happened in the Portage subdivisions. Renters weren't worth it. Saints or serial killers, we'd disappear in six to twelve months. The neighborhood was offering up their worst emissary. But I hadn't seen anyone all day, so I opened up.

"My wife's trying to kill me." Bob pushed through and plopped onto my couch without saying anything about the valances or the Jaipur throw or the series of Cezanne landscapes that surely made his own living room look meager and cheap. A green sweatband strangled the crown of his head, covered the little bit of red hair still clinging to the sides. Matching green sweatbands cuffed his wrists.

"New Year's resolution?" I stuck my head outside and checked the empty driveway for Emma. A few snowflakes skittered through the dark.

"It's this kickboxing workout. Silvy does it facing me to make sure I'm doing it with her. So she's punching and kicking at me the whole time."

Work from Home

"I'd have guessed Silvy for yoga."

"If only the good lord could be so merciful." Neighbor Bob sat up and a bright tube of his gut squeezed over his shorts. "She says that's for hippies. Says we need throbbing hearts, that we need impact. She punches so close I can feel the tiny hairs on her knuckles."

When I first met Silvy, she'd yelled at me for raking their lawn. I was just trying to be neighborly, clearing out those giant golden oak leaves starting to molder brown. I'd filled two bags by the time she shrieked at me from her porch, waving a kitchen knife. She stabbed into my bags, and the leaves hemorrhaged across their yellowed lawn. She flung the bag until she'd expelled every last leaf. Her hands had been slathered in corpse-blue paint. She was one of those artist types. They composted, she informed me. My landfill-happy ass could stay the hell on my side of the property line. Though built like a wire coat hanger, she seemed capable of great violence.

"It's horrifying, Dennis." Neighbor Bob swung his feet up. Dirt sprinkled from his shoe tread onto the polished mahogany coffee table. "She says we're going to be so healthy that we'll live forever. I signed on only until death do us part." He rubbed his glistening thighs. A smooch of silver paint flashed on his hairy bicep. "I'm hiding out here until she calms down."

What kind of neighbor would I be to send him back to his frightening wife? Few had what Emma and I did. We could've been a TV commercial for Windex—a stunning thirty-something couple gazing into each other's eyes, light streaming through windows so clean they looked like nothing. I had never been inside Bob and Silvy's house, but I could imagine: dingy windows and fingerprint-smudged walls. My spotless rooms smelling of bleach and lemon polish must've been a haven for Bob.

I uncorked the Shiraz I'd gotten out for dinner. Roasted red potatoes, bacon-wrapped asparagus, steak medallions. I poured Neighbor Bob a glass and one for myself. He downed it, and I poured him another. Emma still wasn't home when I got him his third.

Neighbor Bob slugged back the Shiraz. He rolled the empty bottle between his naked knees. I asked him about work, and he punched himself in the chest. A ripple swept across his skin-tight tank top. "I'll die in my office. The cleaning lady will find my rotting corpse."

"That bad?"

"You've got it right to stow away at home." He kicked off his sneakers. A hole was forming on the big toe of his black argyle socks. His toenail could pop through any second. "The working world's a killer."

"Hey, I want the work. There's just nothing out there for me."

"Bah! What you do here is better than what's out there." He raised the bottle and squinted through it like a telescope. A tiny drip of wine landed on the couch. "Living it up at home. We should all be so lucky. Stay free of that nine-to-five devil as long as you can, my friend."

Emma's car would be crunching snow in the driveway any moment. I stared at the floor and cleared my throat repeatedly. Bob didn't take the hint. No one notices the small things, and those of us who pride the details get lost in the clutter of taxes and mortgages and marriages and births and burials. No one was left with a clean finger to inspect the lack of dust atop the window frames.

A car door slammed somewhere, and I scrambled toward one of Neighbor Bob's sneakers. The wine and ruin of the evening flushed hotly into my face as I bent to pick it up and then shove it into Bob's hands. He puzzled over it, sniffed the inside. He finally stood, and an outline of Bob traced in sweat remained reclined across the couch cushions. Two wine bottle rings intersected each other like an obese heart stamped on the coffee table.

"I'm just saying," Bob said, "look on the bright side. We should all be so lucky to be off work with the support of a spouse—preferably one not attempting to murder you." I bit the inside of my cheek as he gathered his sweatbands and sashayed out the door.

And then it was just me and Emma, once she got home. She'd recently been promoted from sales to manager at Cable Core. She controlled the programming of nearly every TV set in southwestern Michigan. If I asked

Work from Home   177

her to, she could shut down Silvy and Bob's Tae Bo and PBS. I was proud. Of course I was. I was barely even upset anymore about getting laid off from my construction management job, where we'd gone from developing a hundred houses a year to a big fat nothing. The bubble burst on the whole damn country. And the house the company was building for us burst too. It was now just a gaping foundation in a ghost-town subdivision.

So maybe I had a degree in construction management and no construction to manage. Now I was using my leadership at home, here, where it could mean the most. I was managing our living.

I sat on the couch, waiting for Emma to get home hungry and ravage the fridge. She would find the blackberry cheesecake I'd made. Then she'd smell the garlic in the oven. She'd feel terrible when she realized she'd ruined dinner by coming home so late again. Soon we'd be laughing over a cold meal, scooping it straight from the pans, her swooning over every bite.

I pasted a sticky note to the fridge just before going to bed: "Eat everything. I love you. Don't bother with dishes."

The next morning, I took a tuna noodle casserole over to Bob and Silvy's. It'd been in our fridge for three days now, still undiscovered by Emma and her late homecomings. Before it molded, I could use it as a peace offering. Bob was a buffoon, but maybe I had Silvy wrong. I could befriend a stay-at-home artist. We could commiserate our unrecognized burdens.

When I stepped onto their porch, I heard the sounds of passion inside. My fists tightened to my new secret: Silvy was cheating. But then Silvy cried, "Bob-o, Bob-o, oh Bob-o." Bob grunted out cusses, as if continuously pounding his thumb with a hammer.

I felt myself getting hard and lowered the casserole dish over my crotch. The noon sun winked through the January clouds. For Emma and me, it was the longest moratorium on lovemaking in our seven years together. I wished Emma would suddenly materialize for a surprise lunch visit. The neighbors along my street could all be home for secret lunches of lust right now, a block party of chanting lovers.

178   Work from Home

I should've just left the dish on their doorstep and escaped. Instead,
I lingered. I'd seen my share of porn, but this was different. There was
no camera to make Silvy conscious of how ridiculous and redundant she
sounded as her song splintered into syllables: "Ba-ba-ba, O, O, O, O-Bob."
Emma and I were quiet lovers. We gritted our teeth and bit our lips.
Gasps and seizes. I'd always imagined that near silence was what real
love sounded like, sincere and secretive. I pressed my ear to the door, to
the naked and blaring barks. My casserole dish clinked against it.

"Who's out there?" Silvy's voice struck at me.

I ducked under the peephole. My chest dipped into the casserole
cellophane.

"I'll string you kids over the power lines by your nut sacks when I
catch you."

I sprang to run away. The casserole dish slipped, shattered. Noodles
and tuna and glass polluted the fresh snow. The sun made one last great
surge of bright, and then slipped behind a thick cloud. The earth darkened. I hurdled their porch railing. "You'll be biting curb for dinner
tonight, you little shits," Silvy hollered.

Establishing an alibi was top priority once I got home, so I opened the
want ads. I called on a delivery driver job for Coca-Cola, but I didn't have
a CDL license. I called about a financial consultant gig, but they wanted
at least three years' experience. I'd only overseen the development of hundreds of acres, torn down forests and implanted families by the dozens.
I dealt with tens of millions of dollars, until there were no more dollars.
But that meant no experience to them. I hung up, glanced out the window at snow collapsing from the sky.

I called a housepainter while I diced shallots. He listed off tools I'd
need, liability insurance, all-white uniforms, and he wanted experience
too. I didn't tell him about the hundreds of houses I'd managed from
excavation to the last fleck of paint on the front door. I was a construction
worker who'd never touched a tool. The painter wished me good luck
elsewhere.

Guys like him didn't get me. When I ran the subdivisions, they'd shake their heads and chuckle when I asked them to expedite deadlines or stop smoking in the houses or use the porta-johns instead of pissing against the retaining walls. Or, worse, they'd ignore me, treat me as mute and innocuous as a stack of Sheetrock.

The last place I called, an insurance company needing an assistant, took interest. He said he liked my voice, said he liked my get-to-the-point phone persona, liked how he could tell I was smiling while I talked. I wasn't. He hazed me with First Screening questions: How many times is nine used in one hundred? Is *conversate* a word? What's the capital of Montana? What did you score on the ACT? What year were you born? Now multiply your birth year by your ACT score. That's a big number, huh? What if we lived to be that old? That would be a lot of insurance premiums, he joked.

He wanted to meet in person, said he had high hopes. When he asked my name, I lied and said Robert Avery. Neighbor Bob's name. We planned a time to meet the next day. Then I scrubbed the toilet, the grout lines, caulked the tub surround. I refrained from looking out the window at Bob and Silvy's house. I set the table, used our best china, lit long purple candles. I ironed my best slacks, snugged one of my old ties around my neck. Tonight would be a perfection impossible for Emma to ignore.

I suited up to shovel the sidewalks for Emma. The fresh snow scooped lightly. If I hadn't been home to get a jump on the shoveling, soon it would be clomped solid by pedestrians wandering home from work. It was six o'clock and already dark and I hated how the sun gave up on me before I had everything done.

Just as I was flinging snow toward Neighbor Bob's property line, he popped outside, as if he'd been waiting to pounce. He wore a silvery sauna suit that made him look like a spaceman extra in a low-budget sci-fi movie. He shot me a salute and then high-stepped in place on his porch. Glass and casserole churned up through the snow. I wondered if he was toying with me.

180   Work from Home

"Jogging's safer than kickboxing." Bob reached for his toes, reached for
the clouds, bounced into squats. His ass nearly grazed a dagger-chunk
of frosted casserole glass. "Join me?"

"Emma's home soon," I said. "I don't want to miss her."

"I'd miss Emma too." Bob panted little breath-clouds. "Emma's a catch
and a half. Doesn't make you trim your spare tire or cook or clean, and
she's mighty good looking."

"I make sure she never has to ask," I shot back.

"Yep, she's a bona fide looker." Bob's sneaker toed a hunk of frozen
tuna mush that tumbled down the steps. "Come and join me. Least you
can do, don't you think?"

I couldn't figure out if he was trying to intimidate me. I peered down
our street through the snow falling like fists. Emma was already an hour
late. Her headlights would soon glare through the window across the
unlit candles and shimmering flatware, flash over the clean cement, and
she'd sit in her car thinking of me, of all I provided without asking. Then
she'd click off her lights. Darkness. Nothing. Absent me. She'd feel it like
a blister bursting in her stomach.

"Maybe I will go with you."

"Good. You can call an ambulance when I have a heart attack." He
karate-chopped a snowdrift on his porch rail and said, "Let's hit it."

Two blocks into jogging, my silk tie grated like wire around my neck.
My boots skidded along the unclean sidewalks. I hadn't run since high
school gym class, and even though I must've weighed thirty pounds less
than him, I struggled to keep up with Bob.

"The secret," Bob said falling into pace with me, "is screws. Little
ones. Screw screws into the bottom of your soles, and, wham, instant
crampons."

"What if you screw into your foot?" I asked to no response. I probably
threw away five hundred pounds of dropped screws and bent nails when
we built houses, a hundred thousand mistakes.

Bob's breaths thrummed like a drumbeat. The snow glowed pink
around us. We hit the Corner Bar by the railroad tracks, and Bob stopped.
"Let's have a beer," he said. "On me."

"We should head back."

"Must've burned ten thousand calories by now. We must replenish to battle the elements."

Three people bowed their heads over pint glasses inside. Styx's "Too Much Time on My Hands" mumbled over muffled speakers. An old man with a long yellow beard sat at the bar. Bob landed beside him, even though there were plenty of spots where we could have sat alone. A fishing net hung over our heads, plastic perch trapped in the crosshatch.

Neighbor Bob slapped the bearded fellow on the back so hard he coughed a bead of phlegm onto the bar. "Buy you a beer?"

The man looked ancient with pinhead eyes and sagging earlobes, but he wore a leather vest with a skull stitched on the back. I imagined him flipping open a switchblade and knifing Bob's belly. A corner of the old man's mouth curled. "Wife made me swear off the beer," he said. "Too many calories. And now I get piss-ass drunker than ever on vodka."

Our beers came and Bob turned to me. "How's that dreamy home life?"

"I have something, a job interview tomorrow." I scratched at the bar top with my house key. Under inches of lacquer, they'd encased seashells and seahorses and bottle caps and tackle and bluegills.

"Screw job interviews. You can use one of these." He reached down and plopped one of his wet shoes on the bar, screw side up. "Enough here to screw 'em all." Bob punched the old guy in the shoulder. Some of his vodka sloshed over the lip of his glass. "Isn't that right, Bob?"

I wondered if Bob actually knew this old guy, if he could really be Bob too. When I was a kid, my dad used to yell "Bob" into a crowd, and we'd watch the heads turn. There's at least one in every crowd, he'd say. I was always afraid the whole crowd would turn, and we'd face an army of Bobs. Perhaps every man ended up Bob eventually with a job they hated and a horrifying wife and a personality no neighbor could endure.

Bob ordered more beers for us and vodka for Bearded Bob. He pulled money from the wrist of his shimmering sleeve like a magic trick. I guzzled my pint while Bob and Bob gabbed about how they were both in management before Bearded Bob retired, how Neighbor Bob felt the life draining out of him through his belly button, how Bearded Bob had been there, brother.

Bearded Bob turned to me. "So what do you do, buddy?"

"I was in management too. Before the recession." I dug harder into the groove I'd started on the bar top.

"There it is! Here we are. More managers than anyone could manage," Bob said, and both raised their glasses and drank.

"What did you manage?" Bearded Bob asked.

Houses. Homes. Men. Cigarette butts and dumpsters. I couldn't find the best words to explain. I felt myself blending into a blur of Bob-ness.

"Mimes or coatracks or shower rings or dildos," Bob said. "What does it matter? Every manager tricks himself into believing himself necessary."

"That indeed is a special trick," Bob said and sipped vodka through his beard.

"Just like trying to manage a marriage. Nothing any man can do worthwhile there," Bob said.

"Slow down," Bob said. "I can't drink to your wisdom fast enough."

"But our young buddy here is different." Bob pointed at me without looking my way. "Got one hell of an old lady at home. And he cooks and cleans like a dervish. Right, neighbor?"

"I try." I smiled.

"Don't worry. You'll nail that interview tomorrow. You'll be back at the real life soon, managing a fleet of volcano insurance salesmen in no time."

Then the Bobs downed their drinks in tandem, eyes peering over glass rims at me. I half-expected a synchronized invitation: *Join us.* Back at home, Emma was probably walking into our dark rental at this second.

The next morning, I tried to wake up before Emma to clear off her car, but she was already gone. The snow had pounded us all night. Everything was white and rounded, all the edges of the world smoothed. I got back to work clearing the heaped sidewalks.

Bob burst out his front door. Silvy's voice shrieked behind him. He wore a suit, a navy number with cufflinks that blinked gold. He was a parody of a 1950s banker. He lowered his head like a prayer and fiddled his key into the deadbolt. He was locking Silvy in, and I was grateful.

"Today's the day for the maybe interview, right, big guy?" He plodded down his steps. The snow reached just under his knees. His suit would be soaked. "I'll give you a ride. It'll break up my monotony. Do me a favor."

"Sure. I'll just go like this." I outstretched my arms to model my stained sweatshirt, plaid flannel pants, moon boots.

"It's not the clothes that make the man. Don't be judged on your duds." Bob studied his cufflinks. They had hourglasses stamped into the metal. "That's my problem. I got hired trying to please. Should've gone in there in my underwear."

His front door flung open. Silvy squinted from the porch, yelled, "You still haven't left?"

Bob ducked into his Buick, nodded at me through the open driver's-side door. "Last chance," he said, "or stay here with Silvy forever." He waggled his eyebrows in mock terror. I flipped the shovel over my shoulder and waved him off. He spun his tires down the road in a fury of fishtailing.

I finished shoveling our driveway, our sidewalk. Our rental was perfectly cleared. But I kept going. I worked my way up Silvy's driveway, scraping up the layers of ice underneath. When I finished, their sidewalk flashed like a fresh wound against all the white.

Only the front porch steps and landing remained shrouded in snow. My shovel whined against their warped pine boards. I waited, held my breath. Silvy had to have heard me. I scraped onward. The fourth step's ice ripped off like a car wreck. Glass and casserole chipped into my shovel. I chucked it all into Silvy's yard. She could just try and compost that.

Still, Silvy hadn't come out to scare me back into my home. I clunked my elbow against her door. No stir inside. I rammed the door with my shovel handle. Twice. Three times. The door opened and there was Silvy.

"All right, fine," she said. "Come in already then."

Before I could lower my shovel, Silvy's back was receding down her hallway. "Should I take off my boots?" I asked the dark hallway. There were no lights on inside, and my eyes were still snow blind.

"Coffee?" Silvy said from somewhere. "It's burnt to hell and a day old."

"Okay." I yanked one boot off. "That's okay."

By the time I escaped my second boot, Silvy was standing over me, a mug in each hand. Both were made of lopsided clay. I took one and sipped, then choked. She'd put whiskey in my coffee. A lot. I sipped again, while Silvy observed me, grim as ever, yet somehow more lithe than skeletal in her home. I followed her down the hall. Her walls were brown and smeared. Their darkness made her silver hair glow. Her pale skin sizzled.

We walked through the kitchen, and that's when I realized the smears on her walls were things. Paintings. Crammed over every inch of wall were sparrows in flight, crows on a wire, a jay bullying a robin, a dead hummingbird bleeding out the beak. She'd painted praying mantises and spiders, daisies and rotted tree stumps. Even her kitchen cabinets were scrawled: an opossum's funnel snout, the back of Bob's head, his giant open palm with lifelines like tributaries.

"They're something," I said as we entered the living room.

"Astute." She stepped onto a drop cloth pocked in reds and picked up a large paintbrush with frayed bristles. She resumed painting what I must've interrupted—tree branches weighted with snowdrifts. I recognized the tree from our backyard. She was painting it pink.

"Do you sell these, your art?"

"They're on my walls, so what do you think?"

"Well, I like them," I said. I did, but in the future they'd never be able to sell their house like this. People want to buy clean. Blank. I had managed the painting of thousands of walls, all the same off-white. The point was to make it look so clean you'd think no one had ever been there.

"Thank Christ you like them," she said to the wall.

"Really. You have an eye."

"Two actually. And I have ten fucking toes."

Her walls couldn't distract from the clutter, though. Dirty mugs and wine bottles sprouted from every surface. A celery stalk wilted on an end table. Lemons rotted somewhere. In every corner, slumped pottery spewed spider plants. I guessed Silvy hadn't cleaned in years.

Beside an overgrown wicker planter of ivy, I spotted a painted figure. She was bent at the hips, long bare legs. Her breasts were partially covered by an arm holding open a door. It was Emma. Emma excavating the fridge. She was made of bright orange paint and placed next to the window that faced our house, our kitchen. Silvy had been watching my mostly nude wife. Emma looked beautiful, and here was proof she'd seen the meals I'd made. Maybe. I wanted to ask Silvy when she'd painted this, when she'd witnessed Emma. But I doubted she even knew what day it was. I doubted she knew anything worth knowing. Silvy the voyeur had no right to trace the curves of my wife's body. I wanted to take a sledgehammer to the wall.

"This is what you do all day," I said, "while Bob works?" I plucked up the wilted celery. An ant crawled from the celery onto my wrist. I threw it against a painting of a neon-green mailman. I walked over to orange-painted Emma. "Wonder what Bob thinks. I bet he likes this one."

Silvy and Bob probably screwed on the drop cloth in front of my wife's image. The whole room, all the paintings, became acid burning through Sheetrock, turning solid walls into cheesecloth, gossamer boundaries between our homes.

"They're not for Bob."

"Of course not. Why would you do anything for him?" I said.

"I don't work for Bob. If I did I'd hate him." Silvy hadn't turned from the wall.

"But you have to manage a home," I said, and I felt like an instruction manual for domestic success. Refer to page 38, table B for directions on how to overcome annoying neighbors.

"That sounds like brilliant advice." She spat onto her brush and mashed the foamy saliva into her paint.

"Damn right. Work is part of marriage." I stood in front of Emma's painting, blocking Silvy from her. Behind my back, I pushed on the wall where I imagined Emma's mouth. I pushed harder, strained secretly, would punch a hole through and fall into the darkness between the studs if I could only get it started.

186 Work from Home

Silvy touched her spitty brush to the wall. She said, "In sickness and in mopped floors. 'Til foreclosure do us part."

"I handle needs."

"No one notices needs. Only wants." Silvy slashed a new branch onto the tree, one that wasn't there in real life.

"That's selfish."

"Maybe."

"Well, that's not me. I'm not that," I said.

I left my post at the Emma painting, left Silvy to her pointless doodles and ravaged house and unfulfilling marriage.

Emma would be home in eight hours, or nine, or ten. Whenever she came home, the house would be ready for her, perfect. I'd managed a thousand houses. I was the God hand that oversaw residential Eden before the fall. One home had to be easy.

On my way back through the hallway, I saw him. A painted man waited near the door, stuck on the wall. His skin was the silvery gray of the sun straining to pierce winter clouds. He held a casserole dish over his crotch. He waited for the door to open. Silvy had painted him on this wall, so far from the orange-painted woman. I willed the walls to fold up, for Bob and Silvy's whole house to implode, for the woman to touch the man's casserole and see him.

But I didn't have time to wait for impossible. I had to get home, find a swath of floor I hadn't polished, cook another meal that would keep well in cellophane. Emma was coming home.

THIS PICTURE OF YOUR HOUSE

I snap pictures from the sky out the side window of Tommy's twenty-year-old Cessna 150. The plane's a rickety old bird, but she flies even cheaper than our van can drive ever since Bush decided to invade Iraq and shot gas prices up to four bucks per gallon. My Nikon does most of the work. All I do is aim away from the wing struts and spin the lens until your house turns crisp and then *click, click, click*. I've gotten pretty good at framing your property line from those rose bushes to that row of pines. All so easy that me and Tommy can get toasted up there on a pint of gin. The part requiring real skill, the selling, comes when I touch ground.

Sage always drives the van, and I sit shotgun when we're on the sell. Keeps my hands free for the frames, so I can change out the pictures between driveways. What's on the pictures is what everybody wants: an aerial photograph of your house, of course. Your whole beautiful house and every last square foot of property. A picturesque home is what everyone wants, and your vanity has almost bought Sage and me a new old trailer home.

The last sale of the day, before we close on the trailer, is stashed way out in the boonies on Luce Road, high number territory, 6995. Nice long paved driveway tells me we're not dealing with some hillbilly cheapskate. Big elms and maples all around, lawn mowed in straight stripes, yellow

188   This Picture of Your House

and blue irises blooming near the red brick walls. Sage calls it idyllic while she's turning down the driveway.

I tell Sage to park close to the two-car garage. Probably got a sports car inside waxed up fine for summer driving after another brutal Michigan winter. As I hurry this house's photograph into the frame, I dog-ear one corner, but the frame mostly covers the flaw, and I hope the mister or missus won't notice.

We idle with the windows down, AC full blast. Just when I light a fresh Winston, the homeowner presses his face to the screen door. He's wearing a bright yellow T-shirt, and, sure enough, a silver mustang is galloping across this fella's gut, "Ford" emblazoned on his chest. Trick with these old rich guys is in the waiting. Me and Sage loiter in the van, me smoking, her smiling big with those gorgeous teeth of hers. Just waiting and waiting. Make them come to you. And they always do, when you're staking out their own driveway.

Finally, he struts out in a huff, round belly heaving under all that yellow cotton, and I return his grimace with my grin. Have I got a treat for you, my chompers say. It's not just Sage with the gorgeous teeth. We've both been bleaching. Got a little competition going: we measure every Thursday with these off-white paint swatches from Lowe's, and the winner gets a back massage or fellatio/cunnilingus.

"There a problem?" this guy says, doing a cop script. But he's no cop. I can always tell.

"All you got is blessings," I say, "judging by the majesty of your kingdom here."

"We just love your place," Sage says. "All those tulips, be still my heart."

"She loves it. We love it. Who wouldn't?" I say.

"They're irises," he says.

"You love your house right down to knowing each species. Blessed with beauty and wisdom too," I say, oozing syrupy charm, because I can tell this guy wants to scare us off. I got a sixth sense for assholes, and I never scare. Never. Not even that time I did sell to a cop, and he kept touching his gun the whole time. That cop ended up buying, of course. "For a man who clearly takes pride in every flower on his acreage, I've got a treat for you," I say.

And he says, "What's that?"

And I tell him, "Closer, closer. I can't show you from way over there." I'm still holding my cigarette, and I tuck it by the door, so the smoke rises in wisps toward his nose. Fact that I'm smoking probably just makes him want to get rid of me quicker, and that can work for me.

Once he's close, I lift the photograph of his house. It's squared up just right, the green lawn and flashy flowers popping, and just under the frame is a view of Sage's upper thighs poking out of the denim miniskirt she picked out for today.

"Bet you recognize this place," I say, and when he just keeps staring at the photo, or maybe at Sage's thighs, I finish for him: "It's your lovely home, like you've never seen it before. You're admiring the best aerial photography in the county. Like God snapped the shot."

"We just love your place," Sage repeats.

"Begging to be framed," I say. "And lucky for you, I've already done it." I push the frame into his hands. "That's Amish made, hand crafted, real oak. Can't get a frame like that at Walmart."

But then he says, "There's a crease in the corner."

"Oh, that's barely anything. That'll flatten right out pressed into such a well-made frame, in a day or two tops."

He turns it over, inspects the back, as if he's looking under the hood. Back of a picture, what the hell does that prove?

"Lucky for you, the frame's on sale this week. Makes the whole package an unbeatable deal."

"We just love the work those Amish do," Sage says. "You tried their pies?"

"Sure. I've tried their pies," he says, because we've all tried their pies. They bully them into every local shop and set up lean-tos all over the highways. Every time we drive to scope out the trailer home we're buying, they're waiting to pick us off in their ugly dresses and bonnets, and Sage always stops. Probably could've bought the trailer a month sooner if not for all the pies, and I have to admire their sales techniques.

"Special deal for my friend with the lovely home is only four hundred dollars."

The tight-ass scrunches his nose like Sage just farted. "I can't get anywhere near that."

"What kind of price would please you, sugar?" Sage says. "We want this lovely photo going where it belongs, above your mantel."

"But we can't lose money again, baby," I say to Sage, because that's the pity routine, one I don't love playing. But Sage thinks it's our best move. She can't understand why everyone's heart isn't bursting with pity, like hers. "We gotta eat. Can't just give them away."

"It's not that I can't afford it." He pushes the framed photo back through my window, and the corner digs into my chest. "Obviously, I can afford it. Just on principle, that's a crazy price to pay for a photo."

"A customized aerial portrait set in a hand-crafted frame?" I raise the cigarette, which is mostly all ash now, and I take a nice long puff. He scoots to the side like the smoke might bite him. "Heck, just yesterday, your neighbor a few houses down said I was crazy to be charging *only* four hundred."

"Oh yeah? Which neighbor?"

"I sell way too many of these to remember every name."

"Describe the house for me. Did a dog bark at you? Vinyl siding or painted? What color was the front door?" he says, and I feel like shoving the cigarette's cherry right through his house's picture, right through the chimney, and then flicking it in his face.

That's when Sage says, "Now, what's that?" She's holding the photo close to her nose. She points a tangerine-painted fingernail at a bright glob in the backyard. Truth is no one looks at the pictures too closely between snapping the shot out the Cessna's window and slipping it into the frame.

"That's a sunbather, babe," I say. "Looks like."

"Don't look like they got no clothes on," Sage says.

"Tell me, friend," I say, propping the photo in my van's window frame, "you think that might be you?"

This Picture of Your House

He doesn't say anything, because we've snagged him. Sure, even if you squint, you can't see anything worth seeing, pecker or titties or any good bits. It's the idea that matters. Since photography was invented, it's always been about the impression of being caught in a second, seemingly so real that every painter in the world had to start going abstract. Suddenly, any Joe Schmo could capture any portrait, easy as looking. Lucky me trapped the perfect second.

When he runs inside in a yellow flash of torso, I'm surprised. I grip the door handle, but Sage puts a hand on my knee. "What, you gonna chase after him in his own house?"

That's my lovely Sage, always soothing my impulsive instincts. Indeed, chase him inside and what? Face the barrel of a gun. He wouldn't own some dusty rifle or sensible Glock. He'd have dumped a bunch of dough into a shiny Colt revolver, something that made him feel like a cowboy. He'd probably wear it on a holster while he drove his Mustang around town.

"He'll be back," Sage says, patting my thigh. She lights me a fresh cigarette, presses it between my lips. "You know, I think it probably is him. Gut looks familiar, no? But maybe they got a matching pair." Her tangerine fingernail swirls around the pale blob of someone's body. It gets me wondering how a person ever feels comfortable enough in their backyard to get naked and show God what he made. Sage and I have rented an apartment for three years, a crummy one-bedroom, and the pot-dealing neighbors keep the hallways reeking of skunk. The trailer we've been scouting has red siding and a bay window. But even at the Stars Aligning Estates, where each street is named after a zodiac sign, the lots are slivers of an acre. Give your wang some sun on Sagittarius Drive, and the whole place would be snapping pictures.

"I hope it's her," I say. "Not him."

"That's mean," Sage says.

"I'm just saying, if it were you, I'd pay a bunch more. I'd pay anything to keep you safe."

"Nice try, buster." She prods me with a tangerine nail. "I'm plenty safe."

The yellow-shirted belly bursts through the door, carrying not guns but bottled waters. He passes them through my cigarette smoke. Sage cracks hers and guzzles, beams at the man with a thirst-quenched smile. My water just sits in my lap.

"Suppose I bite," he says. "You got the negatives with you?"

"I don't," I say.

"But you have his word he won't show no one else." Sage takes another grateful guzzle. "And my word too. Two words for the price of one. How about that deal?"

The guy scratches one of his legs with his sneaker heel, balancing his pot belly like a flamingo as he mulls. He digs into his pockets, produces a folded stack of bills. "Unless you'd prefer a check," he says. "But I figured you type of people wouldn't appreciate a check."

Extortionists, he means. Crooks making a lucky break. If making him feel like he's getting robbed opens this tight-ass's wallet, so be it. I count the money in front of him, and there's only ninety dollars, plus a sad, crinkled pair of Washingtons. "You're short," I say.

"That's what I'm giving you," he says. "No more."

"If I was a dishonest man, I could upcharge you for capturing such sensitive subject matter." Truth is, sometimes I get full asking price, though that's rare. The goal is turning the photo into any amount of green. But this guy has pissed me off, and I want to squeeze him for more. I know I can.

"I'm giving you what you get," he says. Just when I'm about to throw the money in his face, Sage pushes the frame over me and through the window. She's saying thank you, saying once again how much she loves the place, backing the van down the driveway. This guy and me stare at each other through the windshield the whole way, the framed photo tucked under his arm, the wad of cash crinkling in mine.

I stretch the resentment out over days. Hate like that is an endless cigarette, a satisfying burn that just ends up killing you. But, damn, sometimes satisfaction is worth the trade. I'd rather live a shorter life burning hot, I guess.

Over the next few days, we sell eight more aerial estate photos, finishing off big-belly-yellow's neighborhood. I keep using him as bait in my pitch.

"Your neighbor down at number 6995 bought one. He snatched it right up. Thought it was a dandy deal." Every time I say it, Sage pinches me with her tangerine nails. Sure, I gave him my word about the photo, but that doesn't mean he can't serve me as a sales prop. I'll inhale that sucker and blow him cold onto his neighbors.

Eventually, 1002, near the end of the block, sets me straight. This lady buys a picture plus frame for $499.99, no questions. She's clutching it with both hands, bobbing her permed, magenta-dyed head, when she says, "I'm surprised Mr. Platt could afford one of these."

"Who's that now?" I say.

"The gentleman with the lovely irises," Sage says.

"The what?" I say.

"You know, the yellow shirt." She makes a big round gesture over her belly.

"Sure, Mr. Platt. He loved his photo," I say.

"His wife just died," the magenta-headed lady from 1002 says. "I'm surprised he could pay, because he's losing the house. Couldn't afford it without her. Life insurance left him hanging out to dry."

"Oh," I say.

"It's a whole thing. The entire neighborhood talks about what a shame it was, her death, the heart attack. But you don't see me gossiping on about it." The lady won't stop ogling the photo of her house to bother looking up at us.

"Oh," I say.

"That's horrible," Sage says from behind me, sounding like she's choking on one of her long nails. "Just horrible."

Finally, Mrs. Bobblehead breaks staring at her photo to flash us her serious face. "Yes. That's what I say too. Horrible."

After we move into the trailer, we become instant homeowners. Maybe we don't own a few fancy acres that frame up nice in a photograph, and maybe if me and Tommy snapped a shot of our place, it would just be a clump of white boxes zigzagging through the trailer lot like broken teeth. Maybe not a house, but sure as hell a home.

First thing we do is gut the place, from cabinets to the orange shag carpet to the chicken-print wallpaper in the kitchen. We strip it to studs. Out front sits a junk mound big enough that Tommy could spot it from the Cessna. Soon enough, Sage and I make the place beautiful: blond cedar paneling, vintage turquoise oven, thick cream curtains hung on reclaimed conduit. We're shabby chic. We're living it up.

But just after we replace all the vent covers with these beautiful black iron pieces from Harold's Antiques Trove, Sage says we're missing something. I feel it too. That sense of missing lingers over the place, as if there's no frame to our photograph.

That night we cruise out to Luce Road again, way out by the six thousands. We drive by the mailboxes and porch-lit home fronts that purchased a picture to fund our new trailer. We roll up to 6995, and the house is dark. Maybe no one lives there yet. Maybe they're sleeping. We park at the road and tiptoe.

Sage works the shovel while I watch. We hope they'll live, but I'm unsure about those delicate spidery roots. She tugs them out of the earth like a pro, and I fumble them into the Hefty bag. I bet her nails are trashed; she just painted them lime green yesterday and will have to start over before we head back out on the road to sell more pictures. The bag full of flowers grows heavier, and I set it aside to reach into my pocket. I brought the negative of yellow-shirt guy's photograph, and I plant it in one of the holes where his irises used to live. He probably wanted the negative to make copies, I realize now, so he could blow up that blink of sunbathing body, but I have no idea where he moved to. Plus, he swindled me down to bones on the price. Leaving the negative here seems like kindness enough. I kick dirt over the hole.

That night, me and Sage screw with dirt on our hands, the scent of it all over our bodies. It's great sex, and it's always great with Sage. After, she struts outside in just a T-shirt, me following in just shorts, and neither of us mind if any of our new neighbors are watching. She lights a cigarette for me, passes it from her lips to mine. She doesn't want me smoking in the new trailer, and that was an easy sacrifice. I'd never tell her, but I'd give up the whole smoking thing for her. I'd give up anything.

She leans into my legs and tips her head up to the stars, and we can see a few more out here than we could in that apartment squeezed into the middle of the city. I blow some smoke up where she's probably looking. Then she says to the sky, "Think those irises will be okay in the bag overnight."

"Sure," I say. "Of course." But I don't know shit about flowers.

"What about him?"

"Who's that?" I say, but I know.

"Yellow belly at 6995. You think he's managing?"

"Baby, that son of a bitch is just fine. How could anyone hurt a grumpy old asshole like that?"

"He's not that much older," Sage says.

"Enough older," I say, and we go to bed in the home we own as much as anyone owns any place. Mortgages and leases and liens and loans—who owns anything? Tommy, even, could lose his plane in a snap if he missed a payment, if we didn't sell enough photographs. But Sage, it seems, can't let it go.

Next morning, we're planting the irises, and she says, "You think he only gave us ninety-two because those were his last dollars?"

"I think he was a cheapskate."

"Sometimes I think about how much he might've needed that money if his wife just died and we pressured him into that photo. Puts my tummy in knots, you know?"

What I don't know is how to plant irises, how deep the hole should be, whether this bag of dirt we bought on clearance has the right nutrients or alkaline balance or whatever. I don't even know if it's the right time of year. I don't know anything. For now, most of them we've planted are standing tall and pretty—this army of color fencing our pretty red trailer home.

"He had a Mustang. He had a nice house. How bad could things be?"

"I bet you're right, Vance. I should leave it alone."

"Bury it right here in our dirt, baby," I say and pass her a blue iris, the prettiest one I can pull from the black trash bag. She lowers it gently and brushes the earth over the top.

I study her hand, the lime nails smeared in clearance dirt. If Sage died first, and some joker showed up with a picture of her sunbathing, her whole body blaring in the sun, even if it was only the size of a petal from way up in the heavens, there's no price I wouldn't pay. Not for that kind of miracle.

EVERY NUMBER ALBERT KNOWS

Albert is measuring Ms. Johanna Posey's house at 119 Palmetto Drive. He clips his tape measurer to one corner of the siding, walks it out. The tick marks extend along their yellow aluminum track, the inches, the feet, all flinging toward the next corner. Albert marks and measures and moves on to the next wall. In a single hour, he's hugged every wall. All that Ms. Johanna Posey has loved over the last thirteen years fits inside fifty-four-by-thirty-five feet.

On his clipboard goes the Posey house's perimeter, which he calculates into square feet, doubles for two stories, subtracts the garage. Within this area, Ronda Posey lost her baby teeth, including the one she accidentally swallowed. Ms. Johanna Posey sometimes wonders about that swallowed tooth, if it might still be milling within her daughter's precious viscera. Or if her stomach acids decayed and absorbed it, what part of Ronda is made up of that incisor? When Johanna pats her shoulder, is it there? When she trims her bangs, does it flutter to the bathroom tile?

The Posey home exterior allows Albert to estimate the interior, reveals more than Ms. Johanna Posey herself knows, since she has imagined her house too small for her family of four crammed inside. Once upon a time, fifty-four-by-thirty-five feet was plenty big enough, but then she spent two years quarantined inside. Outside, bodies struggled to breathe, the virus hardening Grandma Edna's lungs. A cop's knee crushed a man named George's windpipe for eight minutes and forty-six seconds. Meanwhile, the Poseys all kept breathing. And now it's time to go. Time to get gone. There's no work for Ms. Johanna Posey here in Gaffney, South Carolina. Out west they are hiring everyone, will hire a newly single mother, no problem.

Albert wouldn't mind a house like the Posey home for his daughter, Wendy. She's on the market, and her housing interest has broken their long-held pattern of biweekly phone calls that never extended beyond four minutes and broached such topics as weather, Atlanta Braves trades, and streamed sci-fi movies. They are talking now. Wendy asks his thoughts on ranch versus two-story layouts, on septic versus city sewer. Albert waits, abates excitement, like coaxing an opossum from a crawl space. Instead of asking if she remembers the stories they used to make up about her teddy bear they'd named Major Tom and his explorations of distant solar systems, he coaches her on interest rates.

Wendy currently lives sixty-seven miles away from Albert, and if she purchased this house, she'd be only eight miles from his townhouse that's only a fourteen-minute walk from the cemetery where his sister is buried, which he visits every Wednesday to tell her stone all the things he wishes he could say to his daughter. His sister always listens. He will never risk too much distance from the site where her body rests.

Albert admires Ms. Johanna Posey's scalloped siding, which he'll tell Wendy about. He'll tell her it's made of real cedar. That's a fine feature. He's never asked her opinion on wood. He hopes she appreciates it as he does. Almost all homes are wrapped in vinyl these days. He remembers the fad when everyone demanded aluminum siding at the promises of never needing to paint, no rust, ultimate longevity, and now he sees so few aluminum-sided houses. Eventually all construction seems to return to the original materials: wood and wire, brick and brass, glass and gypsum.

A knock on Ms. Johanna Posey's door means it's time for Albert to step inside, check for any surprises. He just needs to glance, really, to identify any qualifying square footage, like the basement that now contains

Mr. Posey's bedroom, ever since the separation where neither party separated, for the children's sake. Instead, Mr. Posey muscled through the basement threshold a mattress, a small desk, and a 65-inch HDTV, big as a bay window cut through concrete foundation. But the 65-inch TV remains blank for Albert, and Mr. Posey stares like a statue at a 13.3-inch screen filled with spreadsheets. Albert doesn't even notice him as he measures the square footage, another eighteen-by-twelve feet to be tallied. Mr. Posey's space is not separate as far as Albert's measurements are concerned. The utility room, too, containing six square feet of blue carpet counts as quantifiable living space. This room is where Ms. Johanna Posey's wedding photos wilt. This is where her father's Gulf War medals reside inside a box once used for diapers.

Albert searches on, opening closets, just in case one might open upon a hallway tunneling toward a snowy night of Narniac proportions, fairy-tale square footage, like he used to read about aloud to Wendy before she grew too old for a father to read to her at night. What Albert does find is every skeleton in every closet. He is expert at willful ignorance, at not noticing the porn stash, the unlocked gun safe, the go-bag ready to jettison Ms. Johanna Posey on her way if this house doesn't sell quickly, and her ex-husband can figure out what the fuck to do with the mortgage. Albert ignores Ronda's closet corner where she hides to pluck hairs from her scalp while reciting the lyrics to "Help Me, Ronda" in a slow, melancholic whisper. Over the years, 2,342 hairs have accumulated into a small stack in the corner.

The attic is rarely a qualifying space in most homes, but Albert finds the attic access opened, a foldable wooden ladder extending its ten steps, and he can see from the hallway carpet that the room appears walled, finished enough to qualify. Every square foot matters when selling a house. Accuracy is Albert's pride. Duty demands he climb the ladder, enter the attic room of Ronda's big sister, Caroline.

The room's drywall is wallpapered with lipstick advertisements cut from glossy magazines. All lipsticks and lips. Every picture. Hundreds of hues of nude pink to fire-engine red. Albert's mind begins estimating the sum total of all of these women's mouths, all of these tubes of wax, oil, pigment. Albert is not here to speculate about the white carpet stained by sporadic brown circumferences—coffee, soda, feces, food. What matters most is that this wall is 125 inches long, this one 98, adding up to a legitimate living space.

He'd be pleased to leave now, but Ms. Johanna Posey has folded the ladder, thrown shut the attic access door. Albert is stuck and soon will be behind schedule. He has two more houses to measure before lunch. And lunch is a sacred time when he eats his three hard-boiled eggs, his carrot sticks, his single Oreo cookie. He's on a diet. It's working. He's lost seven pounds in three weeks. Would work better without the cookie, he knows. But what is life without an occasional Oreo cookie?

The Oreo will be delayed. Ms. Johanna Posey has stymied his progress. She knows Caroline is so rarely home until well past dark, when she parks her battered Volvo in the driveway and trudges up to her dungeon without speaking a word. Ms. Johanna Posey has quit trying to ask about her day. So easily a parent can slip into this path of least resistance that turns silence into chasms. Just ask Albert, who, yes, she forgot was in her house working with silent efficiency, as invisible as the conditioned air whispering through her vents. She was annoyed that Caroline left her attic room door open once again. How many times has she warned her that someone could run right into the ladder, stub a toe, slam a knee? This cathartic lecture is her only communication with her daughter these days.

Albert grows uncomfortable surrounded by so many reddened, waxy lips. He stomps on the floor. He raises his voice to request assistance. He left his phone in the car. Company policy. He carries a clipboard, measuring tape, three pencils, flashlight, calculator—all he should need to complete his measurements. He turns from the lips to face a corner, but the corner features a wadded pile of dirty teenager clothing, underwear, bras, inside-out T-shirts caked in deodorant. Albert returns to the lips. He notices crinkled corners. He never noses around. But what's a measurement man to do with slack time forced upon him? The page he pinches between his fingers is thinner than he expected. It peels away, flimsy as sunburned skin. Beneath, Albert finds a small square cut into the drywall. Inside the hole, he finds a box decoupaged in eyes wearing heavy shadow, liner, mascara. Inside the box, he finds a baggie of marijuana, a small glass pipe, a pink vibrator, a morning-after pill.

His own daughter, Wendy, is twenty-six now, only one year younger than his sister ever was. He adored his daughter through her childhood years, and she looked just like Albert as a kid, perhaps unfortunately so—same mousey brown hair and high forehead and weak chin and yellow eyes. Same small arms and large belly. Same resting expression that most people perceive as annoyance. But, in truth, the world fascinates Albert. The whole universe. His sister had been a physicist, a graduate student, before she died at twenty-seven. She'd told him that the study of physics is embryotic. The science so new they understood barely more than nothing. Her death left Albert floundering in curiosity. Throughout his daughter's childhood, Albert and Wendy spent evenings researching black holes and dark matter and multi-dimensional theories. They'd write science-fiction stories about Major Tom, paint nebulas using thirty-six colors of acrylic paint. But then she turned thirteen. She grew tall, lovely like his sister had been. She became disinterested in physics, fascinated by boys her age, by girls her age. Albert couldn't stave off the creeping resentment toward his daughter. He gave up on her and spent evenings at his sister's grave, sitting in a lawn chair where he'd read Stephen Hawking with his feet propped on her tombstone. It took Wendy's recent interest in buying a house for them to reconnect. He knew every number she'd ever need, the surety so opposite from his sister's physics.

The box from inside the lipstick wall rattles with one last item. Albert's fingertips probe the smooth polish of a .327 Magnum bullet. He initially mistakes it for a lipstick tube. But then Albert lifts it to the light. A swarm of lips pucker behind the bullet.

Albert must escape this room or he'll be late to his next appointment. Albert must escape this room or he'll think too much of the years he avoided his daughter when she could've been collecting similar talismans in secret boxes. Albert must escape or he'll think of his sister and how she passed, and that makes his skin prickle as if it might catch fire. He lifts the window sash wide. He dips through the opening, boots scraping shingles. He knows he stands twenty-three feet above ground. But standing up here feels different from knowing a number. His vision dizzies. He snails across the roof, using both hands and feet. The roof rises at a moderate pitch of four inches per foot, but this feels like falling would be too easy. His body quivers, his legs gone wobbly, his traitorous arms gelatinous.

Once he nears the edge that drops to the garage roof, Albert looks back. He notices a white bag floating against the siding. Its glow against the yellow paint beckons him. Here is another secret stash from this ghostly daughter.

He needs to know despite always obeying the professional commandment of willful ignorance. He didn't notice Ms. Johanna Posey's twenty-eight boxes of sneakers that she can't stop buying. He paid no mind to the love swing that Mr. Posey once convinced her might rekindle their love life. Albert even disregarded the telescope pointed at the neighbor's bathroom. But Albert has been smothered by lips. Pushed onto a roof. Late. Hungry. He's under duress. He's trying not to tally the ways he's failed Wendy. He's straining not to inventory the signs he missed from his sister.

He waddles back toward the bag. His boots slip, scrape, and shake loose asphalt. But he catches himself, keeps his eyes steady on the white plastic bag that hangs from the siding by a nail left undriven by the careless carpenter named Sandy who sided this home in 1954, and no painter has taken the time to set that nail in the five repaints over the years, from white to blue to green to white again to the current yellow. The nail has grown thick, more pigment than steel at this point.

Albert plunges his hand inside the plastic bag Ms. Johanna Posey's daughter Caroline once received with her purchase of a halter top and a tube of lavender lipstick. She hung that bag on this nail to hide what she stole from her mother's room. What she stole, Albert finds now—Ms. Johanna Posey's Ruger revolver from the gun safe she hasn't checked in eleven months and twenty-four days. For now, only Albert and Caroline know the whereabouts of the Ruger revolver. Albert's fingers wrap its grip.

Maybe the Posey family would've moved and separated before Caroline could've gathered the will to use the gun. Maybe a change of scenery could've helped, a smaller house in a nicer suburb out west within walking distance of a community garden. Maybe Caroline could've grown red peppers bright as tubes of lipstick, taking pride in their sheen, gifting them to friends, friends she now lacks but might gain if she had access to plump red peppers. This might have been just enough to stall the bullet from entering the chamber, from meeting the hammer excited by the trigger squeezed by her finger.

If Albert could measure such details, he'd know this bullet isn't meant for someone outside the house. Nor is the bullet meant as revenge for the infidelity committed by her father, whom Caroline still and always will adore. Nor is the bullet meant for her sister, Ronda, who receives the better grades and everyone likes more. Nor is the bullet meant for Ms. Johanna Posey, who bought and stored the gun and forgot about it while worrying about how to salvage a home. This process of elimination narrows the bullet's aim. It points to only one.

But abstractions such as intent remain far outside Albert's job's parameters. Above his pay grade. As conceptual as physics, just as impossible to grasp and pull close. Like dark matter. Like gravity. Like the memory of a sister's arms wrapping for a final hug that no one could know was final. Why speculate when almost everything else can be known and measured? The .327 Magnum bullet is 1.450 inches long. The Ruger revolver is 6.6 inches from muzzle to grip. The drop from the garage roof to the ground is 110 inches. The distance to Albert's truck from his landing is 84 feet. The distance between his truck and his daughter who terrified him through her fragile young adulthood is 67 miles, 947 feet, and 5.2 inches, but it's growing less as Albert's truck drives past his next appointment, onto the freeway where he chucks the gun onto the meridian, and keeps on going. The numbers diminish with each second forward. Just as the time stretches longer from when Albert's sister, the aspiring physicist, used a similar revolver and ended her universe and all of its physics, every infinite cubic foot of its wonder.

THE SALESMEN APPROACH

We're watching your subdivision. The entrance sign reads MEADOW CORNERS, but we know there is no meadow. We know how you all leave at sunup, return in your hatchbacks when the sky melts into copper. We know you avoid us, escape to your office where you hide, knees hugged to your chest and back against the door, biding your time until our working hours ebb away and we turn to husks in two-piece suits, too tired to sweat after a day of lugging briefcases. You imagine that we return to our unfed children, cradle them in our limp arms. Then you tire of imagining our lives, kick your feet up, and we disappear. But you imagine wrong, underestimate your adversary.

We've changed tactics. We're raiding at night. We're storming the lanes, attacking the cul-de-sacs, ambushing from the manicured shrubs. We pour in at twilight, twelve dozen lines of hunched shoulders and swinging briefcases and neckties knotted snug around our perspiring throats. You see us coming, and you try to cover your window, but your designer curtains are too sheer and silky like gossamer, and we see your silhouettes quivering back there. We take aim, stab our fingers at your doorbells, and there's no escaping us now. We buzz and ding and knock and buzz and ding and knock. We'll wait all night if we must. We've been here since before your foundation splashed into the earth. We'll be here long after your mortgage goes sour and the real estate agent stakes a foreclosure sign into your browning lawn.

So answer this door. Face our wrath. Face our bleached smiles that mask the disappointment of ten thousand slammed doors. Open this door, face us face-to-face, and then try to make us disappear.

You give in because you must. You give in because there's only so much guilt one man can take. Because you know what it's like to be turned down for a raise once again, turned down when your family desperately needs it, when that extra $94.35 per pay period could save your Eames lounger nestled in your favorite nook in this house you can't afford in this subdivision that's split into twelve dozen quarter-acre plots that used to be meadow, swamp, cornfield, where a farmer named Enos finally gave in and sold his great-grandfather's land because he just couldn't afford to keep it going any longer. Enos is one of us now. That's him over there, also wearing a blue necktie, also flashing bleached teeth, also knocking, his finger poised over the clasp of his briefcase, waiting for you to open the door just a little farther, because how can we possibly do our job through such a tiny slice? We can make only partial eye contact with your one hazel eye squinting wildly at us. We require full eye contact. We require your fullest attention.

Open fully, we say unto you.

That's better. Hello. My name is H—— and you will forget it by the time I've finished this sentence. But let's not get personal, even though I'm standing two feet from you and your home where you keep your wife and your three children and your English setter, Elvis, where stowed in the attic is your childhood baseball card collection you were sure would make you rich one day, though now it's just kindling printed with the faces of men and you can't remember 98 percent of their names.

Hello. My name is H—— and I'm selling widgets. They are indeed real. After years of algebra problems where you had to solve for widget, you asked Mrs. Dunwoody what a widget actually was and she ignored you, and you asked her again, and she knelt by your desk, hissed in your ear, told you to stop dreaming and focus on the numbers. That stung your twelve-year-old heart, made it impossible to fantasize about marrying Mrs. Dunwoody and someday unbuttoning her beige blouse. So you imagined a widget was the thing your father bought at the bar every night before returning home to you. Next month, your father didn't come home, and your mother said that he loved you and your sister, but he had this problem. That problem and the need for a new Mustang and a twenty-seven-year-old blond named Lindsey Callison. And these problems were a problem of solving for widget, and the problem of widgets may explain why you can't get an erection some nights, why other nights you can't quit holding your wife, why you can't get that raise, why your boss secretly thinks you're a sniveling kiss-ass with a business degree and no business sense.

The widget is not merely a variable for a problem you can't solve. The widget will in fact solve your problems. All of them. Gaze at my briefcase. I'll unclasp, open the lid slowly, creaking hinges echoing through the darkness. All 144 of us are opening our briefcases right now for you and all your neighbors in near-perfect synchronization. Creak, creak, creaking, like the sound of your father's Mustang's door at midnight. Creaking open and, behold, the widget.

What is it made of? Paper, steel, positively charged ions, hope and envy, all-natural herbs, astronaut-grade plastic, limes and lavender, centuries of ingenuity.

How does it work? Just flip the switch, press it to where it hurts, tell it what you want, plug it into a 220-volt outlet, turn the page. You don't need to do anything at all except sit back and let it do the work.

What does it do?

The answer to that is exactly why we marched down your streets. So sorry if the clomp of our loafers woke your daughter. She was having a nightmare anyway. A nightmare where you are a bear and your lips are ringed with blood and you try to open the jar of peanut butter but your paw just keeps spinning the lid, around and around and around, and it never opens.

The widget can erase all bad dreams, if you understand its operational procedure. Consider this: If you buy thirteen widgets for seventy-five dollars and sell them for a house payment, what is your profit margin? If a handsome boy has twelve widgets and is riding in a train from Chicago to Detroit at fifty-seven miles per hour, how many more will it take to make it to Toledo, Ohio, to elope with your daughter? If you're in a canoe with those twelve widgets, and one-third fall out, how many more widgets will you need to buy to save yourself from drowning? Think hard about these problems. Answer slowly. Dip your hand into our briefcase and caress the widget's smooth surface, and we promise not to snap the case shut on your fingers.

A demonstration is required. But you must open your door more fully, invite us in, let us stay with you for the full two weeks and three days necessary to illustrate the effects. Thank you for your trust. How lovely are your valances, your oaken mantelpiece, the vertical stripes on your daughter's walls. It must have taken excruciating hours to get the lines so perfectly straight. When you pulled away the blue tape, how hard did your heart break when you saw the paint bleeding through? How hard did you smack your son when he smudged his palm into a teal stripe? Did you trust your steady hands to touch up the mistakes, to still your son's sobs, even though your steady hands now shake, and you can't stop them, because you know the finality of the mortgage notice the mailman will deliver tomorrow?

Don't worry. Your mailman also works for us. He's three houses down at the Palmers' residence. The Palmers are, as we speak, deciding whether to purchase a bushel or a pallet or the complete library of our widgets. The Palmers are watching right now as your mailman demonstrates how to paint perfect vertical lines with the aid of a widget. The Palmers are learning how to hide children's bruises with seven easy widget strokes. The Palmers have always been a few steps ahead of you. Like when they refinanced and rented out the guest room to Ruta, who fell in love with Mrs. Palmer, who got the kids in the divorce, and now Mr. Palmer is renting out the garage from them. They will not lose their house. And if you simply trust in the widget—in us, in me—neither will you.

Hold your breath while I remove the widget from its protective case, its vacuum-sealed cellophane, its leather-bound cover. If this seems like an excessive amount of packing peanuts and Bubble Wrap, just remember the joy you took as a child in snapping the bubbles and frightening your dog Rudolph. Remember how you filled your hamster's cage with these Styrofoam peanuts because, you told your mother, rodents love nuts, but you understood the difference, understood a steady diet of Styrofoam could lead to nothing but a fuzzy corpse.

Behold how the widget dissolves guilt from hamster homicide. And it lightens that carpet stain in one pass. In three passes it's completely gone, and you won't even remember how after you got the raise that was supposed to fix everything but still didn't make the mortgage you drank all the rum from four New Year's Eves ago and vomited and passed out right there. No matter. That memory's trace is all gone now. The widget has cleansed it. The widget will take over from here, will stand in as the variable to equal the perfect family, the happy home. The widget will hold your head, stroke your cheek with the back of its polycarbonate knuckles, kiss your children good night, and lock the doors after you leave with us.

THE NIGHT THE STARS FELL

The night the stars fell, Jack was inside, watching a Discovery Channel special about walruses. While the rest of the world witnessed an endless black tar seizing the night sky, Jack was chuckling to himself about the bulging torsos roly-polying onto beaches. Those torsos served as a fine distraction from what he'd been working on while Catherine was at her job. He'd been studying up on miscarriages and had learned that they were quite common. They happened all the time, in fact. He was ready, they were ready, to try again, and Catherine just needed convincing. He'd written a little speech he wanted to give her. He'd gone through a dozen drafts.

After eight months of unemployment and meandering sadness, Jack was going to jump-start his life, make it matter, and—just wait and see—he was going to be so good at being a dad. Throughout his employment hiatus, he'd absorbed countless documentaries, and he was confident he could surpass the father failures of the animal kingdom: grizzlies eating their cubs, lions dawdling in the shade while their partners drudged home fresh carcass, sandgobies gobbling up half their eggs just so they could get back to screwing.

But Catherine returned home from her shift pale faced and silent, and Jack couldn't find the moment to start his speech. She was the intake nurse at the town's only ER. Usually, she'd launch into a diatribe about incompetent doctors and bleeding, whining, snot-driveling patients clustering around her desk. Everyone agreed she was the best at her job, despite everyone annoying her. That she could stand only Jack had always made him feel like he'd won a prize, and every night he listened to her and nodded at her rant before he spoke. On the night the stars fell, however, she sat on the couch and began an unfamiliar script.

"I was in my car, and, fuck, they just started falling." She seemed to be studying her palms as if they might catch fire. "I got this urge to try and stop them, to—I don't know—hold them up there with my hands. Like that helpless feeling you get when a patient goes into seizures and all you can do is roll them onto their side and watch. But it was the fucking sky."

"Where did they land?" he asked. "The stars."

Her eyes sharpened toward him. "How the fuck should I know?"

Jack knelt in front of her, removed her orthopedic shoes, and started rubbing her feet, but he kept an eye on the walruses that, it turned out, were vicious carnivores. One ripped into a sea cucumber, and Jack winced, surprised that he could sympathize with such a gelatinous invertebrate. What kind of life could be flashing before its eyes?

Catherine seemed not to notice him kneeling before her. "Just—what can it mean?" she said. "Are we done? That's it for humans? The whole universe?"

Jack snapped from the walruses back to unsheathing a lightly dampened foot from its sock. "We'll get through this together," he said to her toes. "We'll start something even better. We're tough. We endure."

"Are you kidding me?" Catherine's toes clenched. "We snap like twigs. We can't handle anything."

Catherine, it seemed, was referring to her fragile patients, to humanity in general. But Jack had only the two of them in mind, just one couple who'd recently swallowed a litany of baby names: Esther, Elmer, Elizabeth, Matt. The miscarriage had come at ten weeks, before they'd had an ultrasound, before they'd seen anything, when the baby could still be anyone.

"Don't worry." The walruses were licking viscera from their tusks now. He wished they'd hurry up and return to being lethargic oafs. "We always figure it out," he said.

She slapped his face, hard, palm walloping his right eye.

"Hey!"

"This isn't making the mortgage. This isn't returning a car seat to the store. The stars are *gone*. Nothing's ever going to make sense again."

"That's ridiculous," he said, even though a primal shock had already electrified his veins. Denial seemed appropriate. Test the monster. Call its bluff. "Shut up," he said and grinned, and that made her slap him harder.

"What the fuck?"

"Look. See it yourself."

He followed her pointing finger to the drawn curtains. He hadn't seen the sun today, nor the sunset. He preferred the blackout curtains, preferred his cocoon of animal documentaries, Icelandic and Appalachian and sub-Saharan and Himalayan landscapes, all in HD, a justified expense even though he was leaning into eight months of unemployment. If you're going to watch, he'd told her, don't you want to see all the definition possible?

He crept toward the windows and nudged back the curtain, and what he saw was—nothing. A nothing that felt like it might be the most something of all the nothings he'd ever witnessed. This wasn't a cloud-covered night; this was a hard nothing. He couldn't help imagining how great the Discovery documentary would be: *A Blackened Planet*.

"I'll, uh, go get the car," he said.

"For what possible reason?"

"Just in case." A vague response plus action seemed a better plan than hazarding the wrong answer. He hurried out to the car, but he couldn't bring himself to open the garage door. That would imply that he knew what he was doing. Instead, he clicked the key halfway and turned on the radio, preset to NPR, and heard the host talking about the sky, her voice a bit more choked than usual, panic pinching her larynx. He spun the dial, but everyone was talking about it. He switched to a CD. Nirvana. "Heart-Shaped Box." He remembered the controversy over the music video when he was a teenager, all those Christian moms mad because Kurt Cobain had crucified an emaciated old-man Jesus wearing a diaper. That was the world in 1993. He wondered what those moms were thinking about now.

The passenger door opened and Catherine slid onto the seat. "Are we huffing exhaust?"

"No. I just forgot to open the garage door."

She was still wearing her faded blue scrubs from work, her most worn-thin set, decorated with a hole that revealed a pencil-sized dot of bare abdomen. "Start the engine and forget a little longer. It's supposed to be like falling asleep with a big fluffy buzz on, I hear."

Catherine could crack jokes about fingers amputated by hedge trimmers, about parents fretting maniacally over their kids' 102-degree fevers, but she never joked about suicide. When she was in high school, her dad had shot himself with the Beretta he'd kept locked in the gun safe her whole childhood. She still hated him for it, often referred to him as a coward, while at the same time she poured extra care into her patients who failed bridge jumps and carried bullets in their jaws. Cobain had gone out the way her dad had: bullet to brain to blackout.

He could sense the garage's air thickening, his head growing wobbly. All he had to do was open the door. *Throw down your umbilical noose*, Cobain said, and then: *Hey! Wait!* Jack jabbed the garage-door button.

"It won't work if you open the door," Catherine said, her eyes closed. Her hands balled against her chest in a casket pose. He waited for some sign of Catherine's grisly sense of humor to poke through, but her body remained fixed.

"Let's go for a drive, see what's what." Jack dropped into reverse and backed down the driveway.

Once he was facing the windshield again, the sun visor mercifully obstructed his view, and he tapped along to Grohl's snare drum as he drove. He had never felt anything as deeply as Cobain seemed to feel the words he was singing—even the gibberish no one understood. He'd once watched a documentary where Cobain said he could sing the phone book with as much emotion; his lyrics were meaningless, he claimed.

Catherine leaned forward until her forehead pressed against the windshield, her eyes aimed up at the endless black. If it were any other moment, he'd make a joke about her smushed nose. Catherine owned a momentous nose. It had been the feature that had first attracted him to her seven years ago. A Streisand nose. Someone could make a documentary about just that nose.

They drove past a gas station, where a line of cars stretched onto the street, horns shrieking, drivers shouting, red gas cans crowding truck beds. It smelled like fire out the window, out in the world. Jack turned off the main street, into a residential neighborhood, and here a more expected darkness draped the vinyl siding and brick facades. The calm of sleeping suburbia repeated itself down the street. Catherine rolled down her window and half stood so that her body jutted outside the car. From his view, she looked decapitated. A fire flashed orange up ahead.

Jack slowed when they saw a fat column of fire blazing on someone's front lawn. He worried he might be expected to help put it out.

"It's a trampoline," Catherine said, slipping back inside the car. And sure enough—it was a children's trampoline, flames climbing the safety net walls. "Look at that." Something—a flaming basketball, it turned out—bounced across the trampoline. Then another. Dark squares ricocheted through the fire and onto the grass where they sizzled. Someone was tossing books, incinerating a library from the second-floor window. Bibles maybe, L. Ron Hubbard's collected works, Shakespeare, Flannery O'Connor, Fromm's travel guides, cookbooks, constellation maps, *What to Expect When You're Expecting*. Under an erased sky every title probably seemed offensive.

Catherine applauded the general chaos. He hadn't seen her clap for anything in years. He winced behind the wheel, far removed from understanding the joy of this performance. Before they lost the baby, before they'd even considered babies, they'd shared bottles of cheap wine and then attended the local college's plays, all buzzy with lavish ovation. Now, a few other random claps sputtered around them. Someone whistled. Something larger edged out the window, something already burning and about the size and shape of the crib they'd spent hours assembling and then never returned to IKEA. Jack stepped on the gas while Catherine cheered.

They drove onward, Catherine still un-seatbelted but sitting back down, at least. "You know, I was going to leave you," she said. "I just got so sick of being sad."

"Why?" Jack said. "When?"

She didn't answer for a while. He wanted to interrogate her, ask if it was because he couldn't find a job. He'd *tried* to find one—for the first few months. He'd try again. This time, he'd apply even for those minimum-wage jobs that didn't care about his accounting degree and decade-long career with numbers.

"I guess there's not much point now."

"There's a point," Jack said, but the rest of the words in his head jumbled up as incomprehensible as Cobain squealing through the stereo. He couldn't imagine giving his speech now. He also couldn't imagine a future without Catherine. She'd always had the good job while he bounced around seasonal tax-prep gigs. She'd steered their lives, until she lost the baby. It had happened at work, a few stabs of pain, a few spots of blood, and she'd toughed it out, unlike those paranoid expectant moms who cluttered the ER if their urine smelled funny. But then more blood came. She'd been in the right place to have a miscarriage, if you had to have one, but she hadn't told anyone at the time. She'd seen it, she told Jack later, the body so minuscule she'd had to squint. She didn't tell him where that tiny body went, but she'd seen it and he had not. He wanted to get them back on track. A new baby, just one, could lift them out of their rut.

"You think so?" she snapped—as if she'd been reading his thoughts, though he knew she was only reacting to what he'd last said. "We just keep patching things up and limping along?" She looked out her side window at an ice-cream van shooting spotlights from its roof into the heavens. "That's optimistic in the face of cataclysm."

The road out of the neighborhood ended in a T, and Jack recognized the intersection. When they were young, they'd take a right onto the deserted country roads where they'd pass back and forth a cigarillo packed with pot. They hadn't done that in many years, long before Catherine had miscarried and then cheated on him, and then he'd cheated on her, and then they'd reconciled over weeks of tightly gripped coffee mugs and sweaty midnight talks. Then those long talks simmered into the quiet nothing they now endured—their exchanged pleas and insults and apologies replaced by the perpetual chatter of their top-of-the-line HDTV.

"You know," Jack said, "at home, from our yard, we never really could even see too many stars. Just one or two poking through."

"Liar," she said. "We could see dozens."

"It's not a lie. It's just what I remembered."

"You remember wrong."

"When I was a kid, it seemed like my parents' place had so many more," Jack went on, now that he had her talking, desperate to put some sort of positive spin on things. "Who has time for stars these days, anyway?"

"All of them are suns, you know," Catherine said. Out her window, downtown's businesses still glowed. "All of them are huge bodies with endless weight. And what does that mean for our own sun, for tomorrow?"

"Our sun's fine."

"You think? What if we're all that's left?"

"More likely, it's atmospheric effect, an illusion, like a purple sunset. Those colors everyone goes gaga over are just refraction through smog. Discovery did a special on it. Just a pretty nothing."

"You didn't see what I saw."

"Which means I can be more rational about it."

"So ignorance suddenly makes you an expert?" Catherine said, her words drowning out Cobain's distorted strumming.

The shop windows gaped fluorescently, their fully stocked aisles of detergents and almond milk and wine devoid of customers. All the people seemed to have vanished, but the rapture he'd seen on that alarmist evangelical special, *End Times and You: Be Prepared*, promised there'd be plenty of stragglers. Eventually he spotted people. Figures stood on roofs like statues, gazing at the sky. Jack slowed at a JC Penney storefront.

"Should we say something to them?" he asked.

Catherine stuck half her body out the window again.

"See if they know anything," Jack said. Maybe an impartial third party could talk some sense into her. From their rooftop vantages, they could surely tell it wasn't all that bad. But Jack spoke to the pale blue fabric covering Catherine's thigh, the rest of her body lost to him. Then more of her departed through the window. She pulled herself up so her feet balanced on the door, until her feet, too, one by one, lifted away. Catherine became a thudding atop his roof. He imagined her standing up there, probably staring straight into the sky like the transfixed department-store workers, all of them gone lunatic. Jack wondered if the moon was still there. He hadn't thought to look before. He didn't dare look now.

"It's probably just dark matter, clouding things up, hon," he shouted out the window. He listened for Catherine's reply, which didn't come. "Neil deGrasse Tyson told me the vast majority of space's mass is undetectable," Jack said. "Something our best minds can't explain, so they just throw the phrase 'dark matter' at it like woo-woo magic. It's so real we can't even understand it, Catherine. I bet the stars are all still there, just hiding behind dark matter. This could just be the universe's new magic trick. You know?"

The roof banged with a clamor he was pretty sure was only Catherine collapsing into a sitting position. Her voice called from outside, "Go."

He let his foot off the brake and crept forward, slowly so she wouldn't fall. "Hon," he tried again, "did you hear what I said about Neil deGrasse? Doesn't that sound logical? I bet it makes you feel better, huh?"

But Catherine had snapped. Something white darted out in front of his headlights. Then another, and he recognized those darts as Catherine's orthopedic shoes. Her socks followed. She was barefoot up there. Perhaps she'd stripped nude, and maybe all the star-starved roof gawkers were nude now, too, matching their state of dress to the barren sky.

Jack spotted a bonfire ahead, much bigger than the flaming trampoline. The fire blazed in the parking lot of the Food Lion. From the road, he saw darkened silhouettes mingling before the light. He pulled into the lot, parked near the back where he could safely study this wild species in their habitat. But Catherine stomped down from the roof, naked feet thundering his hood, beelining toward the fire. She was barefoot but still clothed, thank God, implying, he hoped, that she'd maintained moderate sanity. He got out and followed her.

Her fire-shadowed shoulders bobbed toward the light. Jack noted a congregation of dark aprons and white shirts near the bonfire, the same cultish outfit on each person, a dozen swarming around the massive fire. One of them thrust a shopping cart full of diapers into the flames. The rest of them hooted at the sparks. Catherine had already entered into a conversation with one of them, a tall man with an unwieldy bush of a beard. Jack had always kept his face clean shaven, even during his unemployment.

"Bernie over there said he pissed himself, then had a panic attack," the tall one was saying to Catherine, "but I thought it was kind of beautiful. In that way that your neighbor's house burning down might be. I couldn't stop staring. Even after the whole thing went to nothing."

"And then what?" she said.

"Then what?" He cradled his hands inside his apron's front pouch. "And then this. This, lady. It's fucked up but still kind of beautiful, don't you think? We got to be the last ones to see it."

"You don't know what you're talking about," Catherine said. "Kind of beautiful? What the fuck could be beautiful about any of this? You're so full of shit." The man appeared cavemanlike wearing that monstrous beard beside the raging bonfire. He could pummel Jack if he liked. But Catherine feared nothing—besides trying again, besides even fucking talking about it.

"Look, gal—"

"Catherine," Jack interrupted. He attempted to crack his knuckles and pressed too hard on his middle finger so that it panged.

"Never mind," the bearded man said. "You and your bodyguard are welcome to the party, to pillage the store, whatever you want. Just don't crap on people who are trying to have a decent time at the end of the world."

"It's my end of the world too," Catherine said.

But the bearded man had already bounded off to the other side of the bonfire.

More hooting erupted over another shopping cart igniting in a whoosh.

"We got a lot to burn before the sun doesn't come up," said a woman standing nearby, older, in her sixties maybe. She was smoking a cigarette in each hand, alternating drags.

"It might," Jack said.

The woman laughed. She placed two packs of cigarettes in Catherine's palm. "Need more, I'm stocked," she said, patting her apron pouch. "I have a lot more smoking to do." She bullied a pack toward Jack.

"It's bad for you," he said. No one needed a documentary to know that.

"I smoked two packs a day for twenty-one years. My habit was old enough to buy booze. Stupidest thing I did was quit a few years ago. Now I'm reuniting with my favorite hobby." The woman flicked a lighter and held the flame out for Catherine's cigarette, the first Jack had seen her smoke since long before they'd started trying to make a baby. Catherine ran three miles every other day now, ate kale. Her paternal grandmother had lived to be ninety-seven, and her dad had been healthy enough that no one would've been surprised if he lived a century, before he'd shot himself. Catherine had been aiming to beat the family record. If she couldn't make a baby, she'd live two lives herself.

Another shopping cart rolled toward the fire and slowed to a stop next to Jack. Tall, dark bottles dressed in foil labels glistened inside the cart—champagne. "Pop them open," someone commanded. Jack looked to Catherine, but she hardly seemed to notice what he was doing. He lifted a bottle, crinkled off the foil, and began the nerve-wracking back-and-forth of the cork. "Shoot it into the fire," someone else said.

The cork popped. Before he could gauge whether it had landed in the fire, someone pulled the bottle from his hand. An aproned worker guzzled from the long neck, passed it to Catherine, who drank too. Jack reached into the cart for another bottle, unsheathed the cork, popped that puppy into the fire. He went on like this, emptying the cart. A circle of aprons formed around him. He felt more useful than he had in months.

While he worked, two more carts splashed into the flames. Jack calculated that just the row of carnival-colored cereal boxes lining up into infinity were enough fuel to burn through the night and beyond. Once Jack had emptied his champagne cart, another nudged his thighs. It was stacked tall with cakes, each on a cardboard platter with a clear, plastic lid.

"Happy Thirtieth Anniversary," he read aloud off the first one. A blond, aproned woman snatched the cake away from him, popped the lid off, and shoveled it into her mouth with a bare hand.

"Congratulations Class of 2025!" he shouted, and more hands carted this cake away.

"Get Well Soon!" he shouted.

The circle around the bonfire cheered and toasted with their champagne bottles. They hand-fed cake to one another.

"Over the Hill," he said. "Happy Birthday, Alison," he said. "Break a Leg! Lupe's Quinceañera!"

The final cake in the cart read, "It's a Girl!" over plowed rows of white-tubed frosting. The ultrasound had been scheduled, but they'd never made it, never found out the sex of their baby, and Jack wouldn't read this one while Catherine was celebrating with the mad crowd. He popped the shell, reached in, and smeared the words. With a blank slate, he could now christen this new holiday: *Happy Blackout* or *Farewell Cruel World* or *Until the Next Life!*

But this crowd had evolved past hope or fear. These witnesses had been initiated into doom, and Jack felt utterly alone. After the miscarriage, he'd kept making errors at work on the tax forms, the numbers curling into questions for him about what he and Catherine had done wrong. Then he'd lost his job and spent eight months out of work, and Catherine had hardly blinked at his meaningless life. She didn't argue about the expensive TV, didn't demand he find a new job, required nothing of him—to the point where her apathy needled at him, more and more pins poking into his skin, until he felt as if he were living on a bed of nails. So, he'd handwritten his speech a dozen times, about how he'd be the best dad, if she was ready, because they'd made it through so much and that had to have made them stronger. The speech he hadn't given only because the stars had fallen out of the damn sky.

"Hallelujah and Amen, We Put This World to Bed," he pretended to read, and the circle of aproned bonfire attendees roared approval. Jack raised the cake high, and before anyone could face its blankness, he hurled it into the fire. And he kept hurling, cake after cake. There was a wonderful recklessness to it—chaotic and liberating. This, maybe, was what Catherine had been feeling ever since their child went away. He widened his eyes and peered straight up as deeply as he could into the nothing that felt like falling, an endless tumble. He squinted into the indiscriminate dark. This was what he'd been missing. Call it doom. Call it oblivion. Now he knew what Catherine had witnessed.

Someone touched his shoulder—the bearded, aproned man. "You can stay long as you like or need or whatever. But, you know," he said, while pointing toward their car in the back of the parking lot, "I just think no one should miss a minute of being with their people." Catherine was alone back there in the dark, separated from the bonfire, and Jack didn't want to leave the festivities but knew he should go to her. Back at the car, when he clicked the key fob to open the locks, she entered wordlessly. She was tired, he knew. He hadn't worked in eight months, had been sitting on his ass watching TV, but he felt as if he were beginning to understand how tired she was—of just about everything.

He asked where she wanted to go, and she told him: "Drive." He headed for home. They weren't that far away. Catherine stared at him while he drove, but she didn't speak. He wanted to commiserate the blank sky with her, the exhilaration and horror they now shared. He said, "I think you're right. I think it's a good thing we didn't try again."

Catherine pinched the bridge of her long, lovely nose.

He said, "Can you imagine this with a baby?"

"I can," she said. "I have."

"How lonely and cruel to start a life right at the end."

"How can you tell, though?"

Cobain was all apologies now. They'd come to the end of the album, and it was about to start over from the beginning.

If the sun did return tomorrow, Jack decided, they would slip back into a routine turned marvel. Catherine would shower, dress, slip on the scrubs she liked to wear on Fridays, the purple ones, still vital with color. Jack would have coffee ready, and she'd peck his cheek on her way out the door. He would flick on the TV to a documentary about climbing Mount Everest, the snowy incline littered with hikers' junk and well-frozen corpses from decades ago. Catherine would step out under their sun, the last star in existence, the last star so close and so bright it could blind the sky. So bright no one needed to worry about anything.

ACKNOWLEDGMENTS

The memories of the tradespeople I built houses with just before the great recession gave me company in the writing of this book. I continue to hope I can honor the voices of the working men and women who broke their bodies to build our homes.

Writing stories can be lonely, but I've been lucky to work within a generous, vibrant community. I owe so much to my brilliant agent, Heather Carr, who has stubbornly and powerfully championed my short stories about working people. Your enthusiasm and tireless labor, Heather, have meant the world to me. The whole Friedrich Agency team has been so wonderful to work with.

Thanks, too, to the lovely journals and their editors who accepted these stories and gave them a first home: "In Darkness Floating" and "The Salesmen Approach" in *The Journal*, "Dad Died in Denim" in *Puerto del Sol*, "Such a Good Man" in *Redivider*, "Essentials" in *SLICE Magazine*, "Too Bad for Marcel Ronk" in *Washington Square Review*, "The Man with the Yellow Hat" in *New Ohio Review*, "The Whites" in *CRAFT*, "Eat Fire" in *BULL*, "Smoke at the End of the World" in *DIAGRAM*, "Orville Killen: Lifetime Stats" in *Alaska Quarterly Review*, "God Chooses the Wheelbarrow" in *Gulf Coast*, "Privy" in *LitMag*, "Bicuspid" in *Ninth Letter*, "The First Woman" in *South Carolina Review*, "Work from Home" in *Jabberwock Review*, "This Picture of Your House" in *Litmosphere*, and "The Night the Stars Fell" in *One Story*. The University of Wisconsin Press has given these stories a perfect forever home, and I couldn't be happier to work with this expert crew.

Thank you to the great writers who read and talked these stories over with me, so generously lending their care, time, and keen editing: Brad Aaron Modlin, Anne Valente, Michael Guidry, Jacqueline Vogtman, Matt Bell, Michael Czyzniejewski, Brad Felver, Seth Fried, and Brandon Davis Jennings. I especially owe heaps of appreciation to my brother in writing, Joseph Celizic, my magic editor.

For the last decade, Winthrop University has given me a working home and community, and I'm so grateful to all my pals in the Department of English, especially the dear folks who have constantly supported my fiction: Amanda Hiner, Ephraim Sommers, Casey Cothran, Gregg Hecimovich, Ronald Parks, and Siobhan Brownson. And I could never ask for better students. Thank you all for occasionally laughing at my bad jokes, for sharing your stories, and for working so hard to make the best art with me.

These stories would not be possible without the gracious people who gave me permission to retire my painter whites and brushes. Who deserves more gratitude than the great teachers? Thank you to my writing mentors: Jaimy Gordon, Adam Schuitema, Thisbe Nissen, and Wendell Mayo whom I miss every day.

My best friend and wife, Carrie, and my amazing daughters, Evelyn and Alison, make this writing life possible and beautiful. Every word I write is always for them. Brilliant, strong women have always surrounded my life: my two smart, cool sisters and my mom, who first taught me to treasure teaching and love language. This book is especially for my dad, the best man I know.